# Making the Cut

SD Hildreth

# DEDICATION

When I was a child of roughly eight years old and living in San Diego, I saw my first motorcycle gang (back then they were called gangs). We were entering the freeway, and as we merged, a thunderous roar from behind the car caught my attention. I spun around and looked. Motorcycle after motorcycle passed us as we sped up to get on the freeway. After literally dozens of bikers blew past us, I sat in awe; staring at what would later become my first love....

"What was that?" I asked.

"Hell's Angels," my father responded.

"What? Hell's what?"

"Hell's Angels. It's a biker gang," he said over his shoulder.

And, at that moment, I knew one day I would have to find out what it was all about.

This book is dedicated to the one percent.

The Outlaw.

# AVERY

I turned to the side and peered over my shoulder. No two mirrors ever give the same reflection. Some provide an accurate likeness; like the really expensive ones in the mall or the one in my doctor's office. Others, including the ones in college bathrooms, don't. I ran my hand along my stomach until it came in contact with the bottom of my bra.

*I have no tits.*

I twisted my hips as I bent at my waist a little, pointing my butt slightly toward the mirror. My ass looked flat and similar to the hipster boys who wore the neon colored pants in my Psych class. I looked like a sixteen year old boy; a sixteen year old boy who was almost six feet tall. The only problem was the fact I was a twenty-two year old woman.

*Yeah, she's got no tits and no ass, but she's got a really cool personality, I think you should meet her...*

"These mirrors suck. Hurry up," I sighed.

"I know, they make me look fat," Sloan's voice echoed through the empty bathroom.

I glanced at my reflection, wondering if they truly were the mirrors which added five pounds. If so, what did I *really* look like? I stood and stared blankly into the mirror wishing I could see myself through the eyes of an honest person. Well, an honest person with perfect eyesight. Frustrated, I pulled a section of paper from the towel dispenser and wadded it into a ball. I glanced at the trash can on the opposite end of the row of sinks. It was easily fifteen feet away. I bit my lower lip slightly and tossed the ball of paper toward the opening. It landed against the

1

leading edge of the can and fell inside.

*Yes!*

I pulled another foot long piece of paper from the dispenser and wadded it up in my hands. As I lifted my right hand to my shoulder, the door opened. A girl wearing sweats, sneakers, and a loose fitting Henley smiled as she made eye contact with me. As she tossed her book bag beside the sink, I forced a smile and clenched the paper in my hand as if embarrassed.

"Hey," she breathed as she turned toward the stall.

*Holy shit, I wish I had your boobs.*

I tilted my head her direction, "Hey."

As she stepped into the stall, I studied her body. Her butt was small but perfectly rounded. She looked like a hippie version of a Victoria's Secret model. She was further proof God had a sense of humor, and I was the joke of this century.

Butterbody.

*She's got a really pretty face, butterbody looks like a fucking boy.*

"I'm never eating at that gross Thai place again," Sloan huffed as she emerged from the stall.

My fist still clenched, I stood and stared blankly at the floor as she washed her hands. As I considered the cost of butt implants and what I may receive for my first *real* tax return, I grabbed my book bag and followed her to the door. While she opened the door and held it for me to pass through, I turned around, pressed my non-existent butt against the door, and raised my right hand into the air.

"Come on, we're going to be late," she complained.

The trash can was at least twenty-five feet away.

"For the championship," I said under my breath.

"No freaking way," she muttered.

I tossed the ball of paper into the air and immediately swung my hips to the right, opening the door for Sloan to witness the feat of accomplishment. A masterpiece of a toss, I watched as the brown blur reached its apex and began to fall toward the receptacle. Magically, the paper disappeared into the center of the can. Satisfied, I released the door and followed Sloan into the hall.

"I can't freaking wait for the Fifty Shades movie to come out," she said as she hurried down the hallway.

As I adjusted the book bag on my shoulders and attempted to catch up to her, I rolled my eyes. I didn't care about some ridiculous movie about billionaires and airplanes. Red rooms of pain and *laters baby* weren't for me. I dreamed of a *real* bad-boy. One I couldn't introduce to my parents. I wanted the type of man they couldn't make a movie about. Not unless it was rated X.

Finding one who liked smart-assed skinny girls would be the trick.

# AXTON

Otis looked over his shoulder as he reached into the refrigerator, "A hundred is a hell of a lot to get gathered up in the next three weeks, Slice."

I glanced up from my notes and pressed my hands into the edge of the table as I flexed my forearms. I knew I didn't *need* to flex on Otis, but it had become habit when someone questioned me. Throwing my size around was second nature, and I was a rather intimidating son-of-a-bitch to most people, Otis included. As he twisted the lid off the bottle of beer and tossed it into the trash, I began to stand from my seat.

"Well, that's what they asked for and I sure as fuck can't change it. So, what's your recommendation, Otis? Give 'em fifty? Seventy? *Fuck that.* We'll look like a bunch of incompetent twats. Get a hundred of 'em found. I don't give a rat's ass if you have to run an ad on Craigslist that says *AK-47's wanted: will pay top dollar*, find a hundred of 'em and get 'em in here," I said as I tapped my finger on the notepad sharply.

"In three weeks?" he asked as he sat down across from me.

I nodded my head and lowered myself into my chair, "Yep."

"God damn, Slice, that's a huge order. We ain't got any AK's right now. Jesus. I'll get Hollywood on it, we'll see how it goes," he paused as he raised the bottle to his lips.

I shook my head from side-to-side, "No, we won't *see*. Not on *this* deal, you'll make it happen. Corndog gets out in six weeks. And these guys are serious players. They're *Sureños*. More specifically, if I even need to say it, a bunch of 'em are from *Calle 18*, mostly from Los Angeles. These motherfuckers are all about respect. They're not an MC, but they operate under the same principles and they even have fucking bylaws. If you're in the gang and fuck something up, they don't shun your ass, they *kill* you. If we do this deal and it goes as planned, we'll be set with these bastards for good. If we don't, Corndog loses his credibility in the joint. Hell, they'll probably kill him. These sons of bitches don't fuck around. They'll cut a motherfucker's head off just for principal. Hell, I'll do about anything to some prick if I don't like him, but cut off a head? Yeah, I'm thinkin' not."

He pressed his beer bottle onto the table, lowered his head, and peered over the top in my direction, "You mean those MS-13 motherfuckers? This is who you're talking about?"

I nodded my head, shrugged, and grinned, "That's them. The *notorious* MS-13. You know those poor motherfuckers started down in Salvador or somewhere. The fucking cops don't even fuck with 'em, they just let 'em run dope. Poor sons of bitches don't have any money down there, so they turned to dope. Now, they're the entire reason we can't go to Mexico and drink coconut flavored drinks with little umbrellas in 'em on the fucking beach. Well, not if you're white anyway. They're cutting off heads of their *own people* in the street. Fuck that, I'll stick around in the good old US of A."

He stood from the table and faced the door. After a short pause, he turned to face me and pressed the web of his hands into his hips, "For fuck's sake, Axton. I hate this shit. We make a good damned sum of money selling guns to everyone else who buys 'em from us. And those MS-13 fuckers are some crazy assed Mexicans. They'll kill an entire family just to prove a point. Do we really need to do this?"

I stood, cleared my throat, and spoke with a tone of authority, "We may not need to for *money*, and we sure as fuck don't need to for *credibility*, but we're gonna do this for Corndog. Did you forget what he's done for us? For the fucking club? Huh Otis? And since when was it *your* fucking place to question *me*?"

He stood silently, narrowed his gaze, and slowly raised his hands to his face. It was a habit he'd had since he was in his early teens when we first became friends. If he was getting ready to agree to something he didn't *naturally* agree with, or when he was preparing to make a move, he always raised his hands to his face first. As he encompassed his temples in his palms I smiled, knowing if I had him on board *mentally*, this deal was in the bag.

Otis was a rather large man by anyone's standards, and outside of a one-on-one meeting with me, he didn't take shit from *anyone*. Our club was large enough that we had small cliques within it of fella's that ran together, but Otis sided with no one except me. He stood alone and he stood tall. At 6'-7" and 275 pounds of muscle, he wasn't someone to argue with. If Otis said to do something, the men never questioned him, they simply moved in the direction he pointed. His size alone was one reason he was the club's *Sergeant at Arms*. Well, that and the fact he was as mean as a fucking snake. Keeping order in the club and protecting or defending the members was as easy as breathing for Otis.

"I didn't forget, and I wasn't questioning you, Slice. I was *thinking*. Fuckin' Mexicans? And MS-13? Son-of-a-bitch. Yeah, I'll get Hollywood on it. I'll have a hundred AK's in *two* weeks, and that'll give you some wiggling room. Hell, even if we've got to steal 'em, I'll have 'em in time," he sighed as he lowered his hands and pulled his chair from the table.

As I heard the door hinge creaking, I immediately stood from my chair and faced the doorway. As it slowly swung open, I saw Cash standing in the narrow opening between the door and the frame.

"Hey Otis, I got a question," he said under his breath.

"Does that fucking door have a sign on it that says *come on in?*" I growled.

Cash shifted his gaze from Otis to me, "Sorry, Slice. I needed to ask…"

*You stupid little cocksucker.*

Before he finished speaking, I interrupted him, "I asked you a fucking question, Prospect. Does that God damned door have a sign on it that says *come on in?*"

Cash slowly shook his head from side to side.

"God damn it, Prospect," Otis breathed as he began to stand.

I extended my arm and raised my hand in Otis' direction to silence him from continuing. A Prospect needed to understand we had rules in place for a reason, and they need to be followed at all times. If he couldn't follow orders during a simple twelve month initiation, he damned sure couldn't be trusted to stand up for the club and it's brethren under any and all circumstances afterward.

"Hold up, Otis. I asked this simple minded little prick a question. Now answer me," I barked.

"No, it doesn't have a *come on in sign*, Slice" Cash sighed.

I shrugged my shoulders and continued to stare in his direction, "But it *does* have a sign on it, *doesn't it?*"

He closed the door momentarily and slowly pushed it open again. As he opened the door, he peered around the wooden frame toward where I stood, "Yes, Slice. It sure does."

I inhaled a long breath and raised one eyebrow, "Tell me what it says."

"Knock before entering," Cash said softly.

"Big red and white motherfucker, gets your fucking attention kinda like a God damned stop sign, huh? Being big and red with huge white letters and all?" I asked in a sarcastic tone.

He nodded his head.

"It's pretty fucking hard to miss, unless you're a stupid fucker or blind. And you know what? I ain't lookin' to add any dumb asses or cripples to this club. You're never gonna make it, kid. *Now fucking knock*," I growled.

The door closed. Three sharp taps immediately echoed into the room.

"Go the fuck away, we're in a closed door meeting," I shouted as I sat down.

As his steps faded down the hallway, I turned toward Otis and shrugged. He had vouched for Cash, who grew up with a bike between his legs, and was a friend of Otis' family. I called him a kid, but he wasn't young. He was thirty years old and an auto mechanic, having him around would bring some benefit to the club, but everyone had to pay their respects and prove themselves through twelve months of being a Prospect. Cash certainly had his shortcomings, and not knowing when to keep his fucking mouth shut was one of them. I was often able to see what others couldn't, and although everyone seemed to warm up to him quickly, to me he seemed weak.

Maybe that's why I was in charge.

"I know you vouched for that little prick, but the kid's got diarrhea of the jaw. I don't trust his little ass any further than I can toss him," I said as I turned around to face Otis.

"I know you don't. He's got six more months, though. He's still learning the ropes," Otis explained as he lifted his beer bottle.

"He's thirty fucking years old, Otis. He acts like an immature kid," I shrugged.

"And another thing about something you said a minute ago, right before shit-for-brains interrupted us. Joking or not, I need to make this clear, you're not *stealing* any guns, we straight on this?" I asked.

"Yep," he nodded.

Six years prior, Corndog had purchased fifty Beretta 9mm pistols. Unbeknownst to him at the time, they were stolen. After selling a few of them, a customer decided to use one in a murder. Local law enforcement traced the firearm back to Corndog, and questioned him on the sale of the weapon and the location of the remaining stolen weapons.

He didn't budge. He lied, stating he found them on the side of the road. Had he provided the information to law enforcement regarding where he obtained them, he could have walked away without so much as a slap on the hand. The club's exposure on the crime was nil. The asshole who sold him the weapons was the one who stole them, and he was the person the cops wanted. Ninety nine out of a hundred men would have given the thief up and walked free.

Not Corndog.

In fact, he refused to tell anyone in the club who sold them to him. He looked at it as something he needed to take care of himself. I always believed after he was prosecuted and sent to prison, he'd say something to one of the members, but after four and a half years, he stood firm on his promise to resolve it himself. Corndog was an old school biker, with old school biker values. In his opinion, he made a mistake by buying the weapons and not knowing they were stolen. He felt as if he had jeopardized the safety and integrity of the club by being under investigation. In his mind, this was something he needed to resolve on his own, and after settling it, he'd without a doubt walk back into the clubhouse as if nothing ever happened. Many of the newer members could learn a lot from him in matters of protecting the club.

Now in prison and almost done with his five year sentence, he had made a deal with a Mexican prison gang to supply guns to their outsiders on the street. Small groups of Mexican gangs had cropped up in the Midwest since the latter 1990's, and most originated from southern California. Drugs were the primary focus of these gangs, and they didn't interfere with our ability to do what we needed to do, so we allowed the drug traffic to proceed without any issues.

Most MC's in this day and age made the decision not to mess with drugs; as the risk is far too great. If caught and convicted, a kilo of cocaine under the RICO act would provide every member of the MC a thirty year sentence. This was damned sure a chance the *Selected Sinners Motorcycle Club* wasn't willing to take. Not on my watch.

Our club chose the Midwest due to the soft state gun laws. Our first chapter developed just south of Wichita, Kansas. The second chapter formed in Oklahoma City five years later. Three years after that, a chapter in Austin, Texas followed. We were of the opinion as long as our focus was *legal* firearms, prosecution would be by *state* officials, and not *federal*. Federal crimes and MC's didn't mesh well, and typically a member of a MC would have the RICO act punishment tacked onto his sentence if he committed a federal crime. The Racketeer Influenced and Corrupt Organizations Act, or RICO as the Feds called it, was developed to thwart organized crime. A criminal didn't have to do anything *extra* to get the additional time on his prison sentence, all he had to do was be in a *gang* and commit a federal crime. The Feds considered an MC a *gang*. We knew as long as the crime committed wasn't a federal offence, we'd never have to worry about the Feds knocking on our door. A state crime for firearms was typically a twenty-four to sixty month sentence in prison. A federal crime with the RICO act attached was typically ten times that amount.

So, in the Midwest we had become an extremely powerful presence. Semi-automatic assault weapons, high capacity pistols, and riot shotguns were our focus. Machineguns, silencers, short barreled weapons, and sawed off shotguns were federally governed, so we stayed away from them.

Keeping up on the federal and state gun laws was my job. Having the local cops on our side didn't hurt matters, and we strived to keep the club out of legal trouble with our gun business. Staying out of jail in general was next to impossible, but outlaw motorcycle clubs weren't known for abiding by the law.

The *Selected Sinners* were no exception.

"If I'm going to get this order filled in two weeks, I better find Hollywood. Got anything else?" Otis asked as he tossed his bottle in the trash.

I pointed toward the trash can and pulled against the rubber band wrapped around my left wrist. As I released it, snapping it into my wrist, I spoke, "Take that stinkin' motherfucker to the shop. I don't want to smell it. And that's all I got, Otis."

He shook his head and leaned over the trash can. As he pulled the empty bottle from the trash he turned to face me and rolled his eyes.

Slowly he began to saunter toward the door. Otis did everything slow and easy until it was time to throw down in a fight, and then everything turned to lightning speed. I always imagined him saving his energy for such occasions. To watch him leisurely make his way through the day was almost exhausting.

"Better yet, smack that Prospect upside the head with it first. Maybe you'll knock some sense into his stupid ass," I laughed.

"Cut him some slack, Slice. He's a good kid," Otis sighed as he reached for the door handle with his free hand

"He may be a good kid, but I have my doubts that he'll make a good *Sinner*," I responded as I looked up at our motto posted on the wall.

*The Devil Looks After His Own.*

"We'll see," Otis said as he walked through the door.

"Damned sure will," I huffed.

*Damned sure will.*

# AXTON

Our club was located in a town twenty miles south of Wichita. We'd chosen the particular town because it was close to the action of the larger city, and easier for us to conduct business without constant scrutiny from local law enforcement. Winfield was small at 13,000 people, but a fifteen minute ride from the largest city in the state, boasting 375,000 people.

We did our best to toe the line in the city, and the local law enforcement looked upon us as a blessing instead of a curse. Frank Downtain was the city's Chief of Police, and he had two underlings to assist him in watching over the city. Winfield wasn't as adventurous as other large cities, but having the club operate from there was easy. Truly a step back in time, living in Winfield was almost as if we were in the 1950's.

Frank was in his mid-forties, overweight, and underpaid. As with most small town cops, lining his pockets with a little money went a long way. As soon as we arrived in the city, filtering money Frank's way began, and it hadn't stopped. Having been in the city almost ten years, we'd developed a relationship allowing him to do his job, and us to do ours. We made every effort to keep our actions civil in the small town, and he looked the other direction if we ever needed him to. To keep matters palatable to both parties, we attempted to minimize our exposure to criminal activity under Frank's watch.

For ten years, everything worked well. From time-to-time, Frank

15

had the club resolve issues he couldn't iron out under the limit of the law. It came as no surprise, and provided support of my belief that *laws are meant to be broken* every time we were asked to assist him in something he wasn't able to do under the watchful eye of the City Attorney or the State Court.

It was three o'clock in the afternoon, and Frank and I shared a booth in the local Mexican restaurant. The only two patrons in the restaurant, we had the luxury of speaking freely. We often chose the establishment for mid-afternoon meetings for the privacy alone. I shoved another forkful of Chile Pork Verde into my mouth, chewed it slowly while I stared at Frank, and as soon as I swallowed, began to speak.

"Fuck, Frank. Child pornography is a federal crime. Why not call in the Feds?" I asked.

I wiped my mouth on the back of my hand and waited for him to respond. After looking over both shoulders, he leaned into the table as much as his beer belly would allow him to. After shuffling his elbows into place and raising his hands to his chin, he looked up. Still somewhat concerned about his little issue with a local photo collector, I fished in my bowl for another piece of elusive pork.

"Alright. I'll tell you the *whole* story," he whispered.

I lifted the empty fork from my bowl, rolled my eyes at the lack of pork, and grinned, "Wouldn't expect otherwise, Frank. Hell, you and I been doin' this for a *bit*, haven't we?"

He nodded his head, "I know, but it's embarrassing. It makes me look incompetent and inexperienced. It's fucking paperwork. This was going to be a good bust. Someone turned scumbag in, and we investigated it in-house. I could have called the Feds, but I don't like those guys any more than you do. The Feds are a bunch of arrogant pricks. You

16

know they always stick their badges in your face and tell you they're on the scene and *head back to the station* like you're some dip-shit and don't know anything. Personally, I have no use for them. I just wish this would have gone smoother," he paused and rubbed his temples with his fingertips.

As he rubbed his face, I nodded my head once in agreement, "Let's hear it."

He closed his eyes, and after a moment's thought, opened them and began to speak softly.

"A middle school kid told his mother he'd been going to this guy's house for a few years posing for pictures. He said the guy told him if he ever spoke of it, he'd cut his dick off and supposedly he gave this kid a schedule to follow to return to his place for...well...you know, blowjobs. And the other kids supported these statements. So this poor kid is scared to death. You know how little kids want to please adults and they look up to them? Well, *that* part makes my skin crawl. That this son-of-a-bitch used the fact he was an adult to manipulate the kid. So, scared to death and wanting to make the man happy that he was doing what the sick fucker wanted him to, the kid did it for years under the fear of being dismembered. Finally, he reached an age that he began to wonder and feel guilty. The shame and guilt as he got older made him come to his mother for help," he hesitated and swallowed heavily.

I dropped my fork onto my plate and pushed my bowl to the center of the table. I felt my blood begin to boil. I reached under the table and stretched the rubber band until it almost snapped. As he began to speak again, I released it; snapping it into my wrist.

*Snap!*

"So, she came to us and we investigated. We held an awareness class at the school. Kids came forth and gave this guy up. Hell, it was almost a perfect investigation. Too damned good to be true is what it was. We typed up the search warrant, and raided his place. On his computer, we uhhm. On his computer, we found. We uhhm," as he struggled to find the words to finish his sentence, his voice began to falter.

I raised my hand and turned my palm toward him, "I've heard enough."

"Axton, you asked. Let me finish the story. I need to say it and you need to hear it anyway. So…" he paused and rubbed his temples with his fingertips.

As he sat quietly, he reached toward his eyes with his pinkie fingers and attempted to wipe tears from his cheeks. Being a cop in a city the size of Winfield, Frank would probably see a case like this one only once.

But that was one time too many.

After he regained his composure he wiped his eyes again and inhaled a deep breath, "Fuck, this is tougher than I thought; saying it and all. He uhhm. He had videos and pictures, Axton. A lot of them, hell they dated back for years and years. What looked like seven and eight year old kids sucking on his, you know…sucking on his dick while he told them how they were doing such a good job. He would ejaculate on their faces and make some of them swallow it. Sharpe puked when he saw it. I tried to hold myself together, being the Chief and all, but I just lost it. Broke down and started crying right as we watched it. I fucked this deal up, Axton, and I need some help."

It was all I could do to keep from standing up and knocking all the shit off the table. Generally a reasonable man when it came to keeping my anger at bay, this was far more than I was able to contain. I wanted the address of the pedophile, and I wanted to skin the son-of-a-bitch alive.

I sat up straight in my seat and raised my hand. As Frank stared at my hand, his lip quivered. I reached into my cut and pulled out the small notepad I carried with me. I scribbled a note onto the page. I slid the open note pad to Frank's side of the table as I held it in my hand.

***Get me the information on where the fuck this motherfucker is. And I mean it this time, Frank. I've heard enough. I'm about to snap.***

As he read the note, I began to speak in complete contrast to what I had written, "Well, you know the club could help you *find* this guy, but we damned sure can't do anything beyond that."

I trusted Frank as much as a biker could trust a cop, but I didn't *trust* him. I wasn't dumb enough to get caught up in some conspiracy to commit murder charge, and if I spoke of the things he was asking of me, it would be all too easy for him - or someone else - to record the conversation and use it against me or the club later. To provide me a little false comfort, I always used my notepad to discuss matters which were contrary to the law.

Frank inhaled a deep breath and exhaled loudly as he lowered his hands to the table, "We made a mistake on the search warrant, Axton. And now the computer, everything – all the fruits of the search warrant – they're gone. Basically we can't use *any* of it. Everything else on this guy is clean. All we really had was the computer and three kids who were willing to testify. Now all we have is the testimony, and the parents are second guessing having the children testify now."

The thought of someone doing such shit to a helpless kid made me feel sick. The pedophile probably selected Winfield for his home because it was small and lacked competent law enforcement, under the belief the small town kids would never say a word to anyone, and he could continue to take advantage of them for as long as he wanted.

I turned my head and stared out the window, "That's a damned shame, Frank. Sounds like a hell of a mess. I feel for those parents and kids."

I stared out the window for a long moment. As I turned from the window to face Frank, I scribbled onto the notepad and held it under his nose.

***Consider it done. I'll take care of it myself. Son-of-a-bitch, Frank. Fucking hell, and in this town, what the fuck, huh?***

Frank reached into his shirt pocket and removed a pen. As he spoke, he scribbled onto the pad.

"I know. It makes me sick. Hell, I *have* kids," he shrugged as he continued to write.

After he finished scribbling, I slid the notepad to my side of the table and looked down at what he had written.

***If this guy disappears, no one will give a shit. And hell, anyone could have done it. I'll write it up as a missing person, and leave it at that. He doesn't have any family, so who cares, right?***

Growing angrier by the second, I clenched my jaw, reached toward my wrist and pulled the rubber band back. After I released it, snapping it into my wrist sharply, I stretched it tight again and released it.

*Snap!*

I looked down at the red welt growing on the inside of my wrist, "Well, I *don't* have kids, but I'm a compassionate man. That's a damn shame, Frank. Maybe a parent will get to him and make him pay, hell who knows."

I picked my pen up from the table and wrote under the note Frank had written. I turned the pad to face Frank.

*Get me the information. I'll need a day or so to figure it out, and we'll get it taken care of. I'll make it clean and as simple as I can.*

As he nodded his head, I slipped the pen and notepad into my cut.

"Now I have a story for you," I sighed.

"What is it?" he asked.

"It's not a big deal, really shouldn't matter. I'm just trying to be respectful to ya, Frank."

He sat back in his chair, crossed his arms, and lowered them onto the top of his stomach, "Okay, what have you got?"

"We're making a deal with a Mexican gang. They're not an MC, but a *gang*. I have no idea if it'll take place here or in Wichita, but it'll be in about a week or so. If they come *here,* we'll have 'em at the clubhouse for a night. Shouldn't be any problem, and they ought to be respectful, coming to our town and all," I paused and considered what might realistically happen.

My experience with Mexican gangs was nil, and I had no idea what they planned to do regarding the delivery of the weapons. We preferred they come to us to pick them up, saving transportation and potential confiscation if stopped by the police. They may have planned on simply sending a man to pick up the weapons. Or, they might plan on coming to Winfield and having a celebration, a fucking fiesta of some sort. As Frank narrowed his gaze and leaned forward, I waited for his response.

"That's it?" he shrugged.

I nodded my head, "I'll keep you posted. Should be an *in and out* deal, and it'll be legitimate. But you know, if a town local sees a gang of cholos rolling into town, they might give you a call."

He leaned into his seat and sighed, "Yeah, you do that. Keep me posted."

"Will do," I said as I reached for my wallet.

Frank shook his head, "I'll get the tip."

"You sure?" I asked.

He nodded his head.

"Well, I've got an ongoing criminal enterprise I need to look after," I chuckled as I stood.

He tossed a twenty dollar bill onto the table and looked up, "And I've got to go set up a speed trap."

I looked over my shoulder and grinned, "Utter hell, ain't it?"

"Sometimes," he responded.

As I began to think of the piece of child molesting shit I was going to rid the city of, I realized nowhere or no one was immune from what the bowels of society had to offer.

Society sees a man like me, wearing my *cut* covered in miscellaneous patches I've earned over the years, and they typically categorize me as scum. I had no doubt whenever the local child molester went to get groceries he was met by the girl at the checkout counter with a smile. As I threw my leg over the rear fender and dropped down onto the seat of my bike, I grinned. I couldn't recall the last time someone smiled at me.

*And I wouldn't trade it for the world.*

# AVERY

The tattooed asshole behind me had reminded me no less than half a dozen times he wanted a Rum and Coke. As empty as the bar was, he could easily see I was taking the order of two nice gentlemen who sat at the end of the bar and ordered bottles of beer. I reached into the cooler for the beers and simultaneously pulled the opener from the back pocket of my jeans.

"Rum and Coke. Coming right up," I hollered over my shoulder.

I opened two Budweiser's, slid them along the side of the bar, and nodded my head toward the two gentlemen who had ordered them. They appeared to be brothers at minimum; potentially twins. Magically, the two bottles slid to a stop directly in front of them. I clenched my fist, pumped it forward slightly and pulled it toward my hip sharply.

*Yes!*

Doing my job and doing it well satisfied me to no end. I loved sliding shit along the bar and having it land where I planned. Dumb little things seemed to provide me the satisfaction I needed to convince myself I was doing a good job. My competitive nature probably fueled the need for measuring my success, but I desperately needed to know I was succeeding at whatever it was I decided to attempt. Without having a goal and reaching it, I'd go completely insane.

*Rum and Coke, behind me.*

I reached for the rum with one hand and a glass with the other. After scooping the glass through the ice bin, I poured a long shot into the glass and shot a splash of coke on top.

"There you go, Rum and Coke," I said as I handed the man standing at the bar behind me his drink.

*Blonde haired guy at the end of the bar.*

*He had a...*

*Gin and Tonic.*

I turned toward the opposite end of the bar, pointed toward the blonde man, and grinned, "You alright on that Gin and Tonic?"

He mouthed the words, *I'm good* as he nodded his head, raised his half-full glass, and smiled. I smiled in return, reached for the bar towel, and began wiping down the end of the bar. I scanned the bar. A typical Tuesday night, slow as fuck. Six people certainly weren't many to try and keep happy.

"You didn't measure the shot," a voice from behind me said flatly.

I turned around. Mr. Rum and Coke stood at the bar with his glass held at chest height. It appeared he hadn't so much as tasted the drink. I made note of a faint tattoo on his neck I hadn't seen before. It looked like some serious garage work or maybe something he got in prison. It looked like someone had taken a ballpoint pen and scribbled over a word they didn't want anyone to read.

*Nice tattoo, douchebag.*

"Nope, sure didn't. You know why?" I snapped.

He shrugged.

I smiled and began to wipe down the bar which separated us, "If I'd have measured it, you'd have about *half* the Rum I gave you. *Taste it.* And I'll be sure to measure your next one, how's that?"

He raised the glass and tipped it to his mouth. After a small sip, his eyes closed and he shook his head.

"Damn, *that's* a Rum and Coke," he said as he raised his glass.

I smiled, winked, and lifted the towel from the bar, "I'll measure the next one."

Working at a bar as a college senior was far more entertaining than anything else I had ever done for work. I had grown up in the small town of Marietta, Ohio, and a volleyball scholarship brought me to Kansas to attend college at Southwestern College in Winfield. Winfield was a shitty little town which reminded me too much of Marietta, so I opted to find a job twenty-five miles north, in the city of Wichita. Roughly half a million people provided a reasonably diverse group of patrons for the bar, and while I worked there I was learning a lot about dealing with people. The bar was small, and seated fifty-two people according to the card the Fire Marshall required we post above the door. A long bar with a return on each end seated twelve total; five high tops, and five booths at four apiece provided the seating. I controlled the music selection, and generally listened to indie rock on Pandora. No juke box, and no dancing, just great drinks and salty bar food. A cook and a dishwasher got off work at midnight, and I worked until two am. Weekends added a second employee, who worked as a waitress and bartender.

I suppose some small town girls would naturally be drawn to *other* small towns, but having grown up in a town of 14,000 people caused me to yearn for more. Living in a small town, to me, seemed counterproductive. I needed significant change in my surroundings to feel as if I had succeeded. A big city was drastically different from what I was used to growing up, and *change* was something I saw as an improvement. My overly religious Baptist parents would rather have me living in a cave, but given the ability to make my own decisions, I'd probably move to Wichita when I graduated.

A few more weeks, and I would be on my own. I couldn't wait. My best friend and roommate Sloan was on the volleyball team, a senior, and would graduate with me. We'd talked about being roommates after college, and if things went the way we had planned we would both move to Wichita and live together; easing the financial burden of trying to live alone. She worked with me at the bar mostly on the weekends, and we were a force to reckon with. She at a little more than six feet tall and me at 5'-11", together we looked like two Amazon women. Men either had a love for tall women, or seemed to hate them. I always thought men were intimidated by my height, but none would ever admit it. Sloan was a little more conservative than I was, but she provided me balance and acted as the angel on the opposite shoulder of my naturally active devil.

My strict parents attempted to raise me as a conservative girl who abided by the rules and regulations they shoved down my throat. It obviously backfired, because I was a little more adventurous than any of the other girls I met in college. Taking risks and having fun was part of my nature. Having Sloan keep me in check was something I probably needed. Without her, I'd make far more shitty decisions without a doubt.

"I'm headed home, Avery. Thanks. What did I have, I can't remember?" Ryan asked.

I turned toward the register and pressed my finger against the screen. After jockeying through the various screens and finding his order, I pressed the *total* button. After the receipt belched out the bottom, I looked down at the total.

"Let's see, you had two Jack and Coke's and a grilled chicken with fries, Ryan. Looks like twenty-three bucks with tax," I said as I printed the ticket and handed it to him.

"Well, here's thirty. Thanks, I'll see you tomorrow," he sighed as he tossed the money on the counter.

I nodded my head, smiled, and waved as I scooped up the money and receipt. Ryan was a regular at the bar, and always ordered Jack and Coke. He was overly nice, but had never hit on me or even said anything alluding to the fact he was interested in me. I always respected him for that, because he was married and had children. Although he had indicated his dissatisfaction with his marriage, he made clear he had no intention of cheating on her. He did, however, come into the bar almost nightly to unwind before he went home.

To me, men were a strange guilty pleasure, and never a necessity. I *wanted* a man, but my desire, as far as men went, was different than almost anyone I had ever met. If a man asked me out on a date, I wasn't interested. I wanted a challenge, and if someone was willing to take me on a date without any work on *my* end, I wasn't interested. I wanted what I couldn't have. I desired a man who wouldn't give me the time of day naturally; or at least at first, and I wanted to *earn* my way into his mind, heart, and life. If a man appeared to be a challenge, I wanted to try my luck at impossibility; and through my cunning ways, good looks, and competitive nature win him over.

For my first three years at Southwestern, a professor was on my to-do list. He was in his late thirties, single, and soooo hot. He had no idea I was even alive. I dressed provocatively, ditched the bra, and bent over a thousand times in front of him. I tried the naïve schoolgirl act, the innocent religious girl, the *I'm an old soul* routine, and even sat popping my gum as I twisted my hair in my index finger for countless hours as I batted my eyelashes at him.

I got absolutely nothing in return.

After my third year of beating my head against the wall, I learned he was gay.

Overall, I considered it a win, because he wasn't *technically* available. It continued to bother me, as *not* having him wasn't an easy loss for me. I even considered trying to make him go straight, but Sloan talked some sense into me. She was right, there was no way I could win that battle.

"Hey, motherfucker, watch where you're walking…"

I turned to face the voice I heard behind me.

*Mr. Rum and Coke.*

At the end of the bar a hallway led to the restrooms. Two men stood at the opening of the hallway. Apparently Rum and Coke had collided with one of the Budweiser twins, and was challenging him on his ability to find the way to his barstool without bumping into him. One thing I didn't stand for on my shift was fighting. My parents worried about me being a bartender at a bar in a city the size of Wichita, and especially working alone. I didn't really worry about it at all. I wasn't big enough to fight men, but I certainly wasn't afraid to break up a fight.

Additionally, I had a false sense of security.

Immediately after taking the job as a bartender, I applied for a concealed weapons permit, took the course, and obtained one. Now, I carried a 9mm Glock in my purse, and I wasn't afraid to use it if I needed to. Using it to settle a dispute in the bar was out of the question, but I made me *feel* more secure. Ultimately, if I ever needed it, I had it as an option.

"You bumped into *me*," the Budweiser twin responded.

Rum and Coke arched his back and clenched his fist. As he blinked his eyes and stared, probably attempting to clear his mind enough to speak legibly, the second twin slipped off the edge of the stool and stepped beside his double.

"Oh, you gonna get your buddy to jump in, huh? Well, I tell you *what*," Rum and Coke howled.

He unclenched his fist and reached for his back pocket.

*You motherfucker, don't you dare.*

As I stepped toward the end of the bar, and my purse, he pulled a knife from his pocket and began swinging it toward the two men.

"What the fuck!" the first twin screeched.

The second twin began stepping backward, away from Rum and Coke. As he slowly stepped rearward, his brother followed, and the knife wielding tattooed idiot was right behind them. I reached for my purse, and rested my hand on the Glock.

"Put the knife up, sir," I hollered over the bar.

Rum and Coke glanced my direction and immediately turned back to face the two men.

"You fucking bumped me on purpose, you big dumb fuck. Do you know who I am? I'll fuck you up," he growled.

*I'm sure you were a bad ass in county jail, but seriously?*

*You're a douche.*

"Sir, put the knife up, come on. Drinks are on the house. Just put up the knife," I said calmly.

Out of the corner of my eye, I noticed Gin and Tonic and my Hamburger and water come up to the side of the bar to watch the fight.

*Fucking people.*

"Listen. I'm going to guess, and this is just a wild assed guess, that you're on parole or probation. Put the knife in your pocket and leave, your drink is on me. If you don't, I'm going to call the cops. They'll be here in about sixty seconds; the sub-station is all of half a mile from here. You don't want the cops in here questioning you, do you?"

He gazed my direction and alternated glances between me and the Budweiser twins. To be honest, I had grown to have minimal respect for cops. Every time I turned around, there was one on the television who had shot someone or choked someone to death for no real reason. *Because I'm a cop and it's within my rights*, in my opinion didn't make it *right*. *Protect and Serve* wasn't necessarily the motto anymore. Although he didn't need to know it, the last thing I wanted was a bar full of cops.

"Fucking bitch," he grunted as he folded the knife and pushed it into his pocket.

*Fucking bitch who makes a bad-ass Rum and Coke, thank you.*

"Pussies," he hissed as he walked past the twins.

*Yes!*

*Another win for Avery.*

As he grumbled to himself and stepped toward the rear exit, I sighed and released my pistol. I wouldn't have shot him for being in a bar fight, but the gun gave me a little more courage than normal. I sighed, smiled at the twins, and shrugged my shoulders. As I raised my hand in the air in my own little imaginary victory pose, I swung the bar towel in a circle and shouted a celebration of sorts for having ended the little disagreement without any bloodshed.

"This round, gentlemen, is on the house!"

*Okay, that's two Budweiser's, a Gin and Tonic, and a glass of water.*

Wichita was a far cry from the quiet town of Marietta, Ohio, but overall I loved it. The wilder the better I have always said.

And, for the most part, I meant it.

# AXTON

I slammed the gavel onto the sound block three times. After dozen or so meetings during the club's inception which had gotten out of hand, the block had been screwed to the table at the end where my seat was positioned.

"I'm calling this meeting to order. Mr. Secretary, have you got anything noteworthy?" I asked.

Fancy flipped through his notepad and traced his finger along the page, "In the last meeting, Kelp made a motion to allow the trade of the old Sporty abandoned years ago in the back lot to the hardware store for Christmas trees, and provide the Christmas trees to the Toys for Tots kids at the ride this fall. It was left that we were unsure as to the value, and whether or not we had legal right to the little Sporty. I checked with the Treasurer, and we had already filed the paperwork for the mechanic's lien against the Sporty, and it is legally ours to sell or trade. We have the title in the safe. The Treasurer further informed me the value of the bike is roughly $2,200.00. I have my doubts it'll be worth that much, but $2,200.00 was his response."

"Second thing, I can't read my fuckin' meeting minutes, and my memory is shit, so who stood opposed to making the Fayetteville ride mandatory?"

Jeb raised his hand, "I did."

"Gotcha. Just needed to make note of it. Hell, I couldn't read my

31

own writing. That's all I got," Fancy sighed.

"Treasurer, where do we stand?" I asked.

"About the same as last time, Slice. $7,402.20 in the club checking, $5,405.00 in the club savings, and $112,500.00 give or take in the safe. We have nothing due out at this point in time," Mike responded.

"Give or take? What the fuck does that mean? How much is in the fucking safe, Mike?" I asked.

"Close as I can tell Slice, we got a hundred and twelve grand. It's all banded in $1,000.00 bundles. Then there's five hundred loose. So, $112,500.00. But I didn't take time to count all the money in the bands, but there's a hundred and twelve of 'em," Mike shrugged.

I nodded my head, "Good enough."

During Church, when I spoke, everyone was attentive. Not once could I recall being interrupted or disrespected in any manner. Our meetings were conducted in as professional of a manner as a Motorcycle Club could expect, and how I was personally treated in the meetings was second to none. I had my doubts, however, as to my being able to maintain order while the particular subject up for discussion was being brought to light. I decided to talk fast and pause for comments or remarks after I was finished speaking.

"Alright, listen up fellas. We got us a little situation. I know *I* don't normally get involved in matters like this, but for this one, I'm going to. I had a meeting with Frank, and he's got a little deal that needs taken care of. I ain't lookin' to go into a bunch of detail on this, because the whole thing makes me sick, but here we go," I paused and stood from my seat.

"There's a child molester in town and he's been making little kids suck his cock; little grade school kids. He made videos of this shit. Cops raided his place on a fucked up search warrant. Bottom line? He's free and they can't charge him. They got all the proof, but they can't use it in court. Frank's asked us to take care of this guy. I need probably three volunteers. So, it'll be me and three others. Who will it be?" I hesitated and reached for the rubber band without thinking.

*Snap!*

The entire room erupted. Every swingin' dick in the meeting was screaming and hollering *me, me, me*. I shook my head and reached toward the table. Before I got the hammer in my hand, Otis screamed.

"Order, God damn it," he hollered.

The room fell *close* to silent.

"Order!" Otis screamed.

*Silence.*

I turned to face Otis and shook my head, "Jesus. I need to get a bike repossessed and I can't get *one* motherfucker to volunteer. Got us a *ChoMo* to kill and every cocksucker here raises his hand and screams like a fucking kindergartner. Now fuck, there are thirty-two of you fuckers. I need four *total*, and one of them is gonna be *me*. Now how we gonna decide this?"

"I think we ought to draw straws, Slice. Cut twenty seven of them the same, and five shorties. The shorties win," Tater responded.

I raised my hands in the air in frustration, "Well?"

"I make a motion we draw straws," Tater growled.

"Second," someone screamed.

"Who seconded it?" Fancy asked.

"Toad," Toad screamed from the back of the room.

"All in favor?"

"Aye," echoed from around the room.

"Opposed?"

*Silence.*

I pressed my hands into my hips and raised my eyebrows, "Only problem I see is *this*. We ain't got any fucking straws."

Following a reasonable amount of groaning and grumbling, Fancy spoke, "I can cut up a few sheets of paper."

"Well, get to cuttin' it," I shrugged.

After a few minutes of dicking around, Fancy produced a hat with wads of paper in it. I looked at him and shook my head in disbelief. As I accepted the hat, I raised it to shoulder height and inhaled a slow breath.

"Listen up. Everyone take one of Fancy's wads of fucking paper from the hat. The three *short*," I paused and turned to face Fancy.

He nodded his head.

I turned to face the fellas, "The three *short* pieces get to go. Everyone else, I appreciate your willingness, but this is how we're doing it."

As soon as Fancy passed the hat around the room, everyone began to compare paper strips. It would stand to reason Fancy would have made the short lengths of paper *significantly* shorter than the rest, but he didn't. Leave it up to the Secretary to cut a half inch off of an eleven inch strip of paper. After ten minutes of comparison, Otis, Tater, and Toad were the *winners*. I couldn't have picked a better crew if I had selected them myself.

"Alright, Otis, Toad, and Tater are the winners of this fiasco. You three stay after Church, and we'll discuss details. Now, *rides*. Saturday's ride is *mandatory* just in case any of you forgot. We'll meet here at seven in the morning, and head out to Wichita at eight. First bike out is at nine. That'll give us plenty of time. After the ride, maybe we'll hit a few bars. Any *new business* need discussed?"

Otis looked around the room, and turned to face me, "I got one thing, Slice."

"Well, let's hear it," I grumbled.

Otis widened his eyes and began to speak, "*Pete's Ol' Lady* came in here the other day, and was turned away. He didn't say anything to *me*, but I've heard some shit talking floating around about how I treated her when I escorted her off the lot. Seems Pete ain't lookin' to take it up with me, so maybe a refresher of the bylaws are in order. What do ya think?"

After placing emphasis on *Pete's Ol' Lady*, Otis' voice quieted to a normal gravely tone. It was apparent he wanted to call Pete out in front of the fellas, but it wasn't necessary for *him* to do so. It was *my* job.

I scanned the room and crossed my arms in front of my chest as I made eye contact with Pete. Forty years old and an ex-con, Pete looked the part of a white supremacist. Tall and muscular, his head was clean shaven and littered with tattoos. Although his head was shaved, he had twelve inches of beard that hung from his chin, making him appear to be more at home on the yard in prison than in the free world. As our eyes locked, I clenched my jaw and flexed my biceps, "God damn, fellas. We've got the bylaws posted up here on the wall for a fucking reason. I know there ain't one of you motherfuckers able to *remember* them all, so I posted 'em up here for you to make reference to. Now Pete, you see the bylaws up on the wall?"

"Yep," he grunted.

"See the part at the very bottom of the board on the right marked *Ol' Ladies*?" I asked as I turned around to face the bylaws.

"Yeah," he mumbled.

"Read it to me if you will," I said.

"All of it, Slice?" he grumbled.

"All of it," I nodded as I turned to face him.

My position on Ol' Ladies wasn't shared by the rest of the club. I believed if the club wanted members to have Ol' Ladies, they'd have one sewn onto the front of their *cut* when they became patched in. In my opinion, Ol' Ladies were a pain in the ass and a risk to the welfare of club. I hadn't had an Ol' Lady since high school, and the chance of that ever changing was absolutely impossible. Every problem man has on this earth begins and ends with women.

Pete stared up at the bylaws and drew a slow breath. After a momentary study of the board, he pulled against his beard and began to read.

*"Ol' Ladies. One,* don't fuck around with another member's Ol' Lady. *Two,* Ol' Lady *Property Of* patches will be voted on by all eligible members of the club. One hundred percent vote or she doesn't wear it. *Sidenote*: as *Property Of* patches are *optional*, be sure before you touch some chick who isn't wearing a patch. *Three,* members are responsible for their Ol' Lady. *Four,* members may have more than one Ol ' Lady. *Five,* member must state who his Ol' Lady is. *Six,* no, your Ol' Lady isn't allowed in the meetings. *Seven,* club business is *club* business. Do not discuss club business with Ol' Ladies. *Eight,"* he paused and exhaled.

After inhaling a short breath, he ran his fingers though the twelve inches of scruffy beard dangling over his chest and read the last rule, *"Eight,* Ol' Ladies are allowed unescorted at the clubhouse only by prior arrangement by their Ol' Man. Arrangement can only be made by placing an "X" beside your name on the board. *No exceptions."*

"Damn fine job, Pete. Now, let me ask you something. You see your name on the membership board behind me?" I asked.

"Yep," Pete grunted.

I didn't bother to turn around and look. I knew we wouldn't be having this conversation if he had an "X" by his name.

"Is there an "X" by your name, Pete?" I asked sarcastically.

Seeming somewhat aggravated, Pete rubbed his bald head with the palms of his hands, "No, Slice, there sure as fuck ain't."

"So, was Otis out of line when he escorted your Ol' Lady off the premises?" I asked as I flexed my biceps again.

"Slice, it wasn't that he escorted her off, it was *how* he did it. He took her by the arm to the gate, and when she bitched, he told her to *get the fuck off the property* or he'd kick her ass," Pete complained.

I uncrossed my arms and raised my right hand to my chin, "Well, Pete. If you didn't put a fucking "X" by your name, Otis was of the opinion you didn't want your Ol' Lady in here. Otis' job is to protect the members of this here club, and protect us he damned sure does. Keepin' some nosy assed Ol' Lady out of this clubhouse is the Sergeant at Arm's fucking job, and Otis *is* the Sergeant at Arm's. If you don't want her here, Otis doesn't want her here. And, if Otis doesn't want her here, and she won't leave, I'd expect Otis to knock her fucking teeth out if he needed to; to protect the club and all. Now, let me have a look up on the board, and see if you want your Ol' Lady here."

I turned slowly toward the board behind me which listed all of the officers and full patched members. Pete's name, as he had stated, did not have an "X" beside it in the *Ol' Lady Allowed* column. I stared at the board and shrugged, "Nope, Pete. It says up on the board you don't want her in here."

I turned toward Otis and smiled, "Good lookin' out, Otis. Next time she gets mouthy, if Pete hasn't put an "X" on the board by his name, bust out a tooth or two. Maybe she'll get the hint."

I leaned over and placed my hands on the edge of the table, "Any *old business?*"

*Silence.*

"Otis, Tater, and Toad stick around. Other than that, *meeting adjourned*," I barked as I tapped the gavel on the sound block.

After the room cleared out, the four of us sat down at the table. The remaining members either went into the shop, hung around drinking beer in the parking lot, or rode off to who knows where. As the three members sat and stared at the walls, I interrupted the silence with the morbid truth about what we were facing.

"Alright, listen up. This fucker, from what I could gather, weighs about three-fifty. And this ain't some random assed guess, he actually weighs three fifty. So it ain't gonna be easy to toss this motherfucker around once he's dead. My problem is this. Frank said he had videos of this ChoMo son-of-a-bitch making those poor kids swallow his load. Hell, he was shootin' cum on their faces and videoing the shit," I paused and clenched my jaw.

"That motherfucker, I can take care of this on my own, Slice. Seriously, tell me where this motherfucker is," Otis growled.

"No, God damn it. I know you don't like this shit any more than I do, but that's what I'm trying to get at, Otis. This prick is a tub of shit, and we're gonna have to move his fat ass around after he's dead. The point I was gonna make is this," I paused and considered what I had planned.

"I want to torture this prick. I want him to know why we got him, and realize what a fucking nuisance he was before we kill his big fat ass. The only place I can think of where we can do it is where the highway south of town turns and goes up toward Wichita. You know, where Highway 77 meets K-15. There's a river west of 77, by the railroad tracks," I stopped speaking and turned to face Otis as he nodded his head.

"Where we go shooting?" Otis asked.

"You got it. Now, here's the deal. I want to make this fat piece of shit pay for what he did to these kids first then we'll get rid of his ass. But to haul him off, we're gonna have to cut him in pieces He's too God damned fat to move in one chunk. And, just to be safe, we'll need to cut the fat prick's head and hands off. If we get rid of his head and hands, they won't be able to prove who he is. I figure we'll bring 'em back to town and pour 'em into some concrete. We'll toss his head and hands in the Winfield Lake. That place ain't dried up in fifty years. And if we don't weigh 'em down, they'll eventually float. We can toss his body, arms, and legs to Stacey's hogs. They'll eat the bones and all," I stopped speaking and waited to see the reaction of the group.

"Why cut off his head and hands? Seems like we're takin' risks we don't need to take, Slice," Otis shrugged.

I realized chopping up a person made the crime of murder a little more personal, but it was an evil necessity. Eliminating the hands and teeth left little means of identifying a body, short of DNA. With no family, DNA matching would be difficult. Dental records and fingerprints were still the only methods of identifying a body, especially in a city Winfield's size.

"Well Otis, if we get rid of his fingerprints and teeth, they won't be able to identify this fat fucker. As much as I want to get rid of this prick, I ain't really lookin' to get caught, if you know what I mean. So, we cut off his head and hands, sneak 'em back here, and put 'em in a five gallon bucket. We fill the bucket with concrete, and it'll sink to the bottom of the lake. That'll end that."

"Yeah, makes sense. I wasn't following ya at first. Sounds good, Slice," Otis nodded.

To me, this was something I simply needed to take care of. I had no ill feelings about ridding the earth of a child molester. It didn't necessarily mean the other members would immediately sign on to cut a man into pieces and haul his body parts around the county to three or four respective places. Although I knew Otis wouldn't mind, I needed to see the reaction of the other men. As I gazed across the table toward Tater and Toad, I was pleased by their reaction.

"I got an old shitty old chain saw we can use to cut him up. We can toss it in the lake with his head and hands. And we can use my truck to haul his ass in," Tater nodded.

"What color is the truck?" I asked.

"Brown, why?" Tater responded.

"Well, I wasn't looking to try and sneak around in the dark if it was fucking white, Tater," I chuckled.

"Yeah, it's dark brown. It'd pass for black in the dark," he grinned.

Tater had been with the club five or so years, and was a man who had spent a lifetime riding a motorcycle. As a younger man, he had done two short bits in prison for robbery and arson. Never quite conforming to what society expected of him, he had spent his life feeling like an outcast. After losing his wife to cancer at forty-five years old, he decided the only family he needed was the brotherhood of the MC. He was as devoted to the club as any man would ever be to his family, and often volunteered to do things others wouldn't dream of.

Toad also had roughly five years with the club. The only thing that kept him from joining earlier was his commitment to the Marine Corps, and the completion of his final tour. He had been around for years as a *Hang Around*, and we all believed as soon as he completed his military commitments, he'd become a Prospect. Having spent almost a decade in Iraq and Afghanistan, he was not new to killing or death. A younger man of roughly thirty years old, he was quiet and mostly kept to himself until asked to participate. Once asked, he was always committed; probably much more than most. Toad was as good of a man as would ever grace this earth. As he sat with his chin slightly resting against his clenched fist and staring at the table, I began to become slightly concerned about what his thoughts might be.

"You good, Toad?" I asked.

He slowly looked up from the table and raised his hands to the head of closely cropped Marine hair he kept maintained in a military perfect manner, "When I joined the Marines I took an oath, Slice. *Against all enemies, foreign and domestic* and it didn't have an expiration date. So, killing this fat fucker?"

He stood from his chair and rubbed his hands against the thighs of his worn baggy jeans, "Little kids, Slice. The dude fucked with helpless little kids. He forced helpless seven year olds or however old they were to suck his dick while he made movies of it. Those kids? Yeah, they'll be fucked up for life. They didn't have a choice; this prick intervened with their path, he fucked with their life; he altered it. They say God works in mysterious ways? I suppose it all depends on how you w~ perceive it or whatever, but check this out; *God* didn't ͻ kids, the *devil* did. That fat prick is Lucifer h: to administer his justice. The judgment day i. finger into the top of the table.

41

As he stared into my eyes, he continued, "He'll pay for his fuckin' sins when we show up. I got paid by Uncle Sam himself to kill Hajis. You know, I never stopped any of 'em to ask 'em what they believed in or if they'd actually done anything wrong. I just shot 'em. This dude? I *know* what he did. So yeah, to answer your question, I'll be fine, but I'll say this…"

With his finger pounding into the top of the table as if he hoped to crush through it, Toad clenched his jaw and narrowed his eyes, "Killing him isn't punishment enough."

Toad lifted his hand from the table and shook his head. As he began to pace back and forth, I decided to end the meeting. There was no real value in continuing to hash out details. Toad seemed to be more than ready, and I had no doubts about the other two men.

"Well, no sense in spending all night going over this. Tater, make sure the lights and turn signals work on the truck. Brake lights, running lights, *everything*. Make sure all the belts and hoses are in good shape, and it's full of gas. I don't want to break down five miles south of town with three hundred pounds of *ChoMo* in the bed. I figure we'll go in the middle of the night, just bust into his place and Tase him. Then we'll just carry his fat ass out and load him up in Tater's truck. We'll go over the rest of the details tomorrow. Is everyone good with doing this tomorrow night?" I asked.

The three men nodded their heads.

"I'm sayin' it for the sake of sayin', but you know the rules. No colors in *cages,* so leave your cuts at home, fellas."

As Otis and Tater stood from their seats and walked toward Toad, I proud to call the three men my brothers. It wasn't common to find ho would volunteer to do such things, but in a *1%er* Motorcycle

Club it was basically second nature for the men to support the club at *any* cost. The brotherhood of the members was much more like having a family than having an *actual* family. It's always tough for an outsider to understand, but these fellas were my family, my life, and my brothers. They were all I had, and damned sure all I needed. I'd give my life to save any one of my brothers, and I know they'd do the same for me.

That's why an Outlaw Motorcycle Club doesn't let men walk in, sign a sheet of paper, and join. The Prospect initiation period separates the men from the boys, and requires a one hundred percent vote. If the entire club doesn't agree the Prospect is an acceptable member, he's turned away. My life is in the hands of my brothers, and theirs is in mine.

I wouldn't have it any other way.

As the three men spoke amongst themselves and filtered toward the door, I looked up at the membership board. Beside Pete's name, a big black "X" was plastered under the *Ol' Lady Allowed* slot. I smiled to myself, knowing my name would *never* have an "X" beside it, to do so would be to admit I was weak and incapable of surviving on my own. I damned sure didn't nor would I ever need a woman to help me get through life. To me, being in a relationship with a woman was similar to having a rattlesnake for a pet. At first it may be entertaining and something cool to show off to your friends, but in the end you realize the danger associated with ownership. Eventually you must get rid of it, because if you play the odds, sooner or later you'll be bit.

I flipped the light switch and pulled the door closed. Tomorrow night would be here soon enough, and I still needed to decide exactly what it was I wanted to do with this fat prick.

As I sauntered toward my bike, I chuckled at the thought of going home and watching *American Psycho* or a few episodes of *Dexter* to get ideas. I flipped the ignition on and pushed the start button and the V-Twin spun into a mellow roar. As the bike warmed up, I decided I didn't need Cable T.V. shows or a movie to give me ideas. It was an eighty degree spring night, a nice relaxing ride home should clear my mind.

And, as I've always said, *if you free the mind, your ass will follow.*

Worrying about the welfare of their children was the last thing I wanted a parent to be concerned about. Not under the watch of the *Selected Sinners*. Not where *my* club was present. The children are our future, and protecting them from harm was something I felt obligated to do. A parent shouldn't have to worry about their kid being safe from harm in small town USA, hell in any town for that matter. I had all the desire I needed to help make our city a safer place for the children to play, and I intended to do so. Ridding this town of a child molester wouldn't require a *plan*; it would be fueled by passion.

If I was nothing else, I was a passionate man about what it was I believed in.

# AVERY

"Did you try any of these while we were in there?" Sloan asked as she shifted her body so she was standing sideways in front of the mirror.

She turned her head and glanced at the reflection of her perfectly curvaceous body. Her small waist, flat stomach, round butt, and overly large boobs made her look like a big black haired Barbie doll. I, on the other hand, looked like a boy with a nice ass and a pretty face.

"No, they're stupid. *Skinny sweats*. What the fuck is a *skinny* sweat?" I laughed.

"Does my ass look fat in them?" she asked as she twisted her body back and forth.

"In *those*? Your ass looks like *your ass*. It's like you painted it grey and put some little black speckeldy shit in the paint," I sighed as I sat up on the bed.

"Does it look *fat*?" she asked as she slapped her hand against it and raised one eyebrow.

I stared at her ass as she looked at herself in the mirror. I wanted to look more like her. Her body was bangin' ass hot. I glanced up at her face. Well, I'd take *some* parts of her body, but not those ratty assed eyebrows. She really needed to do something with those things. They looked like caterpillars.

"Sloan, you're not fat. But those sweats look like shit. They're too tight. You know how I like my sweats, I like 'em loose, it makes me *feel* skinny. I can't believe Victoria's Secret is selling shit like that," I shook my head at the sight of the sweats glued to her skin like *tights*.

She turned to face me, pressed her hands to her hips, and scowled, "So my ass looks fat in them?"

"Your ass isn't fat. *Ever.* It looks like you're naked. And grey. But if it'll make you take those nasty fuckers off, yeah, your ass looks fat," I chuckled.

"What about this bra? Does it *really* lift my boobs? Do they *look* big? Is it worth $60.00?" she asked as she pressed her arms against the sides of her boobs.

"*Look* big?" I shook my head and coughed as I began to laugh.

I was a little more than cheated while standing in line for boobs, but Sloan looked like she got whatever they failed to give me and a little more *just because.* She was not big or even *thick* as the guys liked to call girls. She was just tall. Tall with very large boobs and a nice round butt I secretly wished *I* had. Well, maybe not *all* of her butt, but half of it. If there was one area she had a *little* extra, it would be the perfectly rounded butt of hers.

"Well?" she asked as she continued to squeeze her boobs together with her upper arms.

*God I wish I had boobs like those.*

As they burst out the top of her new *Bombshell Add 2 Cups* bra, I couldn't help myself, "You know, you really didn't need to add two cup sizes, Sloan, I mean *seriously.* Your boobs were huge already. Now they're *ridiculous.* Are you seriously going to wear that thing?"

She turned her head my direction and gave me the stink eye, "Yeah, I was going to wear it Saturday night."

*Perfect.*

I sat up in the bed and tossed my legs over the side, "Perfect, another night of me waiting in the car while you bang some dude in the parking lot."

"I don't bang dudes in the parking lot. I wish you'd quit freaking saying that," she said as she twisted her hips in front of the mirror.

"Well, *whatever*. Come on, get dressed. Let's go out and do something," I sighed.

"What do you want to do?" she asked as she lowered her arms and released her boobs.

Sloan and I, although best friends, differed in our desires for leisure activities. When we were out of school or off work, she liked to do nothing. I, on the other hand, preferred to stay busy doing *anything*. Anything but *nothing*. Winfield wasn't much of a town, but there was always *something* we could do.

"Well, it's not *that* late, let's go to Hot Shotz," I shrugged.

"That bar is stupid. You know I hate going there. It's Wednesday, we should just hang out, we've got school tomorrow," she complained.

The thought of staying home wasn't very appealing. It was five o'clock and early spring. The weather was a gorgeous 75 degrees, and I didn't want to be confined in my 600 square foot apartment any more than I had to be. When I stayed home, I felt as if I was invisible. Other than Sloan, there was really no form of human contact for me. In the last year, since I expressed my intent of staying in Kansas and moving to Wichita, my parents had all but stopped talking to me.

My mother was nothing short of impossible at times. It was as if she felt a useful means of punishment was telling me she was disappointed in me. As a young girl, her disappointments caused me to strive to improve. After a lifetime of her expressed disappointments, I learned she would always be disappointed in me. Or at least she *indicated* she was, whether it was true or not I would never know. No differently than *the boy who cried wolf*, her complaints began to have less and less validity each time I heard them. I learned to roll my eyes each time she sent me a text message stating she was disappointed.

I often wondered if her continued expression of disappointment was what provoked me to be as competitive as I was. If possibly it caused me to be the way I was about men. In recent years, I had begun to believe my mother's hatred toward every decision I made which didn't include coming back to Ohio and being an active participant in *her* Baptist church formed me into the challenge seeking woman I had become.

My major in Criminal Justice was another thing she seemed to always take exception to. When I chose the career path, she said maybe I would *grow up* and change my mind. For my first year in college, she often asked what credits were transferrable to other majors. The same eye roll and *I don't know mother* followed each time. Now almost complete with my major, she took time to tell me each time we spoke that she was disappointed in my choice, and asked what I expected to do for a career.

I really had no idea what I wanted to do for a career, but my original belief of being a law enforcement officer soon vanished. After a few years of studies, I realized I wasn't as interested in the law enforcement side of things as I was the criminal or the criminal activity. Criminals fascinated me. Attempting to figure out the intricacies of their thoughts and how or why they did the things they did was beyond any other form of entertainment I could find.

I walked behind Sloan and looked into the mirror, "Let's go to the park and just relax before it gets dark. We can get some sun."

"*Bum* park? Yeah, you don't want sun. You'll want to talk to the bums hanging out there. I think that's gross the way you're always asking them questions. They're gross. No, not interested," she hissed.

"They're fun to talk to, I feel sorry for them," I responded.

She turned to face me and wrinkled her nose, "They're gross. One day one of them is going to knock you down and rob you or something. I swear, the way you talk to those people, it's nasty."

"She twisted sideways and stared into the mirror as she raised her hand to her stomach, "Let's go eat pizza."

"Sounds good. It's better than sitting here."

"I'm going to wear this and see if anyone notices," Sloan said as she reached down to pick up her flats.

I rolled my eyes at the thought of her boobs being bigger than normal. As I glanced in the mirror at my B-cup, I silently wondered if my lack of boobs was one of the reasons I wasn't more successful at picking up Mr. Nelson.

"You ready?' she asked.

*No, I need a boob job.*

I glanced in her direction and turned to face the mirror. After inhaling a deep breath and exhaling a very audible sigh, I responded.

"I guess I'm as ready as I'll ever be."

# AXTON

I've had a few occasions in my life where I ended up in a situation I wasn't sure I would ever get myself out of. I've had yet other situations where I participated in something willfully I later wished I had the common sense to walk away from. Sometimes *promising* to do something and *actually* doing it when the time came were two very different things altogether. But, as any good man would agree, if I gave my word on something, you could count on me to follow through. Committing to place myself in a situation that later turned out to be a terrible idea made me feel as if sometimes I was all too eager to volunteer in the first place. *Carefully* selecting the events I wanted to participate in seemed to be at least a little more common now that I had a few years under my belt. As an *old timer* in the club, my participation in criminal acts was carefully chosen, and this *particular* event was proving to provide me great satisfaction.

"What did I do? I don't understand what's going on," the fat fucker blubbered.

"You sick piece of shit. Shut the fuck up. Say one more God damned word, and I'll cut off your fucking cock and feed it to you," Toad shouted as he wedged himself between us.

Duct taped to the tree and exhausted from being Tased repeatedly during the ten mile trip to the river, the fat child molester cried and blubbered, but he didn't speak. A second meeting with Frank provided

51

me enough information to allow me to assure myself what we were doing was all for the right reasons.

I stepped between Toad and the molester, "Listen up. I'm going to ask you a question, and you're going to answer me. You need to think really hard before you lie to me, tell me you don't know what I'm talking about, or deny any involvement whatsoever. If you do any of those things, this is going to get really bloody really quick. If you understand me, a simple yes or no will be fucking fine. Do you understand me?"

He continued to cry and slobber, and finally blubbered an almost inaudible *yes.*

It was all I could do to make eye contact with him. The more I looked at him, the more I wanted to just get this over with and just kill him. But, I needed him to admit it first. I got about two feet from him and stared into his eyes. Tears ran down his face as I inhaled a slow breath.

"Alright. I need you to tell me the name of the little boy you molested who had bright red hair. It was pretty recent. All I need is the first name."

"Why, was he related or something?" he cried.

"I'm…"

"I'm sorry…"

I pulled my knife, flicked it open, and shoved it into his stomach as far as I could. As I pulled it out, his eyes widened and he began to scream. I'd seen enough of my fat biker buddies stabbed that I knew a fat fucker like him wouldn't see any *real* damage from a 3" deep puncture wound to his stomach. It was more to let him know I didn't want to have a conversation with his fat ass. I simply wanted a name.

"I told you. I want a name, you fat bastard. The red-headed kid. What was his name? The next one will be in your eye," I growled as I raised the knife to his face.

"Stick his fat ass again," Toad hollered.

I raised my hand in the air, "Let him speak, Toad. Now, tell me the name."

"Timmy, his name was," he inhaled and attempted to look down at his bleeding stomach.

"Timmy."

After some thought, I decided I needed a little more information from Frank, and he provided enough for me to confirm the man we were going to kill was who they believed him to be. Timothy was the name Frank reluctantly provided me. The ChoMo providing me confirmation was all I needed to hear. As much as I wanted to make him pay for his crimes, killing him would end my suffering of looking at him. The more I thought about what he had done to the little boys, the more I wanted to rid the earth of his existence.

"It's him, ain't it Slice? Fat fucker's the one, ain't he?" Toad asked as he stepped between us.

"I didn't ..." fatty began.

"Shut the fuck up, or I'll stick you again," I bellowed.

I wiped my knife on the fat man's pants and folded it. I swallowed hard and nodded my head, "Yep, it's him."

"Let me do him, Slice. I need my patch. Come on. Killin' this fat whale ain't shit. Let me do it," Toad begged.

"But..." fatty blubbered.

I flicked my knife open and stared at the fat bastard. As he began to cry and spit, I closed my eyes and shook my head, "Hand me the tape, Otis."

Otis handed me the roll of duct tape we had used to secure him to the tree. I ripped off a twelve inch strip and pressed it over his mouth and stretched it to the sides of his fat face. After three more strips, he was muffled and as quiet as he was going to get.

A skull and crossbones patch on the lower right hand side of a member's cut indicated he had killed for the club. Otis and I had patches to confirm our participation in such situations. Tater didn't, and at his age, asking him to do something like kill a man wasn't necessarily a good thing. I turned toward Otis and Tater. Otis shrugged as Tater quietly stood holding the lantern.

Otis swallowed hard and raised his hands to his face, "Let him get his patch, Slice. Hell, killin' fuckers is all he's done for the last ten years. But I'm done looking at this fucker, really."

Otis rubbed his temples with the palms of his hands. He was as ready for this to end as I was. I turned toward Toad and nodded my head. As I folded my knife closed, Toad pulled a long straight bladed knife from a sheath on his belt.

"God damn, Toad," I said through my teeth as he raised the large blade in front of his chest.

"Gunshot would be too risky out here in the dark. Someone might hear it," he nodded.

As the fat man began to cry and grunt through the tape, Toad stepped between the blubbering molester and me.

"Shut the fuck up and listen to me," Toad demanded.

The fat prick attempted to stop crying. Between the molester's sobbing and blowing snot out his nose, Toad spoke clearly and as if he'd actually prepared a speech for the occasion.

"Now listen. This world is full of all types of men. Good ones, not so good ones, and bad ones. I believe, and I may be wrong, that I'm one of the good ones. I ain't never hurt a man without having a damned good reason. Never. I killed some fuckers in the war, and I'd do it all over if they'd let me. So, my opinion's this, and you ain't gonna agree for damned sure, but I'll tell you anyway," Toad paused and calmly glanced at each of us before turning to face the fat man again.

"God controls the good on this earth, and Satan controls the bad. In men, sometimes there's a fight between God and the Devil to see who gets control. Sometimes good men do bad things. And sometimes bad men do good things. But what you did? That's not Satan stepping into a man's life and causing him to do something wrong. No sir, it's not. You can't be fixed. That's my justification for what I plan to do to you. *You can't be healed.* I Googled the shit, and I *know.* You're four times more likely to hurt a kid again than any other criminal is to recommit any other crime. So, what I'm gonna do to you, it'll make sure you don't do what you did to those little boys to anyone else. And I'm gonna guess if I gave Timmy's mom this knife, she'd do a lot more to you than I'm goin' to."

Toad reached down, grabbed the man's hand in his, and as he held it, sliced his wrist. After releasing his hand, he sliced the man's other wrist the same way. After dropping his hand, he reached between the man's legs with the knife. With a deep grunt and a tug of the blade, he sliced through the man's pants and deeply into each of his thighs. Quickly, his pant legs began to discolor from the blood he lost.

"Damn, Toad. I thought you'd cut his throat," Otis said under his breath.

"Read it on the internet. The article said it'd take up to thirty minutes from cuttin' the wrists alone. Said maybe he'd last 5 minutes if I cut the femoral in the thighs. I've seen Marines die from having a femoral artery cut, even with a tourniquet. Thought this would give him a few minutes to think about what he'd done," Toad said as he leaned over and wiped the blade on the man's shirt.

Toad was right. If a parent had seen the videos the man had taken while he abused their children, and later been handed the knife, the killing would have been far more brutal. As difficult as it was to allow myself to believe what I watched was real, it was not something I would ever wish a parent to participate in.

Without speaking, we stood and watched the man slowly die. I'd seen several stabbings, and been involved in several shootings where men had died. I had never, however, calmly stood and watched a man die. I'm thoroughly convinced each time I see a man die it takes a little piece of my own soul, bringing me that much closer to death. It must be the price we are required to pay for witnessing the final deterioration of one of God's greatest creations; mankind.

As I crossed my arms and blankly stared until he finally went completely limp, I thought of all the children and what he'd done to them. I silently wondered if God was watching as we kidnapped the man, or as Toad cut him. And, as the man bled until his last breath escaped him, I wondered if God witnessed the entire event; and if so, why he didn't intervene.

As he peacefully drew his last shallow breath, I came to a conclusion. God *did* witness it. And he, not unlike me, had no place in his heart for a man who sexually molested helpless children.

And, God was using the *Selected Sinners* to do what he wasn't able to do.

Because God is forgiving.

And the *Sinners* are not.

# AVERY

Saturday nights at the bar were a pain in the ass. Although I made more in tips during the night than I made the entire rest of the work week combined, at the time I'm working the shift, I always felt like I wanted to quit my job and become a librarian. Today had been a little more busy than usual. A local poker run ended, and bikers filtered in and out all afternoon starting about four o'clock. As Sloan and her *2 added cups* worked the dining area, I tried to keep everyone happy from behind the bar.

"I'll take another Budweiser," the man at the end of the bar said as he raised his hand.

I reached into the cooler and pulled out a bottle of Bud. I grabbed my opener, popped off the lid, and held it in my hand as I handed him the bottle. After he grinned and accepted the beer, I turned toward the trash can, which was roughly fifteen feet away, and tossed the lid in the air. As the lid hit the back side of the can and fell inside, I pumped my fist in victory.

"Nice shot," Budweiser bottle said from behind me.

"I know, right?" I said over my shoulder.

I grabbed my bar rag and began to wipe the bar as I scanned the dining area for Sloan. She stood talking to a table of three college aged guys who were all focused on her tits as she spoke. One of them had ears the size of the palm of my hand. I rolled my eyes and grinned at the three

57

guys as they slobbered on themselves.

*Add the Bud to his tab, Avery.*

I shook my head and turned to the register. As I added the Budweiser bottle to the man at the end of the bar's tab, I wondered how many drinks I forgot over the course of a busy night. I'd like to think I remembered them all, but it seemed I always wondered how many I just might forget, totally. It wasn't my liquor, and it wasn't any money out of my pocket, but I wanted to do my job and do it well. Still staring at the register in deep thought, Sloan's heavy whispering brought me back to reality.

"Did you see the three guys sitting at number eight?"

I turned around and faced Sloan, who was leaning over between two men who were sitting at the bar. Her boobs were smashed all over the place.

"Yeah, I saw 'em. I'm gonna guess they didn't see you, though," I chuckled as I stepped toward the bar.

She was bent over completely, now resting her chin on the bar. Although I couldn't see them, I was sure her boobs were spread all over the bar. Surprised the men on either side of her weren't staring at the sides of her tits, I rolled my eyes and leaned closer to her.

She glanced over her shoulder toward the high top where they were seated. After a long pause of filling her eyes with their disgusting stares, she turned my direction, "Huh? What are you talking about? I talked to them for like ten minutes. The one with the blue tee shirt is hot."

"No, actually he's not. He looks like he's getting ready to fly somewhere with those huge assed ears. And when I looked over there, *you* were talking and *they* were staring at your tits; all three of them," I said quietly.

"Whatever. I like this shirt though," she said as she stood up.

She was wearing a *Southwestern College* tee shirt, and she had cut a slice in the front of it about ten inches long; from the center of the neck opening to the center of her boobs. Her new bra was working overtime to shove her boobs out the top of the oversized opening she had created.

"Yeah, looks great. Looks like your new BF liked it too," I said as I tossed my head toward the big eared weirdo.

After a single finger salute, she rolled her eyes, and turned away. I loved Sloan, but I envied her a little nonetheless. And, within all of the envy, I despised her at times. She was all too eager to allow a guy to hit on her, pick her up, use her, and break another small piece of her heart. She acted like it was all a part of her plan each time a guy used her, but I knew better. No one wants to feel as if they're being used, and Sloan was no exception. Her frequent excuse of *I just wanted some dick, I got what I wanted* was sheer bullshit.

As she walked into the dining area and made her rounds, I stared at her butt and wished it was mine. I turned toward the register and checked to make sure I added the Budweiser before Sloan walked up. As I swiped the screens and got to his tab, I smiled at the fact I had added it. Maybe I never forgot anything. Hell, who knows.

"So, you ever date the customers?" a voice from behind me asked.

I turned around to face Heineken bottle. I smiled as I pushed the bar rag into the corner of my jeans pocket.

"No, I'm taken. And I'm gay. She's my girlfriend," I nodded into the open dining area.

"The girl with the, uhhm," he turned and looked over his shoulder.

"The uhhm black hair?" he said as he turned around.

"Yeah, the black hair and the huge tits. We're lesbians," I smiled.

"That's hot," he said under his breath.

59

"Uh yeah, not so much really. She's got herpes, she's dyslexic, and she's a fucking vegan. Her huge tits make for some interesting times, but we're always eating really weird shit, she never pronounces my name right, and can't balance a checkbook for shit," I sighed.

"Oh fuck, seriously?" he gasped.

I scrunched my nose, looked down at him, and whispered, "Yeah, and we're roommates. I remember once the checkbook said we had $2,102.00. I went shopping. They denied my card after the second pair of jeans. Ends up we had a $122.00. It's kind of a pain in the ass sometimes."

"Oh, yeah. I meant the herpes, that sucks," he whispered.

I shrugged, "Not so much. Hell now that I've got 'em too, at least I don't have to worry about catching it anymore. But the itching is a motherfucker."

I bent down slightly and started rubbing my inner thigh with my left hand as I waited for him to respond.

He looked like he was going to barf. As he pushed himself away from the bar, I smiled and pulled my hand from between my thighs.

"I was joking. She doesn't have herpes," I smiled.

"She don't?" he said as he leaned toward the bar.

"Nope," I responded as I shook my head lightly.

"Dyslexic vegan?" he asked.

I shook my head, "Nope. Actually she's a stripper. She dances at Jezebel's on Sunday nights. You should go see her tomorrow. Her stage name is The Portuguese Princess."

"She's Portuguese?" he asked.

"Yeah, half," I nodded.

As much as I tried to hold it together, I began to laugh. He sat and stared at me as if my head was on fire. Giggling at the thought of Sloan stripping, and the guys tossing dollar bills at her, I attempted to stop and apologize for bullshitting him. At least he was a pretty good sport about listening to it all. As I started to tell him I was joking about *everything*, I heard a thunderous roar from the parking lot, and it seemed as if the walls were vibrating. At the same time as everyone else in the bar, I turned to face the door.

Immediately after the noise and vibration stopped, I turned toward Heineken bottle and blinked my eyes, "What the fuck was that, a tornado?"

He raised his eyebrows slightly, "Sounded like a bunch of bikes; a whole hell of a lot of 'em."

As I noticed the front door open out of my peripheral vision, I turned toward the end of the bar. A guy who appeared to be no less than seven feet tall stood in the opening. Tanned from what I suspected was a lifetime of riding, he stood in the opening and quickly scanned the bar. As he turned and looked over his shoulder, I swallowed heavily at the sight of what appeared to be the three dozen bikes in the parking lot. Something about seeing that many bikes and bikers together was oddly exciting.

The panty scorching kind of exciting.

*Bikers are fucking hot.*

"There ain't anywhere to sit, but there's plenty of places to stand," he shouted into the parking lot.

"I'll take my check," Heineken bottle sighed.

"Ditto," the guy beside him said.

"Yeah, time to get," Budweiser bottle whispered as he tossed a bill onto the bar.

My eyes widened as the men started walking into the bar. They kept coming, and kept coming, and kept coming. All of them were wearing biker vests with patches all over them. Some had patches on the front the others didn't. The backs of the vests all had the same logo; *Selected Sinners* on the top, *Kansas* on the bottom, with a skull and two crossed guns in the middle. The bar was beginning to look like a scene from a movie. One where the bikers walk in and everyone else stands up and leaves.

As the huge biker stood beside the door with his arms crossed, another man walked in and stepped beside him. He was tall, but not as tall as the giant. There was a certain presence about him as he stood and talked, as if he was the one everyone should be paying attention to. He had a few days growth of beard, and short wavy hair with slight specks of grey. Under his vest was a black sleeveless tee shirt with some writing on the front of it which was mostly obstructed by his vest. As he turned and quietly talked to the taller man, I squinted and walked to the end of the bar closest to them. Although a steady stream of bikers continued to stroll into the bar, I couldn't shift my focus from the shorter man who was doing the talking. Now standing amongst a sea of other bikers, I had to get a closer look at him. Something about him commanded my attention.

*Everything* about him commanded my attention.

The muscles on his biceps flared as he raised his left hand to his face and spoke to the tall man. With his head turned and his mouth partially covered by his cupped hand, I looked down at his boots, and slowly up his body until I focused on his leather vest. He was the type of man a girl fantasized about but was afraid to ever admit it to anyone. A small black rectangular patch with red embroidery was over the chest of his vest. I narrowed my gaze and stared. When I finally reached the end of the bar, the writing on it was clear.

President.

Well, *Mr. President*, you're hot as fuck.

*This could be one wild assed night.*

# AXTON

Although being in a bar was part of being a biker, it wasn't one of the things sitting high on my priority list. Being raised at the hand of an alcoholic father and never knowing my mother, I formed an opinion about alcohol early in life. I've heard the children of alcoholics grow up with either an affinity for alcoholic beverages or a hatred for them. As an adult, I was clearly on the side of hatred.

I stood beside Otis and studied the bar, the customers, and the staff. Without much thought, I reached down and snapped the rubber band against my wrist. I pulled it tight, released it again for good measure, and turned to Otis. As we spoke, I noticed the bartender staring in our direction.

*You must be the firecracker.*

"Well, looks like they were right. Nice little joint. And Jesus H. Christ, the tall chick has the biggest titties I've seen in a bit," I said through my teeth.

"How many of 'em you think will actually show up, Axton?" Otis asked.

After the poker run, a local group of riders had expressed interest in our club. They explained about a small local bar with great service, a good atmosphere, and as far as they were concerned, the joint was biker friendly. To top it off, the men described the two typical weekend waitresses as *a tall thin firecracker* and her even taller friend with *tits the size of basketballs.*

The description of the women, in itself, was enough to gain the interest of everyone within earshot; and we voted to try the place out. Contrary to television shows and modern myth, 1%er motorcycle clubs don't walk into a bar and start fighting the patrons and raping the women. The Selected Sinners, at least on my watch, made every effort to conduct themselves in a manner which would *generally* be perceived as respectful and within the limit of *most* laws. We were, however, a group of outlaw bikers; and when alcohol was added things generally got very interesting real quick.

"Hard sayin'. Don't suppose it matters, does it? Guys seemed to me to be a couple of wannabes. Hell, we needed to go somewhere anyway," I paused and looked around the bar.

I cupped my hand and raised it to my face, "It looks like the place is going to clear out anyway. Imagine that."

"Barmaid is coming to the end of the bar, Axe. Little bitch is burnin' holes through your cut. She must be the firecracker, huh?" Otis said as he nodded toward the bar.

"Being the other girl over there has tits the size of Pete's head, I'd guess she's the firecracker, yeah. I'll order the first round," I chuckled as I nodded toward the tall thin bartender.

Her face was thin like a long distance runner who had spent a lifetime eating raw vegetables and tofu sandwiches. Her features were chiseled and she was an attractive young woman. Her hair was a little longer than shoulder length and light brown; about the color of a glass of tea. She sure wasn't too scared to stare, that was for God damned sure. As she stood with her eyes fixed in my direction, I began to walk toward her. As I approached, she leaned onto the edge of the bar, looked up, and smiled.

"I'm Avery. The other girl is Sloan. I only have one rule, no fighting in my bar. What can I get you?" she said without taking a breath or blinking an eye.

"Avery, huh? Damn the luck, we were just getting ready to start an all-out biker brawl. I'll notify my Sergeant at Arm's to try and keep the fellas limited to some light pushing and shoving, maybe a little grab-ass, how's that?" I said jokingly as I tilted my head in Otis' direction.

For a young girl she wasn't easily rattled. As she rested her elbows on the bar and her chin in her hands, she stared into my eyes and waited for what I guessed was my drink order. I smiled lightly, inhaled a short breath and arched my back. As I exhaled, I leaned closer to her and began to speak.

"I'm Axton. For drinks, I'd say to start, I'll just keep it simple. The fellas will start ordering their own here pretty quick, just put it all on one tab. I'll pay it when we're done. So, why don't you get me about thirty-five Budweiser's? That'll leave a couple extras, but some of these fellas are likely to drink theirs in one gulp. It's been a long hot day."

"Thirty-five, huh? Alright. I'll get on that. As far as the fighting goes, we clear?" she asked without expression.

As I stood and thought of something smart-assed to say in response, she raised one eyebrow. Something about a girl who was respectful but not afraid to stand her ground was appealing. *Different.* As much as I tried not to, I smiled slightly as I nodded my head.

"You made yourself clear, yeah. I can't make any promises, but I'll say this. The men are all respectful, as long as they're treated with respect. They won't fight each other, that's for damned sure. So, as long as the few people left in here treat 'em with respect, you'll be pleasantly surprised. If someone says somethin' slick or decides they want to try their luck at fighting one of 'em, I'll say there's not much I can do to stop it. The big man behind me is Otis. It's his job to keep everyone in order. So, if you need anything, don't be afraid to holler at Otis. Now how about those beers?" I slowly raised my eyebrow to match the one she still hadn't lowered.

She lowered her eyebrow and grinned, "Let me get started on those beers, Axton. Hold on for just a second, I've got two questions."

She turned toward the other side of the bar, walked out the end of it, and disappeared around the corner. As I stood and waited for her to return, I wondered what it was about her that made me want to stay. Typically, I'd tell any other waitress or barmaid to go fuck herself. Something about this one was different. Maybe it was the fact that she appeared to have not one ounce of fear in her. I turned toward Otis, shrugged, and winked. As the men all found places to either stand or sit, she returned to behind the bar with a case of beer. A thin kid followed directly behind her and placed another case on the bar. As he turned and walked away, she dropped the case of beer on the bar between us.

"I'll open all of these and just leave 'em here on the bar in the box, it'll keep 'em colder. How's that sound?" she asked as she opened the cardboard box.

"Sounds good," I nodded.

As she pulled an opener from her rear pocket and began popping the lids from the bottles, she looked up and smiled. Without shifting her focus to the bottles, she opened them as she studied me.

"So, the two questions, you ready?" she asked as she continued to open the bottles effortlessly.

Without thinking, I nodded my head, "Yep."

"First question. It says *Slice* on your vest. Is that your name?" she asked.

"Nope. Name's Axton, next question."

She bit her lower lip, stopped opening bottles and stared.

"I want to be on the back of your bike before the summer is over. What are the chances of that?" she asked.

*God damn, this girl's got guts.*

*They were right, she is a little firecracker.*

As she bit her lower lip again and waited for an answer, I gave my response. As I heard myself speak, I realized what I was saying and what I was thinking were in clear contrast of each other. Something about this girl was getting to me, and I didn't like it at all.

"Well, I'd say your chances are two-fold," I paused and stood up straight.

"Pretty God damned slim…"

"And *not at all*," I nodded.

Strangely, I stood and waited for her to respond. What little I'd seen of her I suspected she'd have something smart-assed to say; something immediate, but well thought out. She talked about as fast as Otis swung his fists, which was quicker than most human minds had the ability to comprehend.

She didn't disappoint me.

"Well, I'll take the *pretty God damned slim* option for five hundred, Axton," she paused and began to open the remaining bottles in the case.

"There's something about you…I'm going to guess you haven't got much use for a woman, other than letting her suck your cock or give you a little pussy whenever you want it. You probably don't trust 'em, don't like 'em, or maybe a little of both. I want on the back of that bike of yours. And although I may suck your cock or give you a little pussy, I won't do it until after that ride's over. Think about that. Guess that's all I've got to say; for now anyway. Here's your first twenty-four Bud's," she said as she shoved the case of beer across the bar.

*You're a gutsy little bitch, aren't ya?*

"I'll do that," I nodded.

I turned and slowly walked toward Otis, attempting unsuccessfully to hide the grin on my face. As I stepped in front of him, I literally tried to wipe the smile from my face with the back of my hand.

"God damn, boss. What was all that about?" he asked as he nodded his head toward the bar.

"She's a talkative little bitch," I responded as I gazed her direction.

I watched as she stood there and stared our direction as she opened the remaining beers. I shifted my gaze to the open bar, which was now close to empty; short of *Sinners.* I took a deep breath, held it, and turned to face Otis. After I exhaled, I tilted my head Otis' direction and spoke sternly as I focused on Avery.

"Bartender's off limits. Spread the word to all the fellas. I don't give a shit about the girl with the tits, but the skinny bitch is hands-off."

After a short pause with no response, I turned and looked at Otis, "We clear?"

"Crystal, Slice," he chuckled, "I'll let 'em know."

"One more thing," I breathed.

Otis turned toward me and raised one eyebrow comically.

"Get two of the fellas to get in a fight," I chuckled.

Otis shifted his stance and faced me directly, "Get in a fight?"

I nodded my head, "Yep. I want to see how she reacts. She said her one rule was no fighting in *her* bar. Hell, get Toad and Hollywood to fight. Or Toad and Pete. Shit, Toad'll fight *anyone.* But get two of 'em to fight, and tell 'em to be prepared to stop as soon as you tell 'em to. I'm going to the pisser," I nodded.

Otis shook his head, chuckled, and grinned, "You got it, Slice. One fight, comin' right up."

As I slowly walked toward the bathroom, I smiled to myself.

*Well, I guess we'll see how little Miss. Avery handles herself when things go to shit.*

# AVERY

Axton, after having stepped close enough for me to actually look at him, was as handsome of a man as I had ever seen. He was attractive in an *although I don't know you, I'd let you pin me against the wall, get a fist full of my hair and fuck me* kind of way, not a pretty man with a two hundred dollar haircut and clothes that looked like he was trying just a little too hard. His good looks set aside, who he *appeared* to be made him even more appealing. The outlaw biker garb he was wearing added to his good looks. His jeans were far from new, but not trashy looking. His boots were worn, but not old and shitty. The leather vest over what was left of his tee shirt fit as good as I supposed a leather vest could, but it added to his *don't fuck with me* demeanor, which was a large part of what made him so damned attractive.

At least to me.

One thing I really liked about talking to him was how his mouth curled up into a shitty little smile. More of a smirk really, but it would be my guess it was about as much of a smile as a person could coax from him. Hell, he probably didn't even know he was doing it.

As the various bikers walked up and took bottles from the two cases of beers I had opened, most nodded their heads or said hello in some fashion, but none stood at the bar or spoke to me. Two customers remained at the bar, but not for much longer; they were in the process of paying their bills so they could leave. The two groups who sat at the high tops, as well as the two more sitting in booths looked like they were in for the long haul. I quickly looked around the bar, did the math, and realized there were just about enough spots for all of the bikers to sit, but almost none of them were, at least not at the bar. As the two men who remained at the bar left their payment for their tabs at the same time, I collected their money and walked to the register in hopes their absence would cause the bikers to feel more comfortable about sitting at the bar.

As I closed the register, I noticed Axton leaning on the end of the bar. As I studied him out of the corner of my eye, I quickly remembered I had no tits whatsoever, and probably no chance of ever convincing him to take me for that ride. Bikers love big tits. Hell, everybody loves big tits. I glanced into the dining area and couldn't help but notice half a dozen bikers gathered around Sloan. I crossed my arms over my chest and slowly walked toward Axton. As I got closer to where he stood, he clasped his hands together and leaned into the edge of the bar. I attempted to form my sparse, skinny lips into a duck face and gave up right about the time I was directly in front of him.

'What was with the face?" he asked as I pulled the bar towel out of my pocket.

"What face?" I asked, half embarrassed that he'd noticed.

"Whatever you were doing with your lips while you were walking up," he grinned.

I shrugged and began wiping the bar.

*Jesus, Avery, you probably looked like an idiot. Stick to the overly aggressive 'I wanna fuck you' attitude.*

"Huh. Looked like you were kissing the air," he chuckled.

I continued to wipe the bar where the two men were sitting. As I swirled the bar towel in a circular motion, I attempted to change the subject without looking up.

"Define slim," I said.

"Excuse me?"

I looked up from wiping the bar, "You said *pretty God damned slim* and *not at all* were my two options. I said I'd take the *pretty God damned slim* option. I want you to define it. What's slim?"

He stood up slightly, "You ever give up?"

I pursed my lips and twisted my mouth to the side, "No, not really."

He pressed his forearms into the edge of the bar and leaned forward, "Huh. Well, my pop was a drunken prick but I never figured it was much of an excuse for my mother to walk out like she did. That was my first exposure to a woman. Second would have been the girl I was seeing all through high school. I was a year ahead of her, so after I graduated she was a senior. Well, I stopped by her house to see her one afternoon. Back then although most everyone else did, I didn't have a cell phone, so I didn't call first. Hell I didn't think I needed to. Quarterback on the football team's truck was in the driveway, so I just went on in. He was balls deep when I kicked in the door."

He paused and chuckled as he raised his head a little, "That one got me a trip to jail for a bit. So, let's see…"

"Next, I suppose woulda been just before my pop went to the joint. His girlfriend at the time was considerably younger than he was. I don't know, maybe fifteen years younger. She was closer to my age than she was to his. He passed out drunk, and I'm guessing it was *before* she got what it was she was after. So I was in the garage working on my bike, and she came out through the garage, bitchin' about him passing out," he hesitated and shook his head lightly.

He raised both eyebrows as his mouth formed into his signature smirk, "She stopped half way through the garage and offered to suck my cock."

"So, this list goes on and on. I'm not so dumb that I believe all women are evil or can't be trusted, but I do believe women who are attracted to men like me are a different breed. Finding a woman who can be trusted one hundred percent is like finding a wolf that won't eat the chickens. It's not that they don't exist, but the odds of finding one are slim."

He stood, crossed his arms, and stared for a short moment. As he uncrossed his arms, he pulled against a rubber band on his left wrist. He now stood erect, still focused on me, and snapped the rubber band into his wrist. He acted like he didn't even notice he did it.

*Ouch!*

I tilted my head to the side and grinned, "So your definition of *slim* is compared to the odds of finding a wolf that won't eat the chickens?"

He nodded his head once, "Mmhhm."

"I'm a vegan. Chicken is meat, and I don't eat meat," I grinned.

He shrugged his shoulders, "Doesn't surprise me."

He hesitated for a long moment, gazed past me, and blinked a few times. With him standing there, I had become all but immune to the other men around, the music, and the noise of the overly loud drunken bikers. Hoping he would continue, I stood and admired his handsome features. As I realized for the first time that he had pierced ears, he began to speak again.

"I'm the President of this club. I damned sure don't need a woman to get in the way of me doing what it is I'm supposed to do. And, the long and short of it is this. She'd sure as fuck get in the way," he said flatly.

Somewhat frustrated with his answer, I shrugged my shoulders, "So, it's not about a chicken eating wolf or even the fact that you really don't trust women. It's more that you think a woman would get in the way of you being a biker. Right?"

"Suppose that's pretty close."

I stood, aggravated at his ridiculous beliefs, wondering how much of it was a show and how much of it was the truth. Maybe he liked women, and he simply didn't like me. Maybe he was being as nice as the President of a bike club could be, and just not telling me the *absolute* truth. The problem, for me, was the fact he *didn't* want me. His complete lack of interest fueled every competitive bone in my body. While I inventoried all of the patches on his vest and wondered what they all meant, I also pondered what the *real* reason was behind his denial of my offer.

*Avery, you're skinny, you have a flat ass, no tits, and your lips are skinny. You have one redeeming feature, and it's not even a feature, it's more of a mannerism. You're a 'courageous smart-ass'. That's' all you've got going for you. And to be honest, I'm not interested in fucking courage. I'd prefer fucking someone with meat on their bones. Well, that and a set of nice tits.*

Now wallowing in self-imposed guilt driven by my lack of confidence in boyish body being attractive, I realized something.

I tossed the towel into the towel bin under the bar, "Answer a question."

"Ask it."

"You came over here to the bar," I hesitated and motioned along the bar.

"And it's empty. I'm back here alone. And for some reason, no one is sitting here. So, why'd you stop to talk to me if you weren't interested?"

*Ha, motherfucker. Answer that.*

He gave me his half-assed grin and crossed his arms, "I like talking to you. Hell, what else am I going to do? I talk to these motherfuckers every God damned day. But just because I'm talking to you doesn't mean I want your ass on the back of my fucking bike or stopping by my house wanting to know if I'm interested in a new tofu recipe you wanna try out."

"Why not talk to the girl with the tits?" I asked as I motioned toward Sloan.

"Never been a tit man," he shrugged.

*Bullshit.*

He turned toward Sloan who was surrounded by bikers. As she stood and giggled, she pressed her upper arms into her boobs, forcing them to burst out of her tee shirt even more.

*Seriously?*

He turned to face me and shrugged.

"Bullshit." I snapped.

He tossed his head toward Sloan, "Tell me this. When she's thirty-five, what are her tits going to look like? I'll fucking tell ya. Take off the knee-high school girl gym socks I'm sure she's wearing, and stuff an orange in each one of 'em. That's what. Now, when you're thirty-five, what'll you look like? I'll fucking tell ya that too, just like you do now. Unless she moves to the moon, she's gonna have to deal with the laws of gravity at some point in time. And, it's working against her while we're sitting here bullshittin'."

He no more than finished speaking, and over the music, noise, laughing, and constant hollering, I heard someone scream.

"You cockfucking sucker!"

I twisted my body toward the scream. A tall muscular man with a military buzz cut stood arguing with a bald headed man with a long beard. The bald man was covered in tattoos, including his head, and looked like he shouldn't be fucked with. Not even a little bit. His response to *Buzz cut* calling him a cocksucker was to take a wild swing, which was immediately blocked and countered.

The punch by *Buzz cut* landed on the side of *Baldie's* face, knocking him sideways. As he stumbled, *Buzz cut* bent his knees slightly and took a defensive fighting stance. It was pretty obvious it wasn't his first time in a fight. Actually, he looked pretty experienced at what he was doing. I noticed as he stood with his fists raised that he clearly had a *Marine* tattoo on his very muscular right bicep.

*Well, that explains it.*

Baldy shook off the punch and growled.

*You're growling? What the fuck?*

"Toad, I'm gonna kill you," he grunted.

As much as I really wanted to see the outcome of the fight, I realized I was at work. I needed to stop this from going any further. Without a doubt, before long it would turn into a barroom brawl and someone would be hurt terribly or killed. At best, the bar would be thrashed. As *Baldy* threw another punch, *Buzz cut* blocked it and swung his open right hand toward *Baldie's* nose. The sound of the impact was sickening. Well, sickening in a kind of sexy way. Immediately blood began to drain from *Baldie's* nose like it was a faucet. I turned to face Axton, who was standing and intently watching the fight as if it were something that happened every night.

Hell, maybe it was.

"I said no fighting in my bar," I snapped.

"And I told you if there was a fight, it'd be from someone being disrespectful," he shrugged, "Looks like Pete disrespected Toad. Toad's kind of a hot-head. And he was a Marine. It's a bad combo."

I shook my head, "You said they wouldn't fight *each other*. You *said* that. And, they're both wearing your vests, so they're *each other*. So what, you're word's shit?"

He tilted his head and gave me a look. A look as if I had hit a nerve. Actually not *a nerve*, but *the nerve*. The *big* one. After a few second death stare which had me frozen, he turned toward Otis and whistled a shrill whistle. Immediately, Otis uncrossed his arms, rubbed his face, and took a few steps toward the men who were fighting.

"Pete, Toad, that's it. It's over. Whatever the fuck started this, squash it," Otis barked.

The two men relaxed slightly.

"Squash it," he growled again.

They both lowered their hands and stood up straight. As if nothing had happened, they shook hands, pulled each other into a *bro hug* and patted each other on the back. *Baldy* was still bleeding profusely from his nose. Instinctively, I reached under the bar, grabbed a clean towel, and yelled at Otis.

"Here!"

As he turned my direction, I threw him the folded towel. He nodded his head sharply, and handed the towel to *Baldy*. Shocked at the immediate and effortless ending of the fight, I turned toward Axton.

"So, if I'd have told you to fuck off and let them *go at it*, what would you have done? This is *your* bar after all," he asked in a sarcastic tone.

"Well, when people fight in here, I have three options, let 'em fight, call the cops, or," I paused and reached under the bar and pulled my Glock from my purse.

"This," I twisted my wrist for him to admire the pistol, and slipped it back under the bar.

"Letting them fight isn't a real good option, there's still regular customers in here. It would make me look incompetent and someone might get hurt or killed. And, if someone got killed the cops would come. For what it's worth, I *hate* cops. So, that brings me to option two, calling the cops. That's an *option*, but not one I want to use. Generally, I tell people to pick, call the cops or stop fucking fighting. Realistically, I'm not pulling the pistol. Not *ever*. Well, unless someone's trying to rob me or someone else in here," I paused and waited for him to respond.

"Model 17?" he asked.

I scrunched my brow and stared, "Huh?"

"Your pistol. Glock model 17. It's a nine millimeter, 4th generation. Must be pretty new," he nodded.

"Oh yeah, it's a Model 17. I got it about eighteen months ago when I got my concealed carry permit," I bragged.

"Nice. Well," he paused, reached for the rubber band, and snapped it against his wrist.

*What the fuck with the rubber band?*

"Avery, what night's do you grace the world with your presence here?" he asked.

Shocked at the fact he asked the question, I considered my unpredictable schedule while I mentally formed my response. I wondered why he would ask if he wasn't interested?

*He wouldn't.*

"Tuesday's, Thursday's and Saturday's, *almost* always. It's hard to say, he changes our schedules all the time. And I've got finals coming up, so it's anybody's guess here real quick," I shrugged.

"Finals, huh? College girl? I would have guessed you a little older."

"Nope, senior. Criminal Justice, go figure," I smiled.

"Wichita State?" he asked.

"Nope. Southwestern College, down in Winfield."

"Winfield, huh?" he grinned.

"Yeah, Winfield. You know where it is?"

"Never heard of the place," he shook his head, "I tell ya what, I'll come in next week. If you're here, I'll see ya," he nodded.

I considered giving him my phone number and decided against it. There's a fine line between *acting interested* and *being a stalker*. I definitely had stalker tendencies, and had every intention of stalking Axton, but I didn't want *him* to realize it.

"Sounds good," I said.

*So, I guess this is where you leave, and I spend all of next week sick to my stomach trying to decide what to wear to work, taking water pills by the dozen so I can shed weight, and feeling like I'm fat no matter what, right?*

He glanced toward Otis.

"Otis, have 'em saddle up," he hollered.

*Yep. Women's intuition.*

As much as I wanted to stay and get a few more sentences in, I knew it was time I changed up my game. I hadn't been successful at picking up a man in several years. Not a meaningful one, anyway. I reached under the bar, picked up another clean towel, and walked toward the other end of the bar without saying a word. It was far too late for me to try the *hard to get* routine, but I could act less interested than I truly was. Sometimes, less is more.

I watched the men walk outside in small groups and a few

82

individually. In many respects, it felt as if they had been in the bar for the entire night, if not more. In reality, they had been in the bar roughly thirty minutes. After almost all of the men were gone, Axton and Otis walked toward the bar. It seemed strange, because I would have sworn Otis had already left.

"I appreciate you not calling the cops when the fellas were fighting," Otis said as he reached over the bar.

As I shook his hand, he smiled, "Call me Otis."

"Avery," I sighed.

"What do I owe you for the beers?" Axton asked.

"Well, they drank both cases entirely. So, that's forty-eight times $4.25, let me check," I responded.

"$204.00 even," Axton said under his breath.

I turned to face him, "Excuse me?"

"It's $204.00 even. Forty-eight times $4.25," he nodded as he pulled three hundred dollar bills from his wallet.

"And you know that because?" I asked.

He turned toward Otis, shrugged, and shifted his gaze to meet mine, "I know it because I know how to multiply numbers. Here."

He handed me three one hundred dollars bills.

"Keep this one, two hundred's fine, it's easier."

"Keep it. It's your tip," Axton nodded.

"And one other thing," Otis said.

I widened my eyes and smiled as I tilted my head toward Otis, "Yeah?"

"Your friend, Sloan? She says the only way she can leave here is if you say it's alright. She's out in the parking lot, afraid to come ask. She wanted me to ask you if you'll let her off work?" he asked.

*That fucking bitch.*

*I can't get a fucking ride, and she's going to leave?*

*Like now?*

*Fucking slut.*

"She wanted *you* to ask?"

He nodded his head once.

Axton shrugged.

*That whore.*

I stepped from behind the bar, shoved my way past Axton and Otis, and walked briskly to the door. As I opened it, I saw Sloan in the parking lot, laughing with one of the guys beside what I guessed was his motorcycle. His back was to me, and the vest he wore was different than the rest of them. It said *Selected Sinners* on the top and *Prospect* on the bottom. There was no skull or guns in the center, and no *Kansas* banner on the vest.

I'd seen the shows on T.V. He was a Prospect; a soon to be member. He looked young, and was probably much closer to Sloan's age than any of the others. She forced a smile, narrowed her eyes, and waved. I shook my head and stomped back into the bar. As I stepped inside, Otis and Axton were on the other side of the door.

"So?" Otis' voice trailed along as he waited for an answer.

I looked around the bar. The guy with the ears and his two friends sat at number eight. Another group of four sat at number six, by the back door. The bar, with the exception of them, was empty.

"Fine with me. She's a big girl," I huffed.

"She sure as fuck is," Axton sighed as he walked past me.

*I wonder what he means by that...*

84

# AXTON

My opinion on women hadn't changed. Not at all. I never believed a woman had a place in the club, nor would I ever consider it. Therefore, having a woman become an active part of my life wasn't an option. Women become mentally attached to men through simple exposure and much more so when sex is added to the equation. For me to think for one moment I could have a relationship with a woman, even a friendly one, without her developing some sort of feelings or expectations would be foolish on my part.

I've never considered myself to be a foolish man.

My experience with women and sex in the last ten years had been a mountain of one night stands. I'd made every effort to be certain that each and every woman I had been with understood what we were agreeing to. *I fuck you, I leave, and there's no chance of seeing me again.* Growing up the son of a Hell's Angel father, I quickly learned the value of making rules and following them.

It takes a true outlaw; a person who refuses to be governed by the established rules or practices of any group, a rebel, a nonconformist.

Being a member of a motorcycle club requires that all members adhere strictly to bylaws and rules, yet the men place minimal value on the law. A club filled with and based on contradiction. The absolute adherence to the rules allows each and every member to immediately develop an understanding of one's ability to be trusted. To be dishonest on the side of the law, but brutally honest on the side of being a member of the club takes a different type of man.

Most of the men who rode with the Sinners, or any club for that matter, had their own rules and regulations. Things they hold sacred. At any cost, they'll adhere to the rules they've developed or put in place. Their doing so allows the members of the club to see their strong will, and slowly a trust develops unlike any other.

In the last decade, I had not seen any woman more than once. It was one of my rules. I had not received the phone numbers of any of the women I had sex with. It was another rule of mine. Having the ability to call a woman and have her come suck my cock or fuck me would create temptation to do just that. I'm tempted enough by simply living life, and I wasn't interested in making my life any more difficult than it already was.

Going to see Avery a second time wasn't breaking a rule of mine, but it was certainly out of character for me. As long as I wasn't fucking her, I was convinced I had no rule in place to prevent me from seeing her. I, not unlike other men, tend to try and find a way to manipulate rules to allow a loophole big enough to slide through without being able to be criticized for having broken it.

In being honest with myself, I found Avery to be an extremely interesting person. If she were a man, I could see us developing a solid friendship. The fact she had a pussy between her legs made things fractionally more difficult. A man having a friend with a pussy is like a wolf being friends with a chicken.

Not impossible, but highly fucking unlikely.

"No, she said it was like riding an eight hundred pound vibrator. She said she was soaked when she got to town. And never heard of Winfield, huh? You lying fucker," Avery laughed.

I shook my head lightly, "I was joking. Yeah, we're based out of Winfield. I prefer the small town atmosphere, it makes life simple."

"Well, now you know. Or if you don't, I'll guess I'll tell ya. Sloan and I *both* live there. We're roommates. I drive back and forth to this shit-hole to work, but I'm going to move here when school's out, and she's coming with me. I like the excitement of a large city."

"Grow up in a small town?" I asked.

"Yep, Marietta, Ohio," she nodded.

"Hell, never heard of it. Marietta, Georgia, I've heard of that one, but not Marietta, Ohio. How big is it?"

"About the size of Winfield, 13,000 people maybe," she shrugged.

I felt a little relief knowing she would be moving in a matter of weeks. Having her in Winfield, and knowing it, would make *not* seeing her more difficult. Having her live in a city of 400,000, and being twenty-five miles away would be better for us both.

"Big city life will be an exciting change, I'm sure. And an eight hundred pound vibrator, huh?" I chuckled.

She nodded her head and laughed, "That's what she said. I'd really need to tell you what else she said, but…"

I leaned into the bar and lightly pressed my right fist into my left palm. As I rested my chin on top of my clenched fist, I cocked one eyebrow, "Let's hear it."

She looked around the bar, "Give me a minute, I *might*."

As she held her index finger in the air, she turned and walked away. After mixing a drink, she carried it to the other end of the bar and handed it to a man who was nursing his last sip from the glass on the bar in front of him. Completely the opposite of most every other biker I had ever met, I'd never been a man who preferred *a little meat on the bones* of my women. Given an opportunity to decide on my own, my preference was a thin attractive woman with small tits. Watching Avery walk to the other end of the bar was nothing short of painful. Yet more proof I had almost no business continuing with this little friendship we were developing.

As she turned around from her short visit with the man, she wadded up a napkin, stood firm, and shot it like a basketball at the trashcan which was almost twenty feet away. As the ball of paper fell directly into the center of the can, she pumped her fist alongside her hip.

Early spring in Kansas can bring snow, ninety degree days, or a tornado. It's anyone's guess and changes from day to day. Today, thankfully, was clear skies, sunshine, and almost eighty degrees. Avery was dressed in shorts, a baseball tee, and canvas sneakers. As she quickly walked back to the end of the bar where I was seated, I found myself admiring her.

*Get your shit and go, Slice. This girls gonna cause nothing but trouble for you, and for the club.*

As she stepped in front of me, she pushed her hands into her rear pockets and twisted her hips playfully, "So, wanna hear it?"

*No, truthfully, I want to leave. If I stay here much longer I'm going to make a mistake.*

"Huh?" I stammered as I snapped the rubber band against my wrist twice.

"You want me to tell you what else she said?" she asked as she twisted back and forth.

*You cute little bitch.*

"Sure," I breathed as I continued to stare at her tanned legs and smooth skin.

"Your boy Cash has a choad," she giggled.

"A *what*?" I laughed as I sat up straight.

"A *choad*. It's a short fat cock. I guess it was about as big around as her wrist, and from what she said, it *might* have been an inch long. *Maybe*. Basically, she said it's this huge head, and no shaft at all," she giggled as she clamped her thumb and forefinger around her wrist and made a fist.

"Choad?" I chuckled.

"Yep, a choad. Short fatty. Look it up," she nodded.

"Hell, I believe you. Just haven't heard that one," I responded.

She closed her eyes momentarily and started laughing. As she got the laugh down to a light chuckle, she continued.

"So I guess she's all wet from the ride, and thinking she wants this Cash guy to fuck her. So they go to his house, and he's all acting like he's going to fuck her brains out. He'd been telling her that as they rode slowly through town to his house. *I'm going to fuck you ragged*, he told her. She said he ripped off his pants like he had no idea he had this fat little mushroom head thing going on. She said she looked down at it, thinking it was soft, and when it got hard she'd be in for a hell of a ride, because it's so fucking fat you know?" she paused, shrugged, and started laughing uncontrollably.

Her continued laughing and my thinking of the situation caused me to begin to laugh. As I chuckled at the thought of Cash's *choad*, she finally continued her story.

"So, she said she got down on her knees and started sucking, and realized *that* was it. She said deep throating him would be taking the head in her mouth, because there was *nothing else*. No shaft. Seriously, when she told me the story we were at Taco Bell. I spit out my fucking burrito. No lie, right on the table. I almost pissed my pants. Sloan's my best friend, don't get me wrong. But she really, really, *really* likes cock; the bigger the better. And this dude pulls out the *head*, and it's the size of a fucking apple, but that's *all he's got*.

"So what happened?" I asked as I wiped the tears from my eyes.

"That's the funny part. Sloan's kinda like me. She doesn't really pull any punches. Maybe that's why we're friends. But she's not like *mean*. She said when she realized it *was* hard, and all of an inch long, she spit it out and got like grossed out. She said she stood up and pointed at it, and just started laughing. Like uncontrollably," she paused and began giggling again.

"And your boy Cash acts like he had no idea. So she left; like walked home. *That* kind of left. The *I'm walking home* kind," she chuckled.

"Holy shit," I said as I shook my head.

"Yeah, that's kinda what I said. *Holy shit*. So, anyway. That was her first ride. She'd never been on the back of a bike. And *now*? She's hooked. It's all she can talk about. And, just so you know, she'll probably start stalking your man Otis. She's guessing there's no way he's got a choad."

"Stalking, huh? That's probably not a healthy thing to do. And good luck finding him, he kind of keeps to himself," I said flatly as I looked around the bar.

"Oh, Cash showed her where your clubhouse is," she responded.

*That dumb little cocksucker.*

I tightened my jaw, and leaned into the bar, "Well, it's no fucking secret. We ride in and out of there all damned day, but the clubhouse is off limits to outsiders. Without an invitation, no one's allowed but members. If anyone comes there without prior approval, they'll be escorted off the premises."

"Sore subject?" she shrugged.

I shook my head, "Club business is the *club's business*, not public business. It's a private club. If she finds Otis and fucks him, I don't give a shit. Hell they can run off and get married for all I care, but she can't come to the clubhouse without an invitation."

"Okay, I'll tell her. I didn't know it was like *a secret*," she said apologetically.

To explain to Avery my disappointments in Cash's big mouth would make the club seem to be a little too eager, almost desperate, in the selection of Cash as a Prospect. To me, *any* club business was the *club's* business. It wasn't a huge thing that Cash had told Sloan where the clubhouse was, and we didn't keep the location a secret from the public. It didn't change the fact that I thought Cash was an immature waste of the club's time. He had until August to show his ability to be an asset to the club. In my opinion, he'd need to change quickly.

I took a deep breath through my nose and exhaled. I studied her for a short moment and then responded, "It's not. There are rules and we have bylaws in place. One is admittance into the premises of the club. It's prohibited. The rules are a requirement, not a recommendation. Nothing against Cash, but it probably wasn't very wise of him to show her where the clubhouse was and not tell her the rule regarding visitation."

"Okay. Well, that doesn't sound as bad. I'm not trying to get him in trouble, but I just thought if maybe you had some kind of *new members must have an actual cock* requirement; he'd like be out of the picture," she chuckled.

"We don't. But don't worry, you've done a good job of burning a mental image into my mind of his choad," I chuckled.

More than likely my entire problem with Cash was his immature behavior. Typically, with age comes maturity. Although he was thirty years old, he was extremely immature. As I sat and became angry at his childish decisions and behavior, I realized Avery was a senior in college. She, too, would be immature by mere design. Her lack of exposure in life would cause her to lack the maturity I'd need to even allow me to expose myself to her without placing the club at risk. As much as I enjoyed looking at her, and truly enjoyed talking to her, I knew what was in the club's best interest. I stood from the stool, stretched reached into the pocket of my jeans.

"How much for the burger?" I asked.

Her eyes widened, "You leaving?"

"Yeah, I need to get back. I've got a business deal to finish putting together. Hell, I've been here for two hours. Time got away from me," I sighed as I looked at my watch.

"Wasn't anything I said?" she asked.

I shook my head, "Nope."

"Don't worry about it. It's on the house," she smiled.

I pulled a twenty from my wallet and slid it below the cardboard coaster underneath my glass of water, "Well, this is your tip. Thanks."

"I suppose I'll see ya the next time I see ya," she shrugged a she pushed her hands into the back pockets of her shorts.

*If you only knew...*

As she started twisting her hips again, I almost sat back down. Avery was attractive, and would be so to any man. Her personality and her actions, however, made her almost irresistible. As she rocked from side-to-side and smiled, I started to lose myself in thoughts of my childhood, and my girlfriend at the time, Shellie. She was a cheerleader in school, and until she fucked the quarterback, and I ended up in jail for beating his ass, our time together was all memorable. She was probably my only *real* love. The only recollections I had of actually enjoying time with a woman involved her solely.

I stared at Avery, pulled against the rubber band, and released it into my wrist.

*Snap!*

I pulled against it again, held it, and stared down at her sneakers.

*Snap!*

"I appreciate it," I nodded.

She grinned and nodded her head, unaware of what I truly meant.

I scanned her body from head to toe, and back up again slowly. I pulled the rubber band again, tightened my jaw in anticipation, and released it into my wrist.

With a mental image of her still burned into my brain, I turned and walked to the door.

As I pulled the door open, I chuckled at my increased vocabulary.

*Choad.*

As I walked to my bike I wondered if there was a name for one as big as your wrist and nine inches long. I threw my leg over the bike knowing I'd never know if there was; at least not from Avery.

There was no way in hell I could ever fuck her once and walk away.

*None whatsoever.*

# AVERY

In my observation, I realized Axton snapped the rubber band against his wrist when he was uncomfortable or troubled. Initially I was going to ask why, but later decided there was probably more value in my keeping my mouth shut and seeing if there was some type of pattern to his behavior. After watching for some time, I believed he did it even more when he was tempted to do something he felt would be better left undone.

When he came to the bar the second time, I noticed he did it when I did my innocent little naïve school girl pose. There was no other reason, no awkward discussions, and nothing I said had pissed him off. But each time I put my hands in the pockets of my shorts and swiveled my hips, he snapped his rubber band repeatedly. Probably out of nervous habit more than anything.

I attempted to do as much research on the club as I could, but found very little to read. There was a website for the *Selected Sinners Motorcycle Club*, listing Slice as President, Stacey as Vice President, Mike as Treasurer, Fancy as the Secretary, Hollywood as the Road Captain, and Otis as the Sergeant at Arm's. The website listed the bylaws, and Axton wasn't joking about the clubhouse. The rules regarding Ol' Ladies were pretty clear in that respect. I desperately wanted to know about the club, but even more, I wanted to know as much as I could about Axton.

"I can't believe they've been here all along, and we never knew," I shouted over my shoulder as I closed the window on the computer.

"I know. God, I want another ride. Not with that weirdo Cash, but with one of 'em. I bet that Otis dude is freaking *hung*," Sloan hollered from the bathroom.

I rolled my eyes in agreement, knowing she didn't necessarily expect a response.

"You know," she said.

"They say you can tell about a guy's cock from his hands, feet, and confidence. Otis' hands are huge, and his feet are huge. But Axton? God he's hot. And it freaking creeps me out that he's so confident. The way he walks, he acts like he could just beat anyone's ass that's dumb enough to get in his way. I bet his cock's a freaking foot long," she yelled.

I leaned back into the stool and smiled at what she said. I felt the same way, but hadn't expressed it. Axton's confidence was apparent in his walk alone. The look on his face, his stride, and his demeanor screamed *do not fuck with me*. He looked like a wind-up toy when he walked, there was a certain rhythm to the steps he took, and the process repeated itself roughly every six or so steps. As I watched him walk I wondered if it was a conscious thing, or something that simply happened.

I decided it was just Axton. I liked thinking of him that way.

"What in the fuck is on your nose?" I asked as Sloan walked out of the bathroom.

Although she had attempted to wrap herself in a towel, it was painfully obvious there was far too much of her to try and cover with the shitty little towels we had in the apartment. With all of her ass and a good part of her pussy peeking out the bottom, her boobs were bulging out of the top. She could cover one of the areas, but definitely not both. She stopped and touched the side of her nose with the tip of her finger delicately.

"It's freaking sore," she winced as she pressed her fingertip into the edge of her nose.

"You pierced it? I squealed as I bounced from the chair.

"Uh huh," she responded.

"When? Why?" I asked as I moved my face closer to her nose.

"I went to *Tracy's.*"

I leaned away from her nose and stared at her, "The jewelry shop?"

"Uh huh," she nodded.

"You dumb ass. They pierced it with a gun, didn't they?" I asked.

"Uh huh."

"You dumb ass."

I rolled my eyes and shook my head lightly. We had discussed getting our noses pierced when we moved to Wichita, because they had actual piercing shops which pierced with needles the proper way, and not with guns. From what we had read on the internet, and learned from asking around, having your nose pierced with a gun intended to pierce ears with was a no-no, and could possibly cause infection and trauma.

"Why didn't you wait?" I shrugged.

"I dunno. I wanted those guys to like me. I thought if I had it *now*, maybe they'd see me differently," she whined.

I raised my clenched fist to my mouth, coughed, and rolled my eyes, "You want 'em to like you? Seriously? Wear your new sixty dollar bra, they'll love you. Jesus, go get dressed before something falls out of that towel."

I watched as she stumbled to the bedroom, touching her nose with her finger the entire way. I sat down at the desk and peered through the door as she got dressed, knowing if I had her huge titties, *everyone* would love me.

No doubt.

*God, if I just had half those tits, I'd have Axton begging me...*

I stood up, walked to the bathroom, and stared at myself in the mirror. I turned to the side and tried to imagine myself with boobs. As I sucked in my nonexistent stomach and tried to force my flat ass to look round, she stepped into the doorway.

"What are you freaking doing?" she giggled.

I turned my head and smiled, "Trying to imagine myself with tits and a little ass."

"Your tits are perfect, and you have a cute little ass."

"I look like a boy," I sighed.

"A hot fucking boy," she said as she reached over my shoulder for the blow dryer.

"So I do. I look like a boy, don't I?"

"No," she said as she started drying her hair.

"Why'd you say it?" I asked as I stared into the mirror and twisted my body so my ass faced the mirror.

*It's helpless. I have no ass.*

She shrugged and continued to dry her hair. I sighed and walked out of the bathroom and back to the desk. Frustrated, I lowered myself into the chair and stared at the black computer screen. Convinced I'd graduate from college, move to Wichita, and remain a flat assed and titless single woman for the rest of my life, I silently pouted at the thought of it all.

"What was that?" Sloan hollered over the sound of the hair dryer.

I blinked my eyes and looked around the room, "What was what?"

"Sounded like someone knocked on the door," she shouted over the sound of the hairdryer.

"I didn't hear anything," I responded as I swiveled the chair toward the door.

*Knock, knock, knock.*

"Holy shit, someone's here," I said as I jumped from the chair and ran to the door.

Having someone come over probably wasn't a big deal to the majority of the population of the free world, but to Sloan and me, it was a *huge* deal. In the two years we lived together, we'd had a total of two visitors that I could recall. One knocked on the wrong apartment door, and the other was pushing bibles and religion.

I bounced to the door and looked through the peephole.

*Holy shit!*

# AXTON

After finding out my point of contact could speak English *not very well*, I learned every member of the club spoke Spanish *not at all*. A quick inventory of the Ol' Ladies produced not one single Spanish speaking person. Having the ability to effectively communicate while trying to sell 100 AK-47's to a first time customer was instrumental to the success of the sale. Frustrated, and not willing to lose a deal due to the incompetence of the club, I opted to find someone who *did* speak Spanish; someone who would be willing to go to a simple drop-off site and watch Otis and me sell a few guns to a Mexican street gang. The only drawback was it had to be someone I could trust, and I didn't trust anyone outside the club.

Knowing if this deal fell apart, I was risking the life of one of the strongest members of the club, I decided to go beyond the boundaries of what I would normally do, and *consider* the help of an outsider. After all, the deal we were doing was legal and legitimate. Including an outsider in the transaction didn't expose the club to any real risk. The Sureños may not have legal intentions with the weapons after they receive them from the club, but that was none of my or anyone else's business.

A Google search confirmed a degree in Criminal Justice required a foreign language class, and my guess was Avery's choice would have been Spanish. Contrary to my typical beliefs and behaviors, the club was asked, and they voted in favor of her being my Spanish speaking assistant. It was further agreed Otis and I would be the two members to do the deal with the Sureños. Otis' size alone would be intimidating to a bunch of short Mexicans, which should minimize the potential for anyone trying anything stupid. If she agreed, Avery could simply stand on the side, look pretty, and tell me what the little fuckers were *really* saying. In my opinion, with Otis and Avery participating in the transaction, there was little risk to the club that anything could go wrong with the deal.

We would have brains, brawn, and the ability to communicate clearly.

After much thought and a long mental battle with myself about the inclusion of an outsider in what I believed to be *club* business, I fully accepted the decision the club had already made, and began my journey to find Avery. Frank provided me with Avery's apartment number, and I rode there to discuss matters with her. Even though it was settled with the club, in my mind it was still rather undecided. As she opened the door, the expression on her face made her level of surprise quite clear.

"Got a minute?" I asked.

She stood wide eyed with her mouth agape, "Yeah, come in."

Still standing in the center of the doorway, she stared. I motioned for her to move so I could step into the house, "You're going to need to step aside if you want me to come in."

"Uhhm. How'd you find me?" she stammered.

"I'm resourceful. I told you that," I responded jokingly.

"So, you come by to give me that ride?" she asked as she flopped down on the couch.

The apartment was much smaller than small. Although I hadn't been in the bedrooms, I could see in the doorway of each room. The apartment was approximately six hundred square feet from what I could tell, roughly twenty feet wide and thirty feet deep. Two people living in it was one person too many. A small desk at one side, a bathroom on the opposite wall, a couch, and two chairs were the extent of the furnishings. I sat in the chair beside the couch and turned to face Avery.

"Not exactly," I sighed as the bathroom door opened.

"Hey," Sloan breathed as she walked by.

"How's it going, Sloan?" I responded over my shoulder, somewhat shocked she was at the apartment.

She was dressed in sweats that were too small and a tee shirt that did a half-assed job of covering her torso. Her stomach was exposed, and it was apparent she couldn't pull the shirt down any further. I'd seen a lot of women in my days around the fellas who had big tits, but sitting this close to Sloan and actually *seeing* her, I would have to admit her tits were the biggest I had ever seen. Half embarrassed by her appearance, I quickly turned toward Avery.

"So, what the fuck?" Avery shrugged.

I sat silently and looked around the room. I hadn't planned on Sloan being at Avery's house and she certainly wasn't part of the equation. I've never been a paranoid man, and I wouldn't consider myself a nervous person, but I was always safe; erring on the side of caution. I reached down, pulled the rubber band to the point of breaking it, and released it.

*Snap!*

I stared blankly at my wrist as I snapped it three more times equally as hard. Now feeling as if I could sense my heart beating in my inflamed wrist, I looked up at Avery.

"You got any glasses? Like sunglasses?" I asked.

*God damn it Axton.*

She looked confused, "Yeah, why?"

"Grab 'em. We're going for a ride," I said as I stood.

*It's just a ride Axton, nothing more.*

*You're using her for a mouthpiece on a gun deal, that's it.*

"Seriously?" she squealed as she bounced up from the couch.

I looked around the apartment. Sloan stood in the doorway of the bedroom, looking in the mirror. She was all of ten feet away.

I tilted my head toward the door, "Yeah, grab 'em. Let's get out of here."

"Sloan, I'm going with Axton *on his bike*," Avery hollered across the tiny apartment.

"Okay," Sloan responded slowly, stretching the word along for a good five seconds.

Sloan peered around the frame of the door and gave a half-assed grin. As Avery grabbed her purse, she pulled out her glasses and put them on. She was wearing jean shorts that barely cupped the bottom of her ass cheeks and a tight tee shirt. I glanced down at her feet.

*Sneakers.*

I smiled and reached for the door handle, "Ready?"

"Uh huh," she smiled.

"Alright, listen up. There's a few rules you'll have to follow," I said as I opened the door.

As she stepped into the doorway, she stopped, pulled off the sunglasses, and stared into my eyes. Now sharing the space in the opening of the door, she stood mere inches from me. For the first time, I realized just how tall she was. Our noses not more than an inch apart, we stood in the doorway, our eyes locked. As a light breeze blew, I caught the faint smell of her perfume; a very light floral scent.

*God damn she smells good.*

"You tell me what to do, and I'll do it. It's that simple," she said without expression.

I pursed my lips and narrowed my gaze, "That's a bold statement, you better be careful, little girl."

She stood with her sunglasses dangling from her fingertips, still shoehorned into the small opening of the doorway. I stood with my back against the frame of the door, refusing to be the one who moved out of the way first. She blinked her eyes and tilted her head slightly.

She smiled a shitty little flirtatious smile, "Think about that. Whatever you say, I'll do it. Use your imagination, Axton. I sure am."

I stood and continued to stare at her. Thoughts of shoving her against the wall, pulling her shorts down around her ankles, and fucking her long-legged little ass while she still wore her sneakers began to fill my mind. I sensed my cock beginning to swell at the thought of her doing *whatever* I told her. The fellas from the poker run in Wichita were spot on. She was a little firecracker, and she seemed to know exactly what to do to push my buttons. I had no business with this cute little bitch on the back of my bike, but I had no other alternative. For the sake of the club, this gun deal had to happen. As I felt the fabric of my jeans beginning to stretch from my overly active imagination, I shook my head and stepped out of the doorway.

As I turned and walked to the stairs, she immediately followed behind me. I pressed my hand against my jeans, attempting to force my cock to relax and become a little less noticeable before we got to the motorcycle. As we reached the bottom landing, I turned toward the bike and pushed against my still rigid dick with the heel of my palm and kept my back to Avery.

Generally speaking, I was able to keep my mind focused and prevent my cock from swelling without my approval. Actually, in the last fifteen years, I have had quite the opposite problem; focusing enough to get hard was proving to be difficult. Standing with my back to Avery and pressing down on my slowly rising cock was further proof I had very little control over my mind and what subconscious inner thoughts I had of fucking her. I had no business being in a relationship with a woman, and doing so was still the furthest thing from my mind, but bending her over and fucking her senseless was becoming more and more of a full-fledged desire than in *inner* thought. I felt like I was a pubescent teen again.

"Is there a problem?" she asked.

*Fuck it, just hop on the bike Slice. She won't notice.*

I turned, threw my leg over the bike, and looked down at my rigid but not quite as noticeable cock. I propped my feet up on the pegs and bend my knees a little to provide some relief.

I turned slightly and pointed to the rear passenger pegs, "Nope. Get on, and put your feet on *those* pegs."

"Keep your bare legs away from the exhaust. It'll burn you to the bone," I said as I motioned toward the two exhaust pipes.

"Just relax, and don't flop around. Wrap your arms around my waist and hold on until you're comfortable. And leave the glasses on, it's a requirement and it'll keep bugs out of your eyes. And when you get on, don't drag your shoe over the fender. It ain't scratched now, and I don't want the motherfucker any different when we're done," I said over my shoulder.

"Easy schmeezy," she grinned as she stretched her long leg over the bike.

As she wrapped her arms around me and pressed her inner thighs against the sides of my ass, the heart beat in my pants provided me a little reminder of the fact my outward intentions and my inner mind were worlds apart.

Worlds apart.

# AVERY

I had no idea why Axton *really* came by and picked me up, and I didn't care. Sloan was right; being on the bike was like riding a huge vibrator. I was in some strange state of ecstatic heaven, and we were flying down the road toward who knows where. Nothing I had done to date could compare to riding on the motorcycle. The fact I was on it with Axton made it immeasurably better.

"You alright" he asked over his shoulder as we slowed down for a stop sign.

I rested my chin on his shoulder and breathed into his ear, "Yeah, I'm perfect."

"So where's your favorite place to relax" he asked.

I wondered why he would ask such a thing. Maybe he wanted to talk or get to know me a little more. I really didn't want him to stop riding the motorcycle. Not ever. I was feeling a strange sense of freedom as we rolled down the road; it was as if absolutely nothing else mattered. There were no worries of graduation, no inconsiderate parents, and no feelings of inadequacy about my boyish body. As the road rushed upon us, there was nothing between me and the entire earth except the wind which hadn't hit my face yet. Since I was a child, I've dreamed of flying like a bird, and now I knew what it was like; because I was doing it. I wanted to throw my hands in the air and scream, but I didn't dare.

"The park where you come into town," I responded.

He nodded his head slightly and twisted the throttle. I pressed my thighs into his, holding on tighter as he accelerated. I would absolutely love being a biker bitch. I closed my eyes and smiled.

*What a rush.*

As he slowed down and turned into the park, I exhaled. I felt as if I'd been holding my breath for the entire ride, but I knew I hadn't. Excited for what had happened, and disappointed we were stopping, I began to feel excited about sitting with Axton in my favorite place. Without a doubt, at minimum, he'd have to give me a ride home; so this wasn't over yet. He pulled into a parking spot beside a picnic table, turned the bike to face outward, and stopped. He switched off the engine and told me to get off. I carefully lifted my leg over the rear fender, being careful not to drag my foot over it. I didn't want to give him any reason not to want to do this again. As I stood beside motorcycle, I saw it and Axton in an entirely different light. Rightfully so or not, I felt as if I had become a part of it all.

The experience.

Being a biker.

Ten minutes, and I was transformed.

He kicked down the stand and got off the bike. He looked at me, and smiled his little smirk of a smile, "You enjoy it?"

It was difficult to explain. I fucking loved it. I never wanted to ride in a car again. I assumed he knew and would completely understand, but I didn't want to babble like my normal self. I inhaled a shallow breath, exhaled half of it, and responded as best I could, considering my level of excitement.

"Saying I enjoyed it doesn't do the experience any justice," I said as I admired the motorcycle.

"Good, it'd be disappointing if you hated it."

I shifted my eyes toward Axton and smiled, "So what's up?"

His bicep flexed as he reached for his rubber band and stretched it tight, "We need to talk."

I took the few steps to the picnic table and sat down. Standing and staring at Axton was nice, but standing in front of me, he was a little intimidating. Sitting down was better. I wondered what he wanted to talk about, or what I might have done to cause him to be disappointed with me. Certainly if he was disappointed, he wouldn't have picked me up and taken me for a ride. As he walked around the bike and to the table, I watched his sexy stride as if hypnotized. He stopped a few feet in front of the table and looked down at me as he removed his sunglasses.

"I'm gonna cut right to it. We need to have a serious talk. I need something from you. I'll explain what I need, and then you can give me your thoughts. Sound good?" he asked.

I nodded my head eagerly.

As a little girl, whenever my parents said we needed to *have a talk,* I knew it was something serious. Whether or not it was serious to me, they always believed it to be. Those types of talks, as a kid, always seemed to make me feel uneasy. Immediately prior to the talk, and during, I felt as if my stomach was full of butterflies. I spent the entire time as I waited for the talk wondering what the subject was going to be, or what mistake I had made in trying to live my life. Feeling uneasy and nervous until the talk was over, my mind would become an overflowing mess of ideas on what the topic might be. As he stood over me, I felt as if I was a little girl again.

He crossed his arms and studied me.

"Do you speak Spanish?" he asked blankly.

*That's weird.*

I nodded my head, "Yeah."

"Fluently?' he asked.

*Okay, that's still weird.*

I looked up at him and narrowed my eyes, "Very."

"Alright. I'm going to tell you something. You may or may not be comfortable with what I say or what I ask of you, but no matter what, you can't discuss this conversation with anyone. *Ever.* If you do..." he hesitated and reached toward my face.

His hand gripped my jaw lightly. As he lifted my chin and turned my face to meet his, he continued, "Well, you just can't. Is that understood?"

*Oh God, you just made me wet.*

I nodded my head and swallowed the lump which had risen in my throat, "Yes, I understand."

Having his hand on my face was exciting in itself. Hearing him tell me secrets made me immediately uncomfortable. The good kind of *I'm excited* uncomfortable. I crossed my legs, looked up, and smiled. For a short moment, he stared into my eyes.

*I mean it Axton, please believe me.*

He released my chin and began to pace back and forth, "Here's what I've got. The club is selling a shipment of *legal* firearms to a group of Mexicans who can't speak English very fucking good. Otis and I are doing the deal. I need you to be the interpreter. I may not need you to say anything at all, or I may. I have no way of knowing. But I'd rather have you there and not need you than be there, need you, and have nothing. And, nobody in the club speaks God damned Spanish. So, what do you say?"

*Holy shit. Seriously?*

*A gun deal with a biker gang and a bunch of Mexicans who can't speak English.*

*Fuck yeah I want to do it.*

I stood from my seat, "Are they legal US citizens?"

"How the fuck would I know? They're fucking Mexicans, Avery. I *doubt* it," he shrugged.

I raised my hands to my cheeks and thought. I didn't want to embarrass him or make him feel as if I was some smart-assed college girl. Quietly and calmly, I explained my understanding of the law, "Well, you put emphasis on the fact the firearms were legal. Selling *legal* firearms doesn't make the *transaction* legal. If they're not US citizens, it's a Federal crime."

He wrinkled his brow and looked at me as if I were insane, "According to *who?*"

I closed my eyes and thought. I had done a paper on gun laws my junior year when we were studying law. I had always been fascinated by firearms, and having recently received my concealed carry permit, my fascination with firearms was rekindled. I inhaled a deep breath, opened my eyes, and explained.

"Well, according to the Federal Government. *The Gun Control Act makes it unlawful for certain categories of persons to ship, transport, receive, or possess firearms. Transfers of firearms to any such prohibited persons are also unlawful. Eighteen USC nine twenty-two 'G' is the law.*"

He stopped pacing, "Fucking Feds. You sure?"

"Positive. I did a paper on it last year. But the law's kind of thin in some respects. There's case law to support a person's knowledge and intent. If you sell the firearms *knowing* the recipient or recipients are

113

illegal aliens, you're fucked. If you sell them, and the recipient *is* an illegal alien, and you didn't *know* it before hand, you're fine. It's stupid, but it's the law," I shrugged.

"So, as long as I don't *know*, we're alright?" he asked.

"Yeah, it's grey. But yeah," I nodded.

*Holy shit, this is exciting. Illegal gun deals with Mexicans. If they're the guys who wear the plaid shirts buttoned at the top, khaki pants, and have tattoos on their necks, that'd be even more exciting.*

He turned his palms up and shrugged his shoulders again, "Well, fuck. I didn't know that. It's good to know. I appreciate it. I guess I didn't realize a Criminal Justice degree required you study law."

Pleased I could offer something, I simply stood and smiled.

He pulled his knife from his pocket, flicked out the blade, and began picking at his fingernails, "Well, I don't *know* shit about these fuckers. And I guess I don't want to. Hell, they may all be US citizens, but I won't ask. So, what do you think? You in or you out?"

As he looked down at his hand and drug the blade of his knife under each fingernail, I studied him. Standing there with one knee slightly bent, wearing jeans, a white wife beater, boots, and his biker vest, he was hot as absolute fuck. The thought of him doing illicit gun deals only added to it, making him even more attractive to me. He was a true bad boy in all respects. Fuck yeah, *I was in.* I considered trying to make a deal with him; possibly negotiating a summer full of motorcycle rides, letting me suck his cock, or having him bend me over the park bench and giving me some biker cock in trade for my translation services. After a moment, I came back to reality. With Axton, doing this for him with no expectation or type of agreed upon payment would go much further.

114

With him, it was about *earning* respect.

I decided maybe I'd split the difference and play with the words I'd used earlier, at my apartment. After all, I did win the stand-off in the doorway after I said it.

I pushed my hands into the back pockets of my shorts, and twisted my hips, "You tell me what you want, Axton. I'll do it. I told you that. It's pretty simple. You want this? You need me to do it?"

He folded his knife, clipped it into his jeans pocket, and stared at me. Without looking down, he reached for the rubber band, and snapped it twice really hard.

Fuck yes. I knew it. Stand there and think about fucking me, you gorgeous bad boy biker.

As he rubbed his thumb into his wrist, he responded, "Well, I wouldn't have fucking asked ya if I didn't."

"*I'm in.* Fuck yes, I am. Anything you need, Axton. And don't think I'm saying that in a naïve schoolgirl kind of way. But if you need it, I'll do it. I don't know why, but I will. And what you said before about keeping this between us? Yeah, we don't need to go over that again; I have your best interest at heart. So yeah, I'll do it, and I'll keep it quiet. When is this going to happen?"

He smiled his shitty little smile, "Saturday. Nine o'clock at night, in the barrio in Wichita."

"Sounds good," I grinned as I twisted my hips back and forth.

He turned away from me, and began to walk away. After a few steps, he turned and looked over his shoulder, "You eat yet?"

"Nope," I lied.

"You like Pho?' he asked as he got on the bike.

I had eaten Pho in Wichita with Sloan several times. According to her, it was the only cure for a hangover. There was nowhere to eat it in Winfield, however.

"I Pho-king love it," I chuckled, "but there's nowhere in this town to get it."

"You got a curfew?" he laughed as he flipped the switch on the handlebar with his thumb.

"Nope."

He pressed the button and started the bike. As the engine began to roar, he hollered over his shoulder, "Get on. Let's go eat."

I twisted my hips again, curled up the corner of my mouth in a half-assed smile, and pulled my hands from my pockets.

*Whatever you say, Axton. Whatever you say.*

# AXTON

We pulled the Ryder rental truck into to the poorly lit parking lot. A single street light illuminated the far corner of the parking lot which was approximately 200 feet square. The three other lights in the corners appeared to have been shot out at some point in time. The concrete bases for the parking lot lights remained, but the poles and the wiring were either removed or stolen at some point in time. Considering the neighborhood, my guess was they'd been stolen.

"Looks like the place, huh Slice?" Otis breathed as he slowed the van to a five mile an hour roll.

"Yeah, at least there's only one truck. I wonder where they're going to put these motherfuckers?" I asked as I attempted to focus on the truck positioned under the lamp post.

Thankfully, they had parked under the light. Regardless of who they were, it made me feel more comfortable they had good *intentions*. Otis had a .45 caliber Colt 1911 in a holster under his left armpit, and I carried a Glock .45 caliber. Luckily, the weather had cooled almost twenty-five degrees from the previous week, and the jackets we wore to conceal the guns didn't look out of place. I didn't expect they would anticipate us doing a gun deal for sixty grand without being armed, but out of what little respect I had for these guys, concealing the firearms was a small show of faith.

Avery sat quietly between Otis and me, and stared straight ahead. As we rolled alongside the truck, it was obvious two men in what appeared to be their late twenties or early thirties were seated inside. Both were clearly Mexicans.

"Remember, stand on my left, so I can hear you alright. I can't hear that well out of my right ear. Let me try and do this deal, and if they don't speak as good as we need them to, I'll just tell you what to tell them, and you tell me what they say in response. Understood?" I asked.

She hadn't said three words on the entire forty minute trip from Winfield to the north side of Wichita. Now, truly in the middle of bean town, we were in a parking lot a mile from any other real civilization. Without a doubt, they had chosen this location due to the lack of vehicular traffic and the lack of law enforcement patrol. Cops really didn't come to this part of town unless they were called.

"Understood," she responded.

"You alright?" I asked.

She clutched her purse with her right hand, and responded, "I'm good."

"Showtime," Otis said as he put the van into park.

As Otis opened the door and stepped out, I did the same. The two men stepped out of the truck, and the driver smiled, revealing a gold tooth. Both men appeared to be unarmed, dressed in wife beaters and what seemed to be freshly pressed khaki pants. The driver had a number thirteen tattooed on his left temple. The passenger had a large MS-13 tattooed on his neck, across his Adam's apple. Incapable of being able to deny any gang affiliation, they were both were covered in what seemed to be either prison tats or something one of their members did in the garage.

"Jew must be Otis and Slice. They call me Chapas and theeese is

Gato. Who's the girl?" the driver asked in a thick accent.

Well, fuck. Seems you speak English just fine.

"She's my interpreter. El Palõn said you didn't speak English very well," I nodded.

"He don't speak English for sheet. I work in this sheet-hole seety. I don't have no choices," he grinned as he tossed his head toward the passenger.

The passenger stood stone faced and stared.

Avery stepped to my left side and stood quietly. I inhaled a shallow breath through my nose, surveyed the lot for any movement, and opened my arms in a gesture toward the driver.

"Well, we've got your inventory in the van. Ten crates of ten. They're packaged for movement without any damage. It's sixty grand even, best price you'll find on the street. Let's do this deal before anyone decides to come up here and see what we're doing. So, we good?" I asked.

The driver nodded his head once and whispered to the other man. The passenger turned and walked to the truck, opened the door, and removed a small Mexican blanket rolled into a rectangular bundle. I watched intently as he unfolded the blanket and pointed at bills which appeared to be wrapped in cellophane.

I nodded my head.

He folded the blanket over the money and handed it to Otis.

"So, jew fuckers cold, or just wearing your coats to hide your pistolas?" the driver chuckled.

"You want me to answer that?" I laughed.

"No, eets all good," he nodded.

"Pull jore truck around to my truck and we'll unload these fuckers," he said as he nodded toward the van.

"Otis, back that fucker up to his tailgate, make it tight. We'll slide those fuckers in there and get the fuck out of here," I said under my breath.

"Got it, Slice," Otis responded.

I gripped Avery's upper arm and guided her to the side. Otis started the van and slowly maneuvered it within a few feet of the rear of the truck. After the driver lowered the tailgate of the truck, I guided Otis back until the back of the van and the truck were almost touching. I unlocked the sliding door of the van and slid it upward. The driver slapped his hand against the bed of the truck. The passenger jumped inside like he'd been trained. I laughed to myself as I made a mental note that he must have been the Mexican equivalent to a Prospect.

"You want to open one of these?" I asked as I motioned to the crates.

"No eets all good. El Pelón says jore homie Corndog is good people. If El Pelón is good, I'm good. Jore not going to fuck us eenyway," he grinned.

"We're in the gun business. I sold these fuckers cheap to build a relationship with your boss. Hopefully, we'll do more business," I said as I hoisted myself into the rear of the truck.

I pointed beside the Mexican's truck, "Just stand at the front of the truck and smile, Avery. We'll be done in a minute."

She smiled and nodded her head without speaking. I was surprised at her demeanor. She didn't appear to be nervous, nor was she overly talkative. The thought of having an outsider in the middle of this deal made me initially feel uncomfortable. The fact she was a woman made me even more uneasy as the day approached. But now that we were almost done with it, I was pleasantly surprised at her ability to remain quiet, not be annoying, and stay out of the way.

"Otis get back here and help me," I grunted as I slid a crate toward the rear of the van.

As Otis peered inside, I explained, "I'll slide 'em to the back of the van, you slide 'em to him. He can have his partner pull 'em into the bed of the truck."

"Got it, Slice," Otis nodded as he jumped into the van.

We unloaded nine of the crates. Surprisingly, they all fit in the back of the truck. As I reached for the last wooden box and began to pull it to the rear of the van, I heard a vehicle. It was tough to tell from inside the van, but the exhaust was loud, and it was accelerating rapidly. For a moment I considered it may be on the adjacent road that led to the parking lot, but I didn't need to speak Spanish to know the jabber from the two Mexicans in the back of the truck wasn't one of joy.

"Fuck!" Otis said as he reached the back of the van.

Standing at the front of the dark van with my face covered in sweat, I couldn't see shit. I hustled to the rear of the van to get a glimpse of what was going on, and my vision became perfectly clear. A completely different Mexican was pointing what appeared to be a Street Sweeper shotgun into the back of the van. He began screaming shit at us in Spanish.

"Don't move, Otis. This beaner's got a fucking Street Sweeper. That cocksucker will cut us in two if he starts shootin'," I said sternly as I raised my hands slowly.

*This was a fucking set-up.*

Without responding, Otis took two steps toward the rear of the van and raised his hands to his sides. The Mexican continued to scream.

*Obviously you have no fucking idea who you're fucking with, do you boy?*

121

# AVERY

What seemed to be a very simple transaction had immediately turned into a huge mess. A truck with two Hispanic males came screaming into the lot, and while it was still rolling into place, one jumped out and held a gun on the two men in the back of the truck. The driver jumped out as soon as the truck stopped, and jumped out with a gun. Now he was screaming into the back of the van as he waved the gun into it. Otis and Axton were in the back of the van, and I was standing toward the front of the truck; alone and scared half to death.

It was as if I didn't even exist. No one was paying attention to *me*.

My purse was draped over my right shoulder. In my purse, as always, was my loaded Glock 9 millimeter pistol. The instructor of the concealed carry course drilled the importance into my head of using the weapon as a last resort in a life or death scenario only. This was clearly one of those situations. It didn't make things any easier. The two Hispanic males were focused on the men in the back of the truck the men in the back of the van.

"El dinero. Dónde está el dinero?" the man screamed into the back of the van.

He wanted to know where the money was.

Maybe they'd take the money and leave. That was probably wishful thinking.

"Dónde está el dinero?" he screamed again.

123

Scared beyond comprehension, I quickly glanced at the van and then toward the truck. The robber at the truck stood quietly on the ground with the gun aimed at the two men who were standing in the bed of the truck on top of the crates of guns. The man standing at the van was shaking the gun and appeared to be extremely nervous.

"El Pelón te matará, pendejo," the English speaking Hispanic whispered to the man on the ground with the gun.

*The bald man is going to kill you.*

"Cállate!" the man with the gun shouted.

*Shut up!*

I couldn't see into the van, but it was pretty obvious neither Otis nor Axton were able to pull their guns.

"El dinero o la vida," he screamed as he shook the gun toward the inside of the van.

He was saying, *your money or your life.*

*He's going to kill Axton.*

The one advantage of the Glock pistol was the absence of a safety or any lever that would have to be messed with prior to pulling the trigger. The internal safety is part of the trigger mechanism, and simply required the gun be pointed and fired. No pulling levers or making distracting noises like on television or the movies.

"Ahora!" the man screamed into the back of the van.

*Now!*

The man at the van with Otis and Axton was apparently done trying to negotiate. He wanted the money *now*. Someone must have tipped him off about the deal going down. I wished I could see Axton or Otis, but I could not. The man at the back of the truck stood quietly with the gun pointed at the two Hispanic men in back. It was obvious they were after the money, and nothing else. The man at the van raised the huge gun to his shoulder as if he was going to shoot. Even if Axton wanted to, he couldn't give him the money; Otis put it in the front of the van. Hell, Axton had no idea what he was saying anyway. If I didn't do something immediately, this was going to end, and end badly.

*If you are in fear for your life or for the life of a loved one, and you have no other alternative...*

I knew if I did anything, I had to do it quickly. I was all of fifteen feet from the back of the van, and I was the same distance from the truck. The man at the back of the truck had his back facing me, and the man at the van had no idea I even existed.

The man at the back of the van lowered the shotgun a little and screamed, "Ahora!"

The English speaking Hispanic made eye contact with me. He was able to see me, but the man with the gun was not, as his back was to me. As I pulled my pistol from my purse, he nodded his head slightly. *God I hope this works.* I took aim at the man behind the van, and fired one shot. As the bullet struck him in the side, his body twisted, and he fired the shotgun into the parking lot. As his body absorbed the shock from his gun firing, he fell to the ground.

The English speaking Hispanic immediately grabbed the barrel of the gun the man was pointing at him and was attempting to twist it from his grasp. As I twisted and took aim at the man's back, he screamed from the back of the truck as he fought for possession of the gun.

He nodded his head toward me as he pushed the barrel of the gun upward and away, "Shoot theese motherfucker!"

Scared and without much thought, I fired a shot into the back of the man standing at the truck. Immediately, he fell against the truck and then flopped onto the ground. I turned toward the van. The man I had shot was on the ground moaning.

The entire thing took a few seconds.

Axton jumped from the rear of the van and picked up the gun the man had dropped. He stepped on the man's neck, raised the gun slightly, and pressed the barrel into the man's chest. The man on the ground began to groan.

*He's still alive. They're both still alive.*

*Thank God.*

"Hijo de la chingada! Your chica saved our asses, homie," the man at the truck said toward Axton.

I stood and shook, still holding the pistol in my hand. My ears felt as if they were on fire. Although I had fired my gun several times during training and at the firing range, I had never fired it without hearing protection. Nothing could have prepared me for the sound of the gun being fired without protection.

"Who are these two motherfuckers?" Axton demanded.

"Putos ladrones!" the driver said as he spit on the man lying on the ground.

"He said they're thieves," I whimpered.

"They're not *your* people?" Axton hollered.

"Fuck no, homie. Someone must to told them we going to meeting. They come for the *money*," he responded.

He looked down and spit on the man lying on the ground, "Fucking puta!"

"Jew can do whatever jew want to with heem. I'm going to execute theeese motherfucker," the driver said as he tilted his head toward Axton.

"Avery. Get in the van. You don't need to see this," Axton demanded.

I noticed Otis was standing behind Axton with his pistol drawn. He was pointing at the man on the ground. I didn't remember seeing him even jump out. I was clearly out of it, and probably in shock. I dropped my pistol into my purse and slowly walked toward the van. As I reached the door, and was out Axton's view, I turned to face the Hispanic man.

"If you're going to do it, do it," I heard Axton shout, "Prove to me he isn't one of yours."

The Hispanic man pulled the trigger of the gun. The man on the ground went limp immediately. I heard another shot. Although I couldn't see him, I assumed Axton killed the man on the ground. I stared at the Hispanic man. Without emotion, he raised the barrel and pointed it at the dead man's head. Again, he pulled the trigger. As the gun fired, the man's head disappeared.

*Holy fuck!*

"Grab that other crate of guns for him, Otis. And pick up Avery's brass, there's two on the ground somewhere. Find them," I heard Axton yell.

"Got it, Slice," Otis responded.

Axton walked beside the van and into my view. I stood and stared.

"I'm keeping this," Axton said as he held the gun in the air.

"I'll gave theeese one to jore partner," the Hispanic man said as he raised the other gun to his chest.

Axton quietly walked up to me and leaned the gun against the van. He opened his arms and without much expression, began to speak.

"I had no idea anything like this would happen. I'm sorry you were involved, but I'm God damned glad you were here. Just like the man said, you saved our asses, Avery."

I stood and stared, not knowing what to do or say.

127

"Come here," he said as he held his arms outstretched and curled his fingers into his palms.

I quietly shuffled my way to him and laid my head against his shoulder. As his arms wrapped around me, I exhaled and bit my quivering lower lip. As he pulled me closer and held me tight, I began to feel safe. Although I had just shot two people, and witnessed their execution; something about being in Axton's strong arms was beginning to make me feel as if nothing else mattered.

As he held me, I realized as far as Axton was concerned this was just another day in the life of being an outlaw. For me, this would without a doubt be a life altering experience. As attracted as I was to Axton, we were two totally different people in so many respects.

As Otis walked alongside the van toward us, I lifted my head from Axton's shoulder. I watched as the Hispanic man drug the body of the man with no head toward the other truck. I blinked my eyes, turned toward Otis, and forced myself to smile. Otis extended his blood covered hand. I blinked again and stared.

"*Devil looks after his own*, Slice. I'm tellin' ya, he damned sure does. One in a million chance, but I got the brass *and* both slugs," he said as he turned his palm upward.

His hand was covered in blood and small pieces of fleshy material. In his palm were the two cartridge casings from my pistol, and the lead bullets. He had apparently dug them out of the dead bodies. He was right, finding them was probably a one in a million chance. Strangely, I wasn't disgusted by it all; I was grateful. Without the bullets or brass casings, there would be no way the police could trace the killings to me. As Axton released me and held his hand out, I shook my head and nudged my way between him and Otis.

128

"Give them to me, they're mine," I demanded.

Otis shifted his gaze back and forth between Axton and me, "They're covered in blood and those Mexican's guts."

"I don't give a fuck, they're mine. And I don't trust either of you two with them," I hissed as I opened my hand.

Axton nodded his head and smiled his shitty little smile.

Otis reached out and dropped the items into my hand. I looked down at my blood soaked palm and stared for a moment; as if I expected to wake up from some weird dream. After a few seconds, I realized this was as real as it gets, and I shoved everything into my pocket. As I wiped my hand on my jeans, it dawned on me; I may not ride a motorcycle or be in some club, but after what happened, the three of us *weren't* that much different.

Without a doubt, in the eyes of the law I had become an outlaw.

And in my eyes...

I had become a *Sinner*.

# AXTON

As soon as we become comfortable and relax in living life, something happens to remind us we aren't nearly as in charge of the outcome as we once thought we were; we're simply along for the ride.

My life had been a full throttle all out run toward the sunset from day one, and it has never let up. From time to time I'd exhale; and when I did, life would slap my face and remind me I wasn't in charge. Avery's involvement in the killings wasn't something I planned or expected, but I couldn't do anything to change it. I did, however, have to try and find a way to make it taste good in my mouth.

After taking Avery home, Otis and I were sitting in the clubhouse attempting to figure out what went wrong, and how we ended up in the situation we were in. Without a doubt, Avery had saved our lives, and we both felt indebted to her for doing so. Having someone clearly save your life, and realizing it, was a humbling experience I wasn't necessarily prepared to admit or accept; at least not yet.

Otis leaned forward and rested his forearms on the edge of the table, "I tell ya what, if she hadn't been there, you and I wouldn't be talkin' right now. I can assure you of that."

"I hate to admit it, but I think you're right," I nodded.

"Shit Slice, you *know* I'm right. That fuckin' beaner was about one breath away from shootin' us and finding that money on his own. She said that cocksucker started screamin' *Now! Now!*" he paused and

131

shifted his focus to the floor.

"You know, there at the end, when he was screamin' like a mad man? That's when she knew it was time. That fucker was done askin', and you and I don't speak fuckin' Spanish. Hell, he was talkin' so God damned fast, none of it could have made sense. It's a good thing she speaks that shit," he raised the beer bottle to his lips and took a drink.

Otis' forearms were still covered in blood. As I studied him I thought of what had happened and who might have put the attempted theft into motion. To think of another Mexican gang attempting to rob the MS-13 was almost impossible for me. No one in their right mind would attempt such a thing. To cross them would not only be suicide, but an assurance your entire family and the families of anyone you knew would be murdered. I was having a difficult time believing the two Mexicans knew who they were robbing on *that* end. I had an easier time believing they knew who *we* were.

I rubbed my hands together clenched my teeth. As I felt my jaw muscles flex, I realized my frustration was reaching an unhealthy level. Typically, I tend to try and resolve issues immediately, before they have a chance to fester within me. The longer I wait to find resolution, the more liable I am to make a decision I may later regret. I sat, stared down at my hands and ran the events of the night through my mind.

I hooked my index finger onto the rubber band and began to play with it, "I've been thinking. There ain't a snowball's chance in hell those two fuckers knew they were robbing the MS-13. And, if they didn't know *that*, it leaves me to believe they *did* know they were robbing us. The more I think about it, the more I think it stinks. Someone said something. And that *something* ended up in the lap of a Mexican gang. They didn't come after the *guns*, they came after the *money*. And they knew *we* had the money. They were screaming at you and me, not the Mexicans. Are you following me?"

"Shit. Yeah I see what you're saying. Fuck, you think one of our own said something?" he asked as he stood from his seat.

"If you already know the answer, don't bother asking the question," I said under my breath.

"I hate thinking of that, Slice," he said as he leaned over the trash can.

I snapped the rubber band against my wrist, "Throw that motherfucker in the shop. God damn, Otis. You know by now I don't want to smell that stinkin' fucker. And I sure as fuck don't like thinkin' of it either, but I can't sit here and be blind. It's pretty simple shit to figure out. Well, now that some fucking beaner ain't waving a Street Sweeper in my face. Wash that blood off your arms when you're in the shop. Hell, you get pulled over on the way home, you're gonna be in fucking jail."

Without speaking, he nodded his head and walked out into the shop. We were both exhausted. The level of adrenaline from the situation we escaped from was so elevated, it had brought me to an all-time high. Coming down off of that high left me tired and feeling weak; and the few times in my life when I found myself feeling weak, it eventually left me feeling vulnerable.

As Otis walked into the office, I turned to face him and stared. I had nothing to say, but I wanted answers, and I wanted them immediately. Being in a motorcycle club exposes a person to all types of violence, activities, and situations which will make most people cower in fear. Over the years I had become almost immune to any feeling associated with exposing myself to violence or criminal acts. Being killed was an entirely different story.

"What are we gonna do about the girl?" Otis asked as he sat down. He raised his hands to his face and began to rub his temples.

I sat up in my chair and stared, "What do you mean?"

"We owe her big time, Slice. God damn, she saved our fuckin' lives. I was cleaning all the blood off my arms, and thinkin'. It kinda freaked me out. But if she hadn't gone…"

"We owe her ass big time," he breathed.

I narrowed my eyes and stared, "You want to buy her a thank you card or get her some fucking flowers? Or maybe a box of fucking chocolates?"

Otis stood from his chair, lowered his hands from his face, and shook his head, "You know Slice, you're the president of this club *and* you're my best friend. But I got to be honest on this one. You're a real prick. That fuckin' girl saved us. She didn't wash your sled or have new soles put on your boots. She shot two motherfuckers who were tryin' to shoot us. Hell, she coulda took that sixty grand and ran. And they'd of killed us for sure. But she didn't. I know she was scared to death. Hell, she ain't one of us and she sure as fuck ain't used to being in the shit we are."

I stood up and began to speak, "We can sit here all night…"

Otis raised his hand in the air, "I wasn't done, *Axton*. This is you and me talkin'. *Steve and Axton*. That girl saved my fuckin' life, plain and simple. No real way around it. There's sayin' it, there's understanding it, and then there's *believing* it. And I'm tellin' ya, when I was cleaning the blood off my arms, I come to believe it. Yeah, buy her a box of fuckin' chocolates, you asshole. Send her a fuckin' card. But I can tell you what I'm gonna do."

"I'm gonna make God damned sure nothing ever happens to that little girl, Axton. Ain't no motherfucker on this earth ever gonna harm that little bitch. I owe her my life. You do whatever your heartless ass thinks is best. But you know what's best for the club? Do ya? I *do*, and I have my fuckin' doubts about you," he hesitated and crossed his arms in front of his chest.

I crossed my arms in front of my chest and flexed my biceps, "You doubting me, Otis?"

Otis uncrossed his arms and chuckled, "Keep flexin' on me, Axton. It's just you and me here, remember? I'll wad your fuckin' ass up and toss you in the street. Do I doubt you? No. Not really ever. But on this deal? You fuckin' right I do. That girl needs taken care of. She needs to stay on our good side. Here's the deal…"

"You know why I ain't got an Ol' Lady? You know why?" he asked.

I shrugged.

"Because I ain't found one I can trust. That's it. Now, why ain't you got an Ol' Lady? And before you answer, I'll tell ya. Because you're an asshole, and you don't let yourself believe one won't fuck you over. Hell, those ratty-assed bitches you had in the past were just that, ratty-assed bitches. Ratty-assed bitches can't ever be trusted, but it doesn't mean all bitches can't be trusted. Now *you* tell me the reason," he hesitated and crossed his arms again.

"So now we're talkin' about Ol' Ladies? I'm trying to figure out who fucked us over, and you're talkin' about having an Ol' Lady? And *you* want to question *me*?" I growled.

"You didn't answer my fuckin' question, Axton," he said under his breath.

"Fuck it. I'm tired. I'm going home. But I'll say this," he paused and slowly walked toward the door.

As he reached for the door, he turned to face me, "You said that night in the bar she was off-limits. Well, make a decision, *boss*. I'll remind you, we got bylaws and we got em for a reason. They're posted on the wall behind ya in case you forgot 'em. But you ain't claimed her as your Ol' Lady, you ain't got her wearin' a *Property Of* patch, and you sure as absolute fuck don't have an "X" by your name. So, as far as the club's concerned, she's fair game. If you don't make a move, I sure as hell will. You want to know why?"

He walked through the door and into the shop.

Before I could respond, he stuck his head in the opening between the door and the door frame, widened his eyes, and began telling me his thoughts, "She's gorgeous. She's got guts. She don't take shit from anybody. She stands up for what she believes in. She don't run her mouth like a teenager, and…"

"Because that little bitch has got my back," he nodded his head once and pulled the door closed.

I lowered myself into the chair and removed my notepad from my jacket. I drew a line down the center of the page. I moved the pen to the left side of line and hesitated. I felt the need to make a list of the people I could trust one hundred percent and the people who I wasn't sure of. To think of someone being in the club and not being able to be trusted was a difficult thing for me. At some point in time, I trusted each and every member enough to vote them into the club. Now, to consider one of my brothers turning against me was a difficult thing to imagine.

I faced the wall and stared at the list of members. After studying the board for a few moments, I turned around, closed my note pad, and removed my jacket. I needed to clear my mind. I walked to the door, flipped the light switch, and gazed out into the shop. My bike sat beside

136

the van we had used to make the delivery with my cut hanging from the ape hangers.

I gazed at the cabinet on the left side of the shop and sighed.

*You're tired Axton. Take some time to think.*

I sauntered over to the cabinet, opened it, and removed a lick 'n stick seat and a clean rag. After I methodically wiped the dust from the rear fender of the bike, I cleaned the seat's suction cups and pressed it onto the rear fender. I glanced at my watch. 1:22 am.

If Avery was anything like me, she wouldn't be able to sleep at all. After my first shooting, I didn't sleep for two days. If for whatever reason she *was* able to sleep, maybe she was more valuable than Otis indicated.

There was only one way to find out.

# AXTON

I looked up the landing of the stairs to the upper floor and stared at the windows of Avery's apartment. The flickering light led me to believe the television was on. Quietly, I walked up the steps, to the door, and knocked three times.

Sloan answered the door in grey sweats that were three sizes too small and a wife beater just large enough to cover her tits and a few inches of her extremely long torso. I gazed past her expecting to see Avery watching television. The small living room appeared empty.

"Hey Axton, what's up?" she whispered.

"Is Avery awake?" I asked as I peered over her shoulder.

"Uhhm, no. She went to sleep right after you brought her home. You want me to wake her up?" she asked.

"Asleep, huh?" I sighed as I pushed my hands into my jeans pockets.

I gazed down at the WELCOME mat in front of the door. As I looked up, I smiled, "As a matter of fact, I do. Wake her up. Tell her that her Ol' Man is here to get her."

As soon as I spoke, I couldn't believe those words came out of my mouth. It was one of those things you say by complete accident or some psychologically triggered inner thought and wish you could immediately take it back. For a split-second I considered grabbing Sloan's dumb ass and slapping the shit out of her while I explained not to repeat what I had said.

She narrowed her gaze and stared.

"Ol' Man?" she shrugged.

"Never mind, forget it. Tell her *Slice* is here, and I want to take her for a ride," I responded.

She stared at me and blinked her eyes, "Slice?"

"That's right. Tell her Ol' Slice is here," I said, attempting to force myself to grin.

Sloan stood in the doorway and stared as she pressed her upper arms into the sides of her tits.

"Ol' Slice?" she giggled.

*Step aside, you nasty bitch.*

Sick and tired of dealing with Sloan and her two twins, I stepped past where she was standing and into the apartment, being careful not to brush against her when I did. A few well-placed steps and I stood at the bedroom with the door closed.

I gazed over my shoulder, "The one with the door closed?"

*Buy some clothes that fit, you big bitch.*

"Yeah, that's it," she responded as she dug her thumbs into the waistband of her sweats, lowering them even more.

I rolled my eyes and turned around. I slowly turned the door handle and pushed it open. The room was pitch black. I flipped on the light switch and stared into the small room. Sure enough, Avery was fast asleep in her bed. Otis was right, she was gorgeous. After admiring her for a moment, I paused, turned off the lights, and closed the door.

As I turned to face the living room, I noticed Sloan had taken a seat in front of the couch. Sitting in the chair with her legs crossed and her heels in front of her crotch, she looked up and grinned. Although they weren't when I arrived, her nipples were now as hard as rocks and appeared to be attempting to poke completely through the light fabric of her ribbed wife beater. Without speaking, I walked past her and to the front door.

As I reached for the door handle, she was already standing behind me. Quickly, I stepped through the door and onto the porch. As I turned around, I was greeted by a smile and her increasingly growing nipples.

*Horny bitch...*

"Tell her Slice came by. I'll see her tomorrow," I sighed.

"Okay, *Slice*," she grinned as she ran her thumbs along the waist of the sweats, lowering them enough to expose the top band of her orange panties.

I blinked my eyes and chuckled to myself.

*I'll make sure you get an invite to the barbeque. I'll have half a dozen Sinners with big cocks waiting to gang bang your dumb ass.*

"You like barbeque?" I asked.

"What do you mean?" she shrugged, pressing her upper arms into her tits.

"Meat, Sloan. You ever heard of barbeque? Ribs, brisket, hot links, chicken? Cook the shit over a grill and eat it? Fucking barbeque?"

"Oh, yeah. I freaking love it, why?"

"Well, we have a club barbeque coming up. I'll make sure you're invited. It might give you a chance to meet a few of the fellas. How's that sound?"

"Sounds freaking awesome," she giggled.

"Consider it done," I nodded.

I turned, walked down the stairs, and laughed to myself as I considered what Avery told me about Sloan. *She really, really, really likes cock; the bigger the better.* I threw my leg over the bike and thought of Pete holding her down while Hollywood shoved her twat full of cock and Toad shoved his down her throat. There was something about Sloan I didn't like, but I couldn't put my finger on it. I was pretty damned sure having the fellas fuck her senseless would make me feel a little better about being forced to look at her in the future. I glanced over my shoulder at the lick 'n stick seat on my rear fender. If there was one thing I detested, it was a seat on my bike without someone sitting on it. I sighed, reached up to the ape hangers and rested my hands on the grips. I fired up the bike and considered going back to the shop and tossing the seat in the cabinet. As the sound of the exhaust echoed throughout the parking lot, I pulled in the clutch and kicked the bike into gear.

*Hell, Axton, you won't be able to sleep anyway.*

There was one man in Wichita who may be able to shed some light on the Mexicans trying to rob us. If there was ever a man who slept less than me, it would be him. I glanced over my shoulder at the seat.

*I suppose it won't hurt anything to leave it on there until tomorrow.*

I nodded my head, forcing my glasses down onto the bridge of my nose, and grabbed a handful of throttle. I figured this late at night I could probably make it there in ten minutes. I just needed to make a quick stop and get one person to go with me.

The man who never sleeps.

# AXTON

At three o'clock in the morning, a person knows for certain just how loud his bike really is. At any time of the day, my bike was loud enough to trigger car alarms, and wake the dead. This early in the morning in a neighborhood full of three million dollar homes, my bike was loud enough to get the cops called pretty damned quickly. I shoved my cell phone into my pocket and waited for the gates to open. As they began to swing apart, I held my left hand out with my palm flat, motioning to proceed slowly. Traveling at part throttle was still louder than a horrible thunderstorm, but as quiet as we could possibly be. As I rolled up to the third house on the right, I raised my left arm and motioned into the driveway.

After riding up the long angled driveway, it finally flattened out in front of the house. I killed the engine and quietly rolled in front of the porch. Appearing more like a mansion than a conventional Kansas home, I stared at the huge stone pillars on either side of the front porch. Not my style, but definitely an ornate entry. There was probably only one home like this in the world where I would truly feel comfortable, and this was it. As Toad killed his engine and rolled up beside me, I looked over my shoulder in his direction.

He shook his head as he stared at the front of the home, "You shittin' me, Slice? Are we at the right place?"

"Yep, this is it," I nodded.

The front door opened and King stepped out onto the porch. Six foot tall and built like a professional football player, his cleanly shaved head and goatee made him an intimidating man in appearance. Dressed in a silk robe and slippers, however, he looked as if he belonged in the ritzy neighborhood. Knowing his background, the amount of time he had spent in prison, and his manner of earning the money he used to buy the home, I chuckled at the sight of him.

"Nice robe, King," I laughed.

"Get your tired asses up here and in the house," he said as he waved toward the open front door.

"Place like this makes me nervous," Toad whispered.

"You won't be for long. King's one solid ass dude," I said as I stepped off the bike.

As we followed King into the home, it was apparent he had spared no expense in building the house or decorating it. A large screen Television on the wall in the kitchen had eight split screens depicting various portions of the facility and grounds. Considering the fact it was three in the morning, it was obvious they were taken with infrared cameras. Leave it up to King to take every precaution in making sure he was not being robbed, watched, or eavesdropped on; at least not without him seeing it happen.

"So, a visit from the Sinners makes me nervous. A visit at three am by the President himself makes me *really* God damned nervous. To what do I owe this visit, Slice?" he asked.

"I'll get to that in a minute. King, this is Toad. Toad's a six tour Marine; fought in Afghanistan and Iraq both. Toad, this is Mr. King, but we leave off the mister, don't we King?"

"That we do, there's no mister in front of my name. Good God damn, six fucking tours? Hell, I know now why Slice brought you. I have a soft spot in my heart for men who keep my country free. I appreciate your service, Toad. I see you're flying the colors of a Sinner. Wise choice, if I do say so myself," King nodded as he extended his hand.

Toad shook his hand and nodded his head sharply, "I appreciate it. Just doing my job."

King cleared his throat as he released Toad's hand, "Go sell that humble shit to someone stupid enough to buy it. I'm part gook, part nigger, part Mexican, and part who fucking knows what, but I'm not a dumb man, Toad. If you fought in six tours as a Marine, you did so because you believed in what you were doing, and I appreciate it."

"Thank you," Toad said flatly.

"Slice," King said as he turned and shook my hand.

"King," I nodded.

"So. Have a seat, gentlemen. What can I get you to drink?" he asked.

"I'm straight," Toad said.

"Same," I agreed.

"Alright then. Well, I was up watching Denzel Washington in *The Equalizer* when you called. Hell, it's over now. Have you seen that one yet?" he asked.

I shook my head.

"That motherfucker took care of business. I like it when a man does that. It keeps everyone honest. So, as I asked before, to what do I owe this visit?" King asked as he sat down in a huge chair that resembled an upholstery covered throne.

I sat across from him on a large couch and Toad sat beside me on the loveseat. I had brought Toad along for the exact reason King imagined. It was no secret King admired military men, especially if a man had actually seen combat. I didn't think I needed to make King feel indebted to the club, but having Toad along would convince him in some respects to provide whatever information he could to assist us.

I turned to face King and rubbed my hands against my thighs, "We did a deal with a local MS-13 clique…"

"Stop right there," King said as he stood from his chair.

"Do you know who you're fucking with?" he asked as he began to pace the room.

I nodded my head sharply, "Sure do. Let me finish, it's not what you think. We're good with them, it's something else. Or at least I think it is."

"Those motherfuckers make *me* nervous, and *nobody* makes me nervous," King sighed.

I stood from my seat and faced King, "Well, let me tell you what happened. I'll take your opinion on it, and I'll let you nose around and see what you can find out. I know you know people we don't, and I need all the help I can get here."

"Sit down, Slice. Son-of-a-bitch, a deal with MS-13? Alright, let's hear it," King said as he sat down in his throne.

As King sat, I began to speak and sat back down on the edge of the couch, "So, Corndog is damned near done doing his time. He's got in tight with some Mexicans in prison, the south siders from LA. One thing led to another, and they learned we deal in weapons. After a little negotiation, I made a deal with some of the Mexicans on the outside who were affiliated with the fellas on the inside. We were hoping for a long-term relationship and some support or credibility from these guys. I felt if they supported the club, it'd make us a damned site stronger in everyone's eyes. So, I made a deal. A hundred AK's for sixty grand…"

King's eyes widened as he stood from his seat, "You sold a hundred AK-47's for *sixty grand* to the Mexicans?"

"Sure did."

He shook his head lightly, "First things first, *El Presidente*. Or maybe I should say *El Stupido...*"

"I don't speak Mexican, but I don't think I like what you're saying, King," I chuckled.

"Sixty grand? You *gave* those motherfuckers away. You know that, right?" he shrugged.

I nodded my head, "I do. And I made sure they knew I knew. Also, I made an agreement in advance for the price on the second shipment if they wanted more."

"*Hijo de la chingada.* Shit, at that price, I'll take a few hundred. Jesus, Slice. Go ahead, tell me the rest, I can't wait to see where this went," he sighed as he sat down again.

"So, the club knows of the transaction. And, of course, MS-13's people know, that's it. No discussions with anyone else. We go to do the deal on the north side of town, the old abandoned grocery store over on Arkansas and thirty-second or whatever," I paused as King nodded his head and raised his hand to his chin.

"Well, we're doing the deal, and Otis and I are loading the weapons into the truck. We're in the back of a Ryder moving van, and the Mexicans are in the back of the truck. We're just sliding the crates to the Mexicans and they're humping 'em into the truck. We're parked tailgate to tailgate. I can't see shit because it's dark as fuck, and we're down to the last crate."

I stood from my seat and began to pace the living room.

"So I heard something, and I started walking to the front of the

147

van. I thought it was a truck out in the street, but it seemed closer than that. And I heard the Mexicans talking a hundred miles an hour. And although I got no fucking idea what they're saying, I know they ain't happy. Anyway, I get to the door of the van, and some fucking beaner points a Street Sweeper at Otis and me, and starts screaming. Another one has a gun on the two Mexicans in the back of the truck, but he ain't saying shit."

I turned to face King. Leaning back in his chair with his eyebrows raised, he sat quietly; ready for me to finish the story. As if waiting for the punchline to a joke, he raised his hand to his chin and grinned as he crossed his legs.

"So, now let me back up. It was brought to my attention that my contact was not an English speaking Mexican, so I took someone to interpret for me. And she was standing outside by the Mexican's truck."

King uncrossed his legs and stared my direction, "You took a *girl* to do a gun deal with the MS-13?"

"She was my only option, King."

"You could have called *me*," he responded.

I turned my palms up and shrugged, "I didn't think of it. I'm damned near done, let me get through this."

"So, after this beaner gets mad, maybe two or three minutes of screaming for us to *give him the money*, he's done. He starts screaming he wants it *now*. But Otis and I got no idea what he wants, 'cause we don't speak Spanish. I can't pull my piece, and Otis can't pull his, we got our hands up at our chests, and we're wearing fucking jackets. About this time I hear two quick gunshots. The beaner drops the Street Sweeper, and it discharges into the parking lot. I jump out, and see him and another on the ground. My girl is standing there with her Glock, shaking like she's shittin' stickers. The MS-13 who does speak English tells me these guys aren't his people, and I say *prove it*. Now at this time, they're both on the ground but they're not dead. He shoots one of the guys in the back, and then blows his head clean off. I shoot the other one. He drags them to the side, we shake hands, and it's over," I paused and turned to face King.

"So my questions are one, who were these motherfuckers? And two, how did they know?"

King stood from his chair and shook his head, "Did your girl know where you were meeting?"

"Nope."

"Did your club?" he asked.

"Yep," I nodded.

He raised his hand to his mouth and stared down at the floor for a moment. He looked up and narrowed his eyes, "Did the two you were dealing with before the other two showed up have any *MS* tats? You know those fuckers always seem to. Did they have any you could see?"

"One had a number thirteen tattooed on his face, and the other had *MS-13* tattooed on his neck. Clear as day, why?"

"All those fuckers do; if they're the real deal. They'll have the tats right where you can see them; hands, face, head, neck, forearms. They don't hide the shit. It's a pride thing. If they didn't, I'd say it was a set-up from the start. But, if they did, they're real MS. If someone has the tats and they aren't affiliated, MS will cut their heads off and toss them up on the hood of a car for show. I did time with those crazy pricks in the joint. Okay, so the fellas you were dealing with were legit. Now, the other two, the deceased, did they have any tats?" he asked.

I crossed my arms and thought, "Not MS, no."

"And at the time the other two show up, you've already got the money and the guns are loaded in the Mexicans truck. They come to the truck and ask for the money? They didn't try and take the guns?"

"Correct."

"Well, here's *my* opinion, knowing what I know about MS-13. There isn't a Mexican on the entire planet who would rob the MS-13 *knowing* they were MS-13. They might on accident, but definitely not if they knew who they were. So, these two *ladrones* show up, but they didn't come to rob *them*, they came to rob *you*. Sounds like they knew which direction the sale was going too, the more I think about it. Hell, you wouldn't roll up on a deal like that and know who was loading and who was unloading. If they came to *you* asking for the money, so they knew *you* had it. You said the guy at the Mexican's truck was quiet? Not making demands? Well, that sums it up. They came for the money, and they knew the direction of the deal. Make sense?"

I nodded my head slowly, "Makes sense. Yeah, they guy at the truck didn't say shit that I heard. The guy at our van just started screaming. The girl told me later he was saying, *where is the money?*"

King raised his hands in the air, "Well, if he started screaming, *where is the money* right out of the gate, he knew."

I uncrossed my arms and glanced at Toad, and then back toward King, "I guess that brings us to the same question. Did the tip come from them or from the Sinners? I might need a little help nosing around here, King. Someone in this city knows who those two were, and you know everybody. So, I'm asking for you to do me a solid on this deal. See if you can find out who they were. That's all. I should be able to make a connection from there."

"I'll do that. Let me see what I can find out. Now, I sure as fuck can't tell you how to run your business, but consider this, Slice," King paused and pointed at Toad.

"Does anyone short of Otis and Toad know about this deal and how it went?" he asked.

"Just the girl," I shrugged.

He opened his arms and nodded his head, "Act like the deal went without a hitch, like it was *perfect*. Don't tell a fucking soul what really happened. See if anyone says anything or asks questions. See if someone acts out of place. But don't say one word about the attempted robbery. And start looking into if there's a member who has financial problems or a sick wife, kid, or relative. You know, someone who needs money and might be desperate. A desperate man acts out of desperation. Leave no one out of your in-house investigation. Hell, start with your boy Toad. Oh, and one more thing…"

"Don't be surprised if your contact with MS-13 doesn't call you first with the names and background information of the two dead Mexicans. They won't take an attempted robbery lightly. To them, it'll all be about respect. And he'll look at it as disrespectful to you, and in turn, to him. He'll dig around, you can bet on that."

I extended my hand, "I guess that's all I've got. I appreciate everything, King."

He nodded his head and shook my hand. As he released my hand from his grip, Toad stood from the loveseat and quickly walked toward the door. As he reached the entrance and stopped, King inhaled a shallow breath and laughed as he exhaled.

"Damn, your boy Toad's ready to get the fuck out of here. Doesn't even want to shake my hand," King chuckled.

Toad turned around and stared at King. The look on his face wasn't one of gratitude or thanks. If looks could kill, King was a dead man. *What the fuck, Toad?*

Toad dangled his arms at his side and popped his neck, "I don't know you, *King*. And out of respect, I was going to leave here without embarrassing you. But now that you mentioned it, I'll explain something to you. You called me *boy* twice now. I'm not a boy, and I haven't been for some time now. You might have helped the club, and you might be doing Slice here a solid, but you've got *nothing* coming from me, you disrespectful prick. And, if you don't agree with me, you can step up here on the porch and I'll whip your ass in your own home. Don't disrespect me again, motherfucker."

Toad turned, opened the door, and walked outside. I glanced toward King. He shrugged and lowered his shoulders.

"Shit Slice. He's right. I didn't even realize I'd said it. Now that he mentioned it, I guess I did. I've done time in the joint, and a lot of it. Hell, I *know* better. If you will, explain to him I'm better than that. Hell, just let yourself out, and tell Toad I apologize."

"He's a hot-head, King. And he won't take shit from *any* man. I ain't saying he's wrong. But I didn't even notice. I'll tell him what you said," I said as I slapped King on the back.

"I'll be in touch," he responded.

As I walked toward the door, I considered King's advice. If there were two people I *knew* I didn't need to question regarding the robbery, they were Toad and Otis. Thinking of any of my brothers crossing the club wasn't easy, but King was right. Desperate men make desperate acts. As I stepped onto the porch, I immediately noticed the lick 'n stick seat still on the fender of my bike. I looked down at my watch. Hell, another hour and a half, and the sun would be up. Realistically, I realized

I should get some sleep.
But first things always come first.
I needed to put that seat to use.

# AVERY

Living life is similar to assembling a puzzle without the box to show you what it will look like when you're done. One piece after another pressed into place until eventually you begin to understand just what it is that sits before you. If you don't try to push the pieces into place, no progress is made, and you never truly know if they would have fit. When they do snap into place, everything starts to make sense, one little piece at a time.

I initially became attracted to Axton because he was a very handsome man. Hell, anyone who looks at him would agree, regardless of whether or not they were attracted to other aspects of who he was. He was simply drop dead gorgeous. Now, I was even *more* attracted to him, and for reasons other than his good looks.

More than likely contrary to what most other women would feel in his presence, he caused me to feel safe. I felt as if nothing or no one could or would harm me when I was in his presence. One thing that always fascinated me about carrying my gun was how I felt safe, powerful, and as if no one could penetrate the barrier the gun created. The gun provided me a false sense of hope. Hope of no one stepping into my bubble and snapping a piece of my puzzle into place I didn't necessarily want.

Simply standing next to Axton, I felt invincible.

When he was gone, I felt vulnerable and powerless.

I sat outside a coffeehouse in Riverside, sipping on a cup coffee and wondering just what piece of my puzzle Axton was going to snap into place. I was anxious to step back when he was done and see just what direction my life was headed and if the piece were in a place where I could make sense of what the end result would be.

"So, I rolled that motherfucker up and strapped it to the bottom of the apes. Hell, it's how all those Chicano bikers do it out in California. I figured what the hell, my sixty thousand dollar blanket," he said as he nodded his head toward his bike.

His motorcycle was parked in the street, against the curb. For all practical purposes, it had been stripped of all accessories. It didn't have blinkers on the rear, only a license plate. In the front, it had a headlight, running lights, and blinkers, but only because they were an integral part of the headlight assembly. On the bottom of the ape hanger handlebars, he had strapped the Mexican blanket the money was wrapped in. It truly looked like it belonged there.

"I like it," I smiled.

He stared at the bike and squinted his eyes, "I hate changing shit, but I'm getting used to it. Now that seat? That's a totally different story. I'll never get used to that motherfucker on there, and those suction cups fuck up my paint."

I shrugged my shoulders, "Sorry."

"Price I got to pay," he said as he shifted his gaze to me.

I wanted to ask him what he got in return, but with Axton I'd learned to bite my lip. So far, he and I were making progress. It was minimal for sure, but small measurable improvements nonetheless. Saying something smart-assed was my natural nature, but learning to be quiet was going a long way with him. The old adage, *don't speak unless spoken to* seemed all too applicable around Axton and his group. And, as my father used to say, *if it isn't broken, don't try to fix it.*

"So, we've got a club barbeque coming up. I'd like for you and Sloan to come. You'll be my guest, and Sloan will be..." he hesitated and looked down into his lap.

"Well, I don't know what Sloan will be. She'll be *your* guest," he sighed as he looked up.

I reached down, picked up my coffee cup, and raised it to my mouth as I tried not to smile. Having him invite me to a club *anything* was exciting, and it was a step in the direction I wanted to take with him. Sloan going, on the other hand, didn't excite me too much. I tipped the cup up, took a small drink, and forced myself not to smile.

"Don't invite her on my account. She's a big girl. She can find shit to do on her own."

He looked across the table and clasped his hands together, "Well, I want to talk to you about that. I'm not going to try and bullshit you here. I don't care much for that bitch. I know you two are tight and all, but something about her gets under my fucking skin. Here's why I want her to come..."

He rubbed his palms together eagerly, "I want one or more of the fellas to rip that bitch a new ass."

*What the fuck? Rip her a new ass? What?*

I leaned into the table and narrowed my eyes, "Huh?"

"You know, rip her a new ass. Like Toad and Pete or Otis. Or whoever," he grinned.

"I have no idea what you're talking about, and I'm afraid I don't want to."

He leaned into his seat and crossed his arms, "You said she likes big

157

cocks. In fact, *the bigger the better* is what you said. Well, I wanted her to come to the barbeque and meet some of the fellas. I can guarantee you she'll get some cock at the barbeque. She ain't gonna meet her groom at this motherfucker, but she'll damned sure get herself fucked real good. Especially if she dresses the way she normally does."

I crossed my arms and stared at him. Something about Sloan fucking one of the *other* members of the club appealed to me as well. Maybe more than it did to Axton. In the two weeks since the botched robbery, she hadn't shut up about Axton. *Slice this, Slice that.* She had reminded me no less than two dozen times in the last two weeks that Axton was hotter than any other man she'd ever seen. It reached a point I had to continually remind her, although Axton and I weren't a couple, and we weren't even technically seeing each other, he was still very much off-limits. Her evening attire changed from the typical hoodie to a wife beater and no bra. Typically I'm not a jealous person, but I'd reached my limit on her unintended *nipple salutes* as well as her verbal advancements.

"So, just out of curiosity, what satisfaction do you get out of this? Oh, and before I forget, yeah, count *me* in. I can't wait. Now, answer the question, please."

He leaned forward and rested his forearms on the table. As I studied him, I realized I had only seen him wear two different outfits. One was jeans and a jacket the night of the gun deal. Other than that, I'd only seen him in jeans, boots, and his cut. No doubt it was fine with me, but I'd never really thought about it before.

"Well, I guess knowing the fellas won't show her any mercy. Even if a bitch *wants* some cock, if she fucks a drunk biker, she's gonna get more cock than she really ever thought possible. She'll have a hard time walking for a week. Knowing one of the fellas beat her pussy to a pulp and walked away without so much as a hand shake would suit me just fine," he smiled.

I rolled my eyes, "I can't believe I'm agreeing to this. Seriously, it's just wrong. But yeah, I'll talk her into going. It won't take much. Oh, and she says she loves sucking cocks, tell them that, too."

"Doesn't really matter if she likes to or not, she'll be doing it anyway," he chuckled.

It's strange how a woman changes when a man steps into the picture, but thinking of any other girl flirting with, hitting on, talking to, or even thinking about Axton was enough to make me angry; Sloan included. I wanted to either win Axton's heart, or lose him entirely, but I didn't want anyone interfering with the process. Lately, hearing Sloan talk about how *smoking hot* he was caused enough tension between us to make me uncomfortable having him come by to take me for a ride. Maybe the barbeque would be just the right thing for her.

I smiled and picked up my coffee cup, "Sounds good to me. I'll tell her. She'll be excited. I know I am."

"You done?" he asked as he motioned to my cup.

I nodded my head and shook my cup, "Yep. This fucker's empty."

"Toss it. Let's ride," he responded.

"Don't have to tell me twice," I said as I jumped from my seat and tossed the cup into the trash.

Something about being on the back of Axton's bike made me feel special. It was as if when we rode together, I was actually *his*. I knew I wasn't, but when I was on the back, and my arms were wrapped around him, it seemed as if we were one; a part of each other. Flying around the roads together having people look at us like we were different. Seeing people at stoplights giving him the *thumbs up* out of either fear, jealousy, or some type of appreciation; and being a part of it made me feel as if I was something or someone I always wanted to be.

To be irreplaceable, we have to clearly stand out as being different.

And when I was on the back of Axton's bike, I was just that.

"Ready?" he asked.

I gripped his waist in my hands and pressed my feet onto the foot pegs. I leaned forward and rested my chin lightly on his shoulder and breathed into his ear, "Always."

And I meant it.

*Always.*

# AVERY

There's the being honest and not necessarily saying *everything*, and then there's being honest in everything you say. The former was what I was attempting to accomplish. So far, I was doing pretty well, and hoping the conversation shifted before I was tempted to say something I may very well later regret.

"No, what he said was this. *See if you can talk her into going, it'll be fun*," I said over the sound of Sloan's hairdryer.

She switched off the hairdryer, bent over, and flipped her hair over her shoulders as she quickly stood, "I think it'll be a freaking blast. And all those guys from the bar? God, there's like fifty of them."

I rolled my eyes and pressed *play* on the remote. Although I had never seen them in the past, I was on season three of Sons of Anarchy on Netflix. To me, Axton was Jax Teller; only bigger, meaner, and better looking. I had become an instant fan of the show, and really didn't want it to end, but I knew it already had. I was doing my best to make the series last, but found it difficult not to watch them as fast as I could.

"You know he kind of already asked me a few weeks ago, when he came over that night looking for you. We were standing out on the porch talking, and he asked me if I liked barbeque. I told him I did. He probably remembered it from when I told him that night. He looked really tired and like he hadn't slept in a while. I felt sorry for him. You know, I should have offered to let him sleep on the couch," she said as she pulled her hair into a ponytail.

*You overweight fucking bitch. You couldn't even fit that fat ass of yours on his bike.*

I closed my eyes and bit my lower lip. It was all I could do to not go absolutely psycho on her ass. Hopefully after the barbeque, someone would be fucking her regularly and she'd leave Axton out of her future thoughts. As the scene in SOA shifted to the lady strapped in the wheelchair in the basement, I chuckled at the thought of strapping Sloan to a chair and having ten of Axton's biker brothers slap her around and teach her a lesson.

"What's so funny" she asked over her shoulder as she walked past.

"It's Sons of Anarchy. Nothing, just a funny part," I shrugged as I looked up.

*Gain weight much?*

"I love that show," she said as she stepped into the room.

I alternated glances between the television and the bedroom door as Sloan stood in front of the mirror. She appeared to be bigger and her face looked fat. It seemed as if I hadn't seen her in the few weeks Axton and I had been spending more time together, but she never seemed to just *get fat* before. As she disappeared into the room, I turned to the television. Opie was standing in the street talking to Jax. I realized if Opie's head was shaved, he'd look just like Pete. As Sloan walked in front of the mirror again, I shifted my gaze to the doorway. My eyes widened to the point I was afraid they'd fall out of the sockets.

*Holy shit.*

She stood in front of the mirror with her hands cupped over her bare boobs. She wore a thong, and nothing else. It wasn't a pose I had never seen, because it was pretty common for her to stand in front of

162

the mirror half-naked. I had never, however, seen her look as big as she did. Her ass was huge, her thighs looked like tree trunks, and her boobs looked like a one-layer round cake flattened against her chest.

I pushed *pause* on the remote and walked to the bathroom. I turned on the water and stood in front of the sink, looking in the mirror. I turned to my side. I glanced up and down the length of my body from head to toe. I turned half way around. I faced the mirror and turned off the water. I reached for my wrist and removed my hair tie and pulled my hair into a ponytail. It was one week before graduation, and for the first time since I began to attend college, the girl looking back at me was the one I always wanted to be. I flushed the toilet and walked out into the living room.

As I sat down and grabbed the remote, I gazed toward Sloan's bedroom. She stood in front of the mirror in a pair of shorts and a volleyball tee.

"You look fucking *hot*," I shouted.

"Really? Do you like these shorts?" she asked.

I nodded my head eagerly, "Fuck yeah I like 'em. They make your ass look *perfect*. Have you like, lost weight for graduation?"

"Do I look like it?" she asked over her shoulder as she gazed into the mirror.

"Uhh, *yeah*. You look fucking hot," I lied.

"Thanks, you look good too," she grinned.

And, for the first time since Sloan and I had met, I smiled knowing she was right.

I looked good.

# AXTON

I had no real way of knowing if it was the arrival of summer, the fact Corndog was getting out of prison, or some subconscious feeling of accomplishment from living through the botched robbery, but my moods in the last week or so had changed from my typical asshole self to an asshole with a sense of humor. Almost as if I was witnessing someone else go through the motions of living life, I was enjoying my exposure to myself throughout the course of each day.

"Take 'em off, Prospect," I howled.

Cash surveyed the crowd. Every member of the club wasn't present, but there were twelve watching and waiting, including me. He gazed at Otis as if the big man was his salvation, his way out, his only hope.

I crossed my arms and flexed my biceps, "Hey motherfucker, look at me when I'm talking to you. That big son-of-a-bitch can't help you. It's me you got to worry about. Now, I told you to drop your pants and get your cock out. You don't have a choice. Drop 'em."

He reached for his belt and unbuckled it. As he unbuttoned his jeans and pulled them past his boxers, everyone started pointing and talking shit. Not a one of us had any *proof* of the alleged *choad*, but we wanted to know just what he was packing before the barbeque. There were a number of single women who would be coming to the party, and having Cash trying to pick up on them and embarrassing the club by pulling out a one-inch cock would be a disaster. After a short discussion, I decided to have him pull it out so we could see if it was something that belonged in a circus.

His jeans now bunched around his knees, and standing in his boxers, he hooked his thumbs into the waistband and stood as if waiting on directions.

"Prospect, if I tell you to go find a fucking dog turd and eat it, you better start sniffing. If I tell you to go cut the toe off a North Korean Communist and bring it to me on a chain, you better get on a fucking boat and start rowing straight west of here. And if I tell you to whip out your cock for me and the fellas to do a cock inspection, you better whip that motherfucker out. Drop 'em, Prospect," I demanded.

Cash sighed, pushed his boxers down to his thighs, and leaned back as he pressed the web of his hands into his hips. Several of the men started clapping and whistling as he pushed his shorts down. Otis and I stared in wait. As Cash stood with his hands on his hips, he lowered his gaze to the ground as if embarrassed. Slowly, his cock began to rise to attention. The crowd gathered erupted into either laughter or cat-calls. Somewhat shocked, but probably more prepared after Avery's description than the rest of the crowd, I stood and stared as if it were a six car wreck on the freeway.

"Jesus God damned Christ, Slice. Kid's got a cock like a mule," Pete screeched.

"Send his ass to Hollywood and pimp him to the porn industry, Slice," Hollywood chuckled.

Toad pushed his way between Otis and I, "Excuse me fellas, I need to see what we got here."

Toad stood between Cash and I and bent at the waist. His hands now resting on his thighs, he was a matter of two feet in front of Cash staring down at his cock. After a short study of the merchandise, Toad stood up, turned to the crowd and shook his head.

"Don't know that I call it a *choad*, but it damned sure ain't much to brag about," he chuckled.

"Shit, Toad. Kid's got a cock like a horse," Pete chuckled.

Toad shook his head and laughed, "Bullshit. Fucker's three and a half inches long. And that's a big maybe. It's hard to tell, because half of it's that huge fucking head. Shit, the head of that fucker's as big as a Washington apple. I'm not impressed."

"Somebody grab the tape measure out of the toolbox," I hollered over my shoulder.

The head of Cash's cock was the size of a teenager's clenched fist. It made everything else seem disproportionate and rather strange. There was no doubt he belonged in a circus, but not for having the shortest cock on the planet. Sloan's description was on track, but somewhat inaccurate. If nothing else, it was entertaining to look at. To me, it was similar to a hairless cat or a pug-nosed puppy, you stare at them in the pet store in amazement, but you'd never dare to take one home. As Stacey stepped beside me, he handed me a tape measure.

"Good lookin' out, Stacey," I nodded as I grabbed the tape measure.

"Now hold still," I said as I pulled the blade out to 24" and locked the tape measure in place.

I leaned down and pressed the end of the tape into Cash's lower abdomen and looked down at the tape measure.

3-3/4".

I pressed the lock and reeled the tape measure back into the case, "Three and three quarters inches fellas, from base to tip."

"Looks bigger; it's probably that huge fucking head. That's the biggest cock head I ever seen, short of on a Shetland pony," Stacey chuckled.

I shook my head and grinned as I pointed down at Cash's jeans, "Pull 'em up, Prospect."

As he jerked his pants up, he expressed his displeasure, "Fucking bitch."

"Well, what'd you expect? My source told me you told the girl you were gonna *fuck her senseless*. Now for you to do anything like that with what *you're* packing would have required that she have a pussy attached to the bottom of her foot or the palm of her hand. But you God damned sure weren't gonna fuck her senseless with *that*, with her being built the way she is," I chuckled as I tossed the tape measure to Stacey.

"Listen up, fellas. Now, the girl with the big titties from the bar, the one who rode back with Cash; she's coming to the barbeque. I need," I paused and raised my right hand in the air.

"Oh hell, why don't we say three volunteers? I need three of ya to agree to fuck this girl, and fuck her hard. I don't want her to be able to walk for a week, nothing less. She says she likes big cocks, *the bigger the better*. Prospect, you're out. Patches only. Who's hung like a horse and wants in on this deal?" I hollered.

Damn near everyone started hollering like a bunch of idiots. I raised both hands in the air and rolled my eyes in disbelief, "Hold up. Quiet the fuck down. Jesus. We're going to have to go on seniority or something. Maybe draw straws again, fuck."

Toad stepped between Otis and I, bit the neck of his beer bottle in his teeth, and reached for his belt. In one effortless motion, he pulled the belt, unbuckled it, and dropped his three sizes too big jeans to the tops of his boots. No boxer shorts for Toad, he was obviously going

168

commando. Now standing in the center of the crowd with the beer bottle still clenched in his teeth, he slapped his palms against his butt cheeks and stared straight ahead, stone faced.

His cock was soft and about eight inches long. It looked like it weighed five fucking pounds. Without a doubt, when hard, he'd have a ten inch cock. I've never been one to actually want to see another man's cock, but the baggy-assed jeans he always wore began to make sense. I raised my hands and slowly began to clap.

Toad raised his right hand slightly and curled his fingers and thumb to form a "C". Holding his hand at chest height and still staring straight ahead, he released the beer bottle from his teeth. As if he'd performed this trick in the bar a thousand times, as it fell toward the ground, he caught the bottle in his grasp without looking down. Standing expressionless, he raised it to his lips and finished drinking it. His pants still around his ankles, he tossed the bottle fifteen feet toward the trash. I shifted my gaze to the trash can as he released the bottle, aggravated he'd thrown it in the first place. Broken glass on the shop floor was one of my pet peeves. The bottle fell right into place in the center of the can.

Toad bent down, pulled his pants up, and buckled his belt. With both index fingers, he pointed to his crotch, "Any of you fellas can fuck with *that*, get in line. I say we go off cock length, boss. You said the bigger the better; let's give this girl a good solid Sinner fuckin'."

"Agreed," I shouted, "If you're hung like Toad, step up."

I crossed my arms and glanced at Otis. He raised his hands to his face and rubbed his temples.

*Shit, Otis, I know you don't have a moral bone in your body. Don't act like you're thinking about this.*

He lowered his hands and shrugged his shoulders, "I'll do it."

*No shit.*

"Alright. I've got Otis and Toad. Who else is hung like Toad here?"

The fellas mumbled and grumbled, but not one volunteer stepped forward.

Shocked, I raised my hands in the air and glanced at each of the members, "Come on. A shot at a God damned college girl the week before she graduates? Black hair, tight pussy, and tits the size of fucking watermelons? Says she loves sucking cocks too. Hell, I forgot all that part. I need one more, fellas. Who will it be?"

Pete stood with his hands in his pockets, staring down at his feet. As he looked up, he raised his right hand and stroked his beard, "I'll do it if we got some rules to this deal, Slice."

Hollywood chuckled, "Rules? If it ain't covered in the bylaws, it don't matter."

I narrowed my gaze and turned my palms upward, "What the fuck are you talking about, Pete? What kind of fucking rules are there to a gang bang?"

Pete released his beard and raised his hands, "I can't do a gang bang, Slice. Hell, everyone here knows I'm hung like a mule, but I got a bad case a stage fright, Slice."

"What the *fuck* does that mean?" I chuckled.

"Can't piss or get a stiffy in front of another man," he shrugged.

I wrinkled my nose and stared, "No shit?"

"Nope. Tried a time or two, and it don't work. Not at all. I can go first, or in the middle, or hell, I'd even go last. But I can't be all up in it at the same time one of the other fellas is, and I can't have 'em standing by me watchin' either. If we're taking turns, hell yeah, I'll hurt that bitch," he grinned.

I glanced toward Otis and Toad.

"I don't need to watch that ugly prick fuck," Toad snarled.

"Same," Otis sighed.

"Your Ol' Lady okay with this, Pete?" I asked.

"She's at her folks up in Milwaukee. I ain't gonna bother askin'," he grinned.

I looked into the crowd, "Anybody else?"

*Silence.*

"Well, it's settled; Otis, Toad, and Pete. I don't want anyone else fucking with this girl. And I don't want any one talking shit to her about it *before* it happens. I want it to be a surprise. Like it just *happened.* Understood?"

Most of the fellas nodded or began to tell how they would have torn her to shreds if their Ol' Ladies weren't coming. I grinned and slapped Toad on the shoulder.

"Don't be throwing beer bottles around the shop. One of 'em breaks, and *you'll* be sweeping it up, not the Prospect," I growled.

"Gotta miss the can to bust, Slice. I don't miss," he responded.

Considering the amount of grenades he'd thrown in Afghanistan and Iraq, he probably didn't miss. As the men all began to filter out of the shop and hop on their bikes, I glanced at my bike. Sitting in the rear of the shop with my new blanket strapped to the bars, it looked good. The lick 'n stick was still on the rear fender from the night before. I shook my head and slowly walked toward the bike. I reached down and gripped the seat in my hands. As I lightly pulled against it to release the suction cups, I turned my wrist and looked at my watch.

12:48.

I pressed the seat back into place and threw my leg over the seat. As

I relaxed into the seat, I raised my hands to the apes and rested them on the grips. As if programmed to do so, I twisted the throttle twice, pulled the choke, flipped the ignition, and hit the *start* button. As I pulled out of the shop and toward the gate, several of the fellas turned and stared.

"Last man out lock up the shop," I hollered over my shoulder.

*Because this might be an all-nighter.*

# AVERY

For a woman to accurately determine what a man is *really* thinking would be similar to a man having a full understanding of what it's like to go through a menstrual cycle. It's never going to be completely clear to either party no matter how much a person tries to explain.

"So, let me get this straight. I'm not trying to play with words, or be a smart-ass; I'm really not. But let me see," I paused, and as I stood from the park bench I forced my hands into the rear pockets of my shorts.

I twisted myself into my best naïve schoolgirl pose just to throw him off a little. The shorts I was wearing were absolutely killing my pussy without any underwear, but they looked hot as fuck. As much as I wanted some relief, I pulled back on the pockets and tried to give him just a little of a show up front. He sat quietly on the park bench and stretched his rubber band to the point of complete failure.

*Snap!*

*Good. Now, if you like it, take it.*

I pulled my hands from my pockets and tossed my hair, "So, I'm going to stick by your side and stay quiet. If someone talks to me, I will respond. If they don't, I stand, smile, and look pretty. If anyone asks if I'm available, I say *no*, and if they ask if you and I are together, I say *no*. And if someone asks if I'm your Ol' Lady, I say *hell to the no*. Lastly, if anyone fucks with me, I find you or if I can't find you, I find Otis. So, technically I'm not spoken for, but I'm not available either. Right?"

"You coulda left the last part out, but that's it. You got it," he nodded as he played with the rubber band on his wrist.

I lowered my hands and stuffed them into my rear pockets again.

*Holy fuck that's uncomfortable.*

I bent my knees slightly and rocked my hips back and forth. After he snapped the rubber band again, I lifted my right shoe slightly and dug the toe into the dirt, twisting it back and forth as I watched the impression I was leaving in the sandy soil. No one knew better than I did that I didn't have any tits, but what little I did have was exposed to the world through the opening of my vee neck tee shirt. As I felt the early evening breeze across my nipples, I glanced in his direction. His eyes were fixed on the opening of my shirt.

*Get an eyeful, Axton.*

"You want to sit the fuck down, you're making me nervous," he grunted as he shifted his gaze upward.

As I tilted my head and gave my best duck face, he snapped the rubber band twice.

*Good, all that practicing I've been doing in front of the mirror worked.*

"My legs are cramping. I need to stand," I lied.

He stood from the park bench and pulled his knife from his pocket. As he raised it to his other hand, he flicked the blade open. Now focusing on his fingernails, he fidgeted with his knife and stopped paying attention to me altogether. Frustrated, I turned away from him and dug the denim out of my sore pussy.

"What are you afraid of, Axton?" I asked over my shoulder as I turned to face him.

He looked up from the half-assed manicure he was performing,

"What the fuck are you talking about?"

"With *us*. You and me? What are you afraid of?" I shrugged.

He folded his knife, clipped it to his pocket and lowered his chin slightly, "A lot of motherfuckers will claim it, but only a handful actually mean what they say; I'm one of that handful. I'm not afraid of a God damned thing on this earth."

"So what's keeping you from making progress with me?" I asked.

He turned and stared at me as if I were absolutely insane. As he crossed his arms and continued to stare, it was obvious I'd touched on a subject he really wasn't ready to discuss. The muscles in his biceps pulsated. As soon as he began speaking, the tone of his voice was sterner than before.

"You just don't *get it*, do you? I *am* making progress with you. More than I've made with anyone in the last fifteen God damned years. It'll probably come as no fucking secret, but I fucking *hate* women. Last I checked, Avery, you're a woman," he paused and tilted his head toward the bike.

"I absolutely hate, and I do mean *hate* having that seat on the fender of my bike. About every ten minutes when you think I'm rubbing my cheek, I'm not. I'm looking over at that God damned lick 'n stick and wondering if it's eating through the clear coat on my fender. But I've left that motherfucker on there for what seems like a month straight. Do you want to know why?" he rested his hands on his belt and raised both eyebrows while he waited for me to respond.

I was beginning to feel small. I swallowed heavily and nodded. A very inaudible *yes* puffed from my lips.

"Because I like having you on the back of my bike. I have no fucking idea why, I really don't, because I hate bitches on the back of my bike.

175

But for some God damned reason, having *you* back there makes me feel, at least for as long as we're riding, like I'm normal. Well, Avery, I got a news flash for you. I'm *far* from normal," he hesitated and snapped the rubber band more times than I could count.

*Yeah, that's not the 'I think you're way too cute' snap, is it?*

"I've been shot at and missed, and I've been shot at and hit. I've been beaten, burned, cut, stabbed, and I've gone long enough without food and fucking water that I should have died. I've been in more fucking fights than any professional boxer, and my left arm is pinned back together with metal screws - because the third time it broke, I didn't have time or the money to fix it. I've been to jail more times than I can count on my fingers and toes. No, Avery, I'm far from normal. You want to know why they call me *Slice*?" he growled.

I stood and stared. I suppose I should have been scared or surprised. For some reason I was neither. I was beginning to like him more. For the first time since we had been spending time together, he was coming out of his shell. I attempted to swallow the rock in my throat, but couldn't, so I simply nodded my head once. He reached down and grabbed each side of his cut, and pulled upward, unsnapping it.

He leaned over, hung the vest from his ape hangers, and turned toward me. As he stood facing me, he reached down and pulled his tee shirt over his head. He quickly turned, tossed it over his shoulder and onto the seat of the bike. As he turned around, now shirtless, I gazed like an idiot at his upper body.

*Oh my God.*

His chest was massive, and far more defined than I would have imagined. His stomach didn't have an ounce of fat on it. In fact, it was chiseled to perfection. His upper arms were solid muscle, and now that he was angry, were quite swollen. But my focus wasn't solely on his muscles or well-proportioned body. My focus, at least now, was on the twelve inch long scar on his stomach.

And the one below it that was eight or so inches long.

And the one across his chest.

And the one that went from his rib cage toward his back and appeared to never end.

The wounds didn't seem to have ever been stitched or taken care of by a medical professional. It looked as if he'd been tortured by a chainsaw wielding maniac. As I stood and stared, he slowly shuffled his feet and turned around.

On his back were smaller scars, but there were more than I could count. They ranged in size from an inch to several inches long. Without speaking, he turned around again and grabbed his tee shirt. As I stood and stared, he pulled it over his head and covered his body.

"That's why they call me Slice. Now, before you ask, about three or four of them came from fights. The other thirty or so?" he paused and ran his fingers through his hair.

"My Ol' Man. You wanna know why I don't have any on my arms? Because a shirt wouldn't hide 'em when I went to school, that is on the days he would let me go. And none of them ever got stitched because I couldn't let the doctors see 'em or he'd have been arrested. When I was a kid he'd already been to the joint twice. One more time, and it'd been life in prison. Well, now he's doing life in prison, and I've got *these* to remember him by," he hesitated and held his hands at waist height.

"Turn around," he demanded and he stepped toward me.

"Axton, I..."

"Turn the fuck around you question asking bitch," he demanded.

177

Reluctantly, I turned around. The park bench was only a few inches in front of me. I felt as if I was trapped, but I faced it anyway. As he positioned himself behind me, he raised his hand to the left side of my jaw, clenched it between his thumb and forefinger, and tilted my head to the right. As he breathed into my ear, he pressed his hips into the back of my ass.

His breath against my ear caused goose bumps to rise along the length of my arms.

"You feel that?" he breathed.

All I could feel was his warm breath against my face. I swallowed heavily.

"Feel what?" I squeaked.

"That stiff cock of mine, Avery. It's pressing against your ass. You feel it?" he asked as he pressed his hips against me with a little more force.

I nodded my head and whimpered.

"That lump you feel rising against that little round ass of yours, you want to know what I call it?" he growled.

Still holding my jaw firmly, his control of me was apparent. His strong hand not only held my face in the position he wanted it to be, but provided me a sense of ownership and restraint. Had he released me, I would have melted into a puddle right then and there. I nodded my head again and puffed out another dry *yes*.

"I call it *progress*," he said as he bit my earlobe between his teeth.

With my ear still clenched firmly between his teeth, he continued, "For the last fifteen years, my cock ain't been much good; probably either from my Ol' Man beating me, or from all the women who fucked me over, hell who knows."

"Reach back there with your right hand," he demanded.

I stood in shock and trembled. Not from fear, but from nothing other than one hundred percent alpha male arousal.

Although we were standing in the hot sun, his breath against my ear caused me to shiver, "You little tease. You said whatever I told you to do, you'd do. Now reach your skinny little arm back here and grab that big fucking cock of mine."

I reached behind me, slid my hand along the thigh of his jeans, and felt around until…

*Oh God.*

"I said *grab* it. If you can't grab it any harder than that, I'll toss your little ass in the dirt and ride the fuck out of here. Now *grab* it," he growled.

Staring straight ahead with my eyes closed, I squeezed his cock firm in my hand. It felt as if I were gripping a baseball bat.

"Now tell me just what it is you feel." he breathed as he released my ear from his teeth.

"Progress?" I squeaked.

He released my jaw, spun me around, and stared into my eyes.

"You're God damned right. That's *progress.*"

"Now you want to know *why* that motherfuckers hard?"

I bit my lower lip and lowered my head.

"Because every time you stick your hands in your pockets and twist around like you're some innocent little farm girl, it makes me want to fuck you. *Bad.* And for *right now*," he reached down and grabbed the rubber band.

*Snap!*

*Snap!*

*Snap!*

"For right now, I'm exercising *patience*," he huffed.

"Now, you got any more God damned questions?" he snapped.

I shifted my gaze to meet his. My eyes now trained on his, I reached toward my left hand. As my fingers found the hair tie which was wrapped around my wrist, I pulled against it and released it sharply into my skin.

*Snap!*

Incapable of speaking, I simply stood and lightly shook my head.

Again, I pulled against the hair tie.

*Snap!*

*Officially head over motherfucking heels, sir.*

# AXTON

Respect. In the hustle and bustle world of the modern age, the general population has forgotten how to be respectful. Most of what would make us more courteous as adults was drilled into our heads as children. Don't touch it if it isn't yours. Don't lie. Don't cheat. Don't steal. Use the words *please, thank you,* and *excuse me* in everything you do. Think before you act. If someone serves you something, eat it out of respect without complaint. Stand up for what you believe in. If you make a mistake, be man enough to admit it. Don't say you're going to do something unless you have every intention of following through with your promise.

No, it's not okay to cut me off on the highway because you're late for your son's soccer game. There is never a good time to text a picture of the soup you ate for lunch to your girlfriend while you're on the highway.

People assume because I look tough, I'm covered in tattoos, and I ride a motorcycle I must be disrespectful. Nothing could be further from the truth. I treat others with respect, and I expect the same in return. For me to walk this earth smiling at every person I see and shaking the hands of strangers would be the same as living a lie. Most people on this planet aren't the caliber of person I want to know, be friends with, or allow to the luxury of even saying they've ever met me.

"Damned near graduation day, huh?" I asked as I slid my empty water glass to the center of the table.

181

"Yep," Avery nodded.

She sure didn't seem to be excited about the fact she was graduating from college. Hell, I barely made it through high school. As much school as I missed, it was a miracle I even graduated. I learned more in my post-graduation reading than I ever did in school. I wouldn't trade who I had become for anything, but it sure would have been nice to get a degree in mechanical engineering. Applying the education of a technical degree to building bikes would be far more efficient than reading books every night.

"Can I get you some more water?" the waitress asked.

"No thank you," I nodded.

She turned and smiled at Avery, "You ma'am?"

"No thank you," Avery responded.

"Anything else?" she asked.

I shook my head and grinned, "The food was great. We're stuffed."

"Okay, I'll leave this here. No hurry, whenever you're ready," she said as she placed the bill on the table.

I looked at the bill. $17.22. I reached for my wallet and placed thirty dollars on the table. I've always believed if I couldn't leave a ten dollar tip for a meal, regardless of the cost, I shouldn't be eating in public.

"Ready?" I asked.

She stood from her chair and slid her glasses onto her nose. Avery had changed from talking a hundred miles an hour about any and everything to being a woman of a few words. In a conversation about a particular subject she'd talk for as long as I was interested in doing so. Through the course of a normal day, she now spoke very little unless I encouraged her to do so. Seeing the change in her caused me to believe she was willing to modify her behavior to attempt to please me.

"You don't talk much anymore," I chuckled as I stood.

She shrugged her shoulders, "Don't have to."

I opened the door and waited for her to walk through. As I stepped to the sidewalk and turned toward my bike, a man was standing beside it taking pictures. I reached down and pulled the rubber band away from my wrist.

"What are you doing?" I growled.

*Snap!*

He looked up, grinned, and took another picture, "Just taking a few pics of this bike."

"Is it yours?" I shrugged as I stopped in front of the bike.

He shook his head and stood, "Nope. Probably yours, huh?"

Avery stood quietly by my side with her hands in her pockets. It was probably a good thing she was with me, as I had found myself fractionally more reserved in her company. I rested my hands on my belt and stared as he continued to try and take the perfect photo of *my* bike.

"Probably."

Dressed in nice jeans, a button down shirt, and dress shoes, he looked like a thirty-something year old business man. I would have expected him to have had enough common sense to at least, in my presence, ask permission to continue.

"You have any kids?" I asked.

He looked up and smiled, "Yeah, two."

"What's your address?" I asked.

He shoved his cell phone into his front pocket and narrowed his eyes, "Excuse me?"

I crossed my arms and began flexing my pectoral muscles, causing my chest to flare, "Your address? I need your address."

"Uhhm, I don't think so, why?"

"I want to come over sometime when you're gone and take some pictures of your fucking kids, you idiot."

"Uhhm. Listen, I was just..." he began.

"You were just fucking with something that wasn't yours is what you were doing. I don't have a family, that bike is all I've got. It's like my kid. It sure as fuck isn't on a pedestal in a museum, is it? It's not on display out here for you to take fucking pictures of, that's for God damned sure," I shook my head lightly and inhaled a deep breath.

I looked up and down the block and then shifted my gaze to him, "You know, this is the only restaurant around. There isn't another place of business for two fucking blocks. It was pretty fucking obvious where we were. It would have been a lot different if you'd have stuck your head in the restaurant and said, *hey, I'm building a Heritage Softail and I'd like to use yours as a template.* Hell, I'd have agreed and probably been fucking flattered."

"I uhhm. I'm sorry, I didn't mean to..."

"Get out of here. I'm done talking to you," I grunted as I raised my hand and waved toward the end of the block.

As he walked away, I glanced at Avery, "I fucking hate people."

She grinned and lowered her chin slightly.

"So, what? Now I talk like a motherfucker, and you smile and nod?" I shrugged.

She grinned and tossed her leg over the rear fender, "Yep."

I stood beside the motorcycle and admired her. As much as I hated to admit it, she looked damned good sitting on the bike. Having Avery accompany me for the last month allowed me to become fractionally more civil. I was still myself, but a little less rough around the edges.

184

"Well, it's a good thing you were here. Balance. You give me fucking balance," I said as I stepped over the seat.

"Progress," she sighed.

I raised my right hand to the apes and rested my hand on the grip. Across the street a new Lexus was parked; probably the amateur photographer's car. I grinned, twisted the throttle twice, flipped the ignition, and hit the *start* button. As the engine warmed up to temperature, I released the throttle, reached over the ape hangers and snapped my rubber band against my left wrist.

*Snap!*

I gazed at the new Lexus.

*Snap!*

"Ready?" I asked as I moved my right hand to the throttle.

"Always," she responded.

As we slowly rode past the Lexus, I grinned.

*Progress.*

# AVERY

Setting and achieving goals has driven me to succeed at almost everything I intended to accomplish. Graduating from college was my most difficult goal to date; therefore I looked at it as a huge accomplishment. Considering my mother's disappointment in my choices in the last few years, it came as no surprise that I didn't hear from my family prior to graduation. As stubborn as I am, I wasn't about to call her and remind her, and as disappointed as she was, she certainly wasn't going to naturally offer. Either way, graduating from college and having no one in attendance made me, once again, feel invisible.

"Avery Taylor," the voice crackled over the loudspeakers.

Already in position on the right side of the stage, I stepped up the three stairs and onto the platform. As I walked across the stage, it was almost as if I was in a trance. Deaf and blind to what surrounded me, with my left hand I accepted the diploma and shook his hand with my right. I shuffled to the next handshake, and the next. Quiet and feeling tiny, I walked back to my seat with my shoulders slumped. As I found my chair, I opened the diploma.

A fake. A phony. Not having the actual certificate made me feel even more uneasy. They had advised us we would receive the actual document in the mail. Knowing it didn't make me feel any better. I slid forward in my seat, knowing this was almost over. I wanted to see Axton, ride on his bike, and let the wind against my face allow me to feel as if none of this really mattered. Instead, I was scheduled to meet Sloan's parents for dinner. I hadn't even reminded Axton I was graduating. I knew he would have bigger and better things to do than come to some bullshit like a college graduation.

*At least my name starts with a "T". This is almost over.*

"I now present you with the Southwestern College graduating class of 2014!"

As I watched everyone stand and scream, I turned and walked along the row of seats toward the aisle. Students stood hugging their friends, family, parents, brothers and sisters. It was a joyous occasion for all. I've never been a person to wallow in self-pity or feel sorry for myself, but I felt alone. My throat felt dry and my eyes felt wet. As I stumbled toward the parking lot still in a fog, I heard my name being called.

"Avery! God damn, girl. Are you fucking deaf?"

I glanced up and toward the voice. A large black mob of Sinner cuts stood before me.

*Holy shit!*

Axton, Otis, Hollywood, Toad, Pete, Stacey, Mike, Fancy, and several other members I didn't recognize were all standing shoulder to shoulder with their arms crossed. Axton stood in the center with his arms outstretched and open wide. Immediately, I felt as if nothing else mattered. I wanted to rush toward him and have him pick me up and swing me in the air. Instead, I walked slowly as if it wasn't that big of a deal.

"I'm proud of you," Axton said as he wrapped his arms around me.

As he squeezed me and lifted my feet from the ground, I closed my eyes.

*You. Just. Made. My. Day.*

Continued 'good jobs', 'congratulations', and 'fuck yeah, you did it, girl's' came from the crowd as Axton held me in his arms. When he finally lowered me to the ground, Otis reached into his cut and removed a wrapped gift. After handing it to Axton, Axton, in turn, handed it to me.

"What…"

"It's from the fellas, it ain't from me. Well, it's from all of us. Open it," he nodded.

I unwrapped the gift carefully and clutched the wrapping paper in my hand. As I opened the small black box, I wanted the moment to last forever. The excitement, the men, the hug, the attention, the fact that there were hundreds of people graduating, and the only men to ride motorcycles to the ceremony and wear their cuts to graduation were all waiting for me. I tilted the top back and peered inside.

A wide silver bracelet, beveled on each side with ornate engraving on the face was positioned in the center of the box on a velvet pedestal. I glanced toward Axton.

*Don't fucking cry. Just don't.*

I nodded my head once and reached inside the box.

"Turn it over," he whispered, "Look inside."

I picked the bracelet up and looked inside. Engraved in elegant script, the words were clear.

***The Devil Looks After His Own.***

I naturally attempted to inhale a breath. My breathing was choppy. I was about to lose my composure and start sobbing. With shaking hands, I removed the bracelet, pressed it over my left wrist, and looked at it down in admiration.

"You like it?" Otis asked.

189

I looked up and nodded my head.

"The bracelet is from the Sinners. The engraving on the inside? It's from Otis and me," Axton winked.

*The Devil Looks After His Own.*

"Where's Sloan?" Axton asked.

I shrugged, "Supposed to meet her in the parking lot. Her parents are here and stuff. We were all going to go to dinner or something, I don't know."

Axton shrugged, "I guess you getting on the back of that sled of mine is out of the question?"

I pulled my gown over my shoulders and lifted it over my head. After carefully folding the fake diploma, cap, and gift box into the gown, I walked to the trash can a few feet away and tossed them inside.

"Glasses?" he asked.

I unzipped my clutch and pulled out my glasses, "Always."

"Ready?" he asked.

I pushed my hands into the rear pockets of my shorts and looked down at my sneakers. What started out as an awful day had quickly turned into the best day of my life. I glanced up and smiled.

"Always," I grinned.

Axton turned toward Toad and nodded his head.

"On it, boss," Toad responded.

*Secretive fuckers.*

As the rest of us methodically walked to the parking lot, Toad stayed behind. Something about being in the presence of all of the men made me feel powerful. I watched as girls I'd went to school with for four years craned their necks and whipped their heads to the side to catch a glimpse of us as we walked through the parking lot.

*That's right bitches.*

*The Devil Looks After His Own. Yep, the fellas came to congratulate me and take me for a ride.*

"We were thinking of riding out to Stearman Field Airport in Benton and meeting up with another club. About an hour ride there, stay an hour or two, and an hour back. It'll kill the rest of the day, you alright with that?" Axton asked over his shoulder.

I may not officially have been Axton's Ol' Lady, and we may not be fucking, but I knew him having me along for the ride with twelve other members, meeting another club, and being the only *bitch* in attendance didn't go without notice from all of the other men. He might not have been ready to admit it, but he was taking me along because he wanted to, not out a feeling of obligation.

I grinned and nodded my head.

"Now, listen up. When we ride with these fellas, it ain't like when we ride alone. These guys are gonna ride hard, so be ready," he smiled.

I started to say something smart-assed, and bit my lip instead.

*Awwe, what the hell.*

"The harder the better. That's what I've always said," I grinned.

As Axton glared at me and continued to walk his mechanical walk of *don't fuck with me* swagger, he reached toward his left wrist. I didn't need to see what he was doing, I knew. I waited to hear the sound.

*Snap!*

I grinned and threw my leg over the back of his fender.

*Mission accomplished.*

# AXTON

"So this motherfucker looks up at the television and says, I'm gonna go take a shower, and when I get back, it better be on Family Feud."

"You see, in the joint, it's just like it is in the club, it's all about respect. They vote on what to watch, and whatever wins the vote is what they watch. Everything's put on a list. You know a week in advance what you're gonna watch. Family Feud is on the list, but big boy is watching Jerry fuckin' Springer. And in the joint it don't matter how big a motherfucker is or how small he is. Now the fella watching the T.V. was about three fucking hundred and six foot six; he was bigger'n Otis. And the fella headed to the shower was maybe five foot five and a buck twenty."

"So big boy keeps watching Jerry Springer or whatever it was. I sat back at my table and watched. I knew what time it was. Little man comes out of the shower and walks over between us. He looked up at the T.V. and shook his head. When he walked back to his cell, I stood up and got my back to the wall. Hell, you never know in the joint when one fight will pop off a riot. So, I'm watchin' over to little man's cell, and here he comes. Got a tube sock danglin' from his fist."

"A fucking sock?" Hollywood shrugged.

Corndog nodded his head, "Yep. *Lock in a sock.* You take the padlock off your locker and put it in a fuckin' tube sock. Now, that lock ain't much, but in the bottom of a sock when you're swinging it, that'll

193

knock the biggest motherfucker to his knees."

"Let the man finish his story, you rude prick," Otis chuckled as he tilted his beer toward Hollywood.

"So little man walks up behind the big fella in a wide sweep, and swings the fucking sock. Funniest fuckin' thing I ever seen. You see, a two foot sock stretches to about three feet when it's got a three pound lock in the bottom of it and you're swinging that fucker about sixty miles an hour. So the sock stretches, and just wraps around big boys head coming back and hittin' little man's wrist," Corndog stopped talking and raised his bottle of beer to his mouth.

After a long drink, Corndog lowered the bottle to his waist, and rested his thumb on his belt, "Now big fella gets up and his eyes are as wide as a motherfucker. That little prick recovers from the first swing, leans back and…"

"WHACK! The fucking lock hits this motherfucker on the temple and down this bastard goes like a sack of shit. And little man steps on his chest with one foot and just pummels this prick into a bloody pile of toothless shit. He finally gets satisfied that his work is done, and he looks over to me and nods his head. I nod back. He walks over to his cell, washes the lock, flushes the sock down the shitter, and walks back out," Corndog paused and took another drink of beer.

"So guess what the little fucker does now?" Corndog asked.

I shrugged, expecting I already knew the answer.

"Drags that big fucker over about ten feet, sits down, and switches the television to Family Feud. Like nothin' happened. When the Goon Squad shows up, he says he didn't even notice the fucker layin' there. Here's the other thing. Nobody saw shit. That's how it works in there. No fucking snitches. *Snitches get stitches for being punk ass bitches*,"

194

Corndog nodded.

"Well, I'm just glad you're out," I said as I slapped him on the back.

"Feels like I never left, Slice. Shit, time in that bitch goes slow as fuck, but once you're out, it's all good. Little ol' five year bit? Shit I'll do the next five standing on my head," he chuckled.

"Well, this little barbeque is for you, brother," I nodded.

"Appreciate it, brother. I'm gonna wander around. Hell there's a hundred fuckers here I ain't seen in a bit," he grinned.

"Stay out of trouble, Dog," I smiled.

As long as I had waited for him to be released, and as much as I anticipated his arrival at the barbeque, it seemed odd having him back. Five years is a long time. In his eyes nothing changed. It was as if he stepped out of a meeting and stepped right back in. In my eyes, he'd been gone for five years. A lot happened in the time he was gone. New members, members retiring, some being locked up, and others died. Be as it may, Corndog was out of prison, and I was glad to have him back.

As I stood amongst the few men who had surrounded Corndog to listen to his story, I glanced around, looking for Avery. I hadn't seen her since she walked away with Sloan fifteen minutes prior. Not necessarily worried, but a little uncomfortable about her wandering around a hundred bikers without a *Property Of* patch, I had my doubts even she would walk around for long without someone doing or saying *something*.

"Anybody seen Sloan?" I asked into the crowd.

"In the dyno room with Toad. Has been for half hour," Otis responded.

"Hasn't been half a fucking hour, Otis," I hissed as I looked down at my watch.

"Fuck it hasn't. It's ten o' clock," Otis responded.

"Why the fuck ain't you in there with Toad? And where the fuck is

Pete?" I growled.

"Toad's alone with that bitch. He wanted *first in*, so he got it. That chic's nuts, Slice. Toad told her he wanted to fuck her until she'd have to be hauled off in a wheel chair. *That* was his pick-up line. And what's she say? *Bring it.* That was her response. *Bring it.* So, that crazy fucker Toad snaps his fingers like a high school cheerleader and does that deal with his head, and says, *it's been brought*," Otis laughed as he swerved his head from side-to-side.

Unamused, I looked around the crowd for Avery. There were probably fifty people in the shop talking or gathered around the kegs drinking and another fifty or so in the paved parking lot outside. I scoured the crowd in the shop.

*Nothing.*

Let's go out in the lot, Otis. I need to see what the fuck Avery's up to.

"Got it, Slice," Otis said as he began to push his way past the people standing by the door.

As we wandered into the parking lot, I noticed there was a small crowd gathered in the corner near the street. It appeared two men were fighting. Nothing out of the ordinary for a biker get together, but I still needed to find out who it was and what the fuck was going on. The crowd surrounding the two men was pretty quiet while one of the two was talking mad shit to the other. I didn't recognize the voice, so I assumed it was someone from Wichita who I didn't necessarily know.

Our typical *open* gatherings were used to invite outsiders to see what the club was like, what we did, and what we stood for. The Sinners did not recruit talent. Potential prospects came to us and asked questions about becoming a member. As a result, we often invited outsiders to our parties to let them see what we were all about. If they were interested,

196

and asked the question *so what's it take to be a member?* We'd take time to explain. Some outsiders later became *hang-arounds*, some lost interest, and others become *prospects*. Having people I didn't necessarily recognize or know at parties wasn't anything new.

I followed Otis toward the group. As we got closer to the two arguing men, I noticed Avery was standing on the side watching the fight intently. Otis tapped me on the shoulder and pointed toward Avery. I nodded my head in acknowledgement, walked to her side, and rested my hand on her shoulder. She spun around nervously and widened her eyes.

"What the fuck are you doing?" I asked.

"Watching these two dip-shits," she responded as she tilted her head toward the two men.

I crossed my arms in front of my chest, "What fucking part of *stay by my side* didn't you underfuckingstand?"

"I'm sorry Axton, but you were talking to Corndog and the rest of the fellas, and some asshole walked up to me and started being a total dick. I tried to get away from him, and I tapped you on the shoulder like twice but you never paid attention, so I figured you were busy. I just wanted him to leave me alone, so I wandered out here to get away from him. Then he found me again. When he wouldn't let up, the other guy told him to shut the fuck up. Now they're in an argument."

"God damn it. I told you if anyone fucked with you, to find me or Otis, didn't I?" I said under my breath.

She nodded her head sheepishly.

"Uhhm. That's the one who told the other guy to shut the fuck up," Avery whispered as she pointed toward the bigger of the two men.

*Neither of you two would bust a grape in a food fight. Stop trying to impress the ladies, fellas, no one cares.*

"Break it up, fellas," I shouted uncaringly toward the two men.

As soon as I spoke, the bigger man's gaze shifted to where I stood. I didn't recognize either of the two men. Neither of them wore a cut or colors from a club. They appeared to be two bikers from out of town somewhere who were invited by someone in the club to come enjoy the fun. The bigger of the two had shoulder length hair, and was doing all of the shit-talking to the other man.

"This asshole was being disrespectful. Everything's just fine. Now why don't you get your hand off of *my bitch?*" the bigger man said over his shoulder.

*Are you fucking shittin' me?*

I pushed my way through the crowd, "*Your* bitch?"

"Let me explain something, *motherfucker,*" I said as I pushed the smaller man to the side.

As I grabbed the sides of his hair in my hands, his eyes widened. Without any notice or saying a single word, I thrust the top of my head into his nose. As I felt it shatter from the force of my head crushing down on his face, I released his hair from my grip and swung a right uppercut into his jaw.

He collapsed onto the concrete.

"*God damn,*" I heard someone holler.

"*That's the President of the Sinners,*" I heard someone else say.

"You just need to pick him up and get him on out of here," Otis said as he stepped through the crowd and into the area where I stood.

I pointed down at the man who was laying silently on the concrete, "Him?" I snapped.

"I'm just getting started," I said under my breath.

I swung my right foot into his stomach, "Get up you worthless piece of shit."

"Slice, he's *done*. That right hand knocked him the fuck out," Otis chuckled.

I shook my head, "No. I'm nowhere near done with this mouthy prick."

"I said get up," I growled as I kicked him in the stomach again.

"Where's the other motherfucker, the one who was fucking with Avery?" I asked.

Otis shrugged his shoulders. I stared down at the motionless body. I reached down and pulled him to his feet by his hair and belt. The thought of *anyone* fucking with Avery angered me to an unhealthy level. Adding salt to the wound came from the stupid fucker claiming Avery as *his bitch* because he had stepped in and *saved* her from the mouthy prick who started the problem in the first place. Everything around me became a haze. The sound of the music, people, talking - it all felt distant.

I felt a hand on my shoulder.

"Slice!"

I spun in the direction of the voice with my hands raised, ready to fight.

"Slice, drag him out to the street. Come on, it's over. You beat that poor fucker half to death. Someone's gonna call the fucking cops. You made your point. We got the other guy out of here," Otis explained.

I looked down at the man on the concrete. His face was almost unrecognizable. Blood covered his face, hair, and shirt. His lips looked like hamburger and both eyes were swollen partially shut. I glanced down at my hands. Both were covered in blood, and the knuckles on my right hand were beginning to swell.

"God damn, I think I just lost it. Where's the other guy?" I sighed as I raised my hands to my face.

"Toad got him. Wasn't too pretty. Kinda broke up the little party," Otis chuckled.

I looked around the parking lot. Roughly to-thirds of the people were gone. Somehow, I had no memory of what had happened. Although this wasn't the first time something similar had happened, it hadn't happened since I was a kid. When I found the quarterback fucking my girlfriend, I ended up in jail for the beating I gave him. I didn't remember any of it. I learned in court he had a broken jaw, fractured skull, and a few broken ribs as a result. Another time, when I was in my early twenties, my father and I were in a terrible fight. It was the first time I stood up to him, and the last time we really spoke. I have no doubt he'll remember what I did to him for the remainder of his miserable life.

I glanced down at the heap of shit on the concrete. I shook my head and rubbed my knuckles as I shifted my gaze to Otis, "So what happened to the other dude?"

"Can we drag this fucker to the street? You done, boss?" Otis laughed.

"Yeah, I'm done," I breathed.

Otis waved toward the fellas who were standing off to the side, obviously afraid to intervene. Hollywood and Pete stepped in front of me, picked the man up, carried him past the entrance gate, and laid him on the curb. Luckily, the clubhouse was in an industrial area of the city, and away from the general population, at least at night. Although he could probably use medical attention, he sure as fuck wasn't going to get it from any of us. When he woke up, he'd realize how he fucked up. More than likely when he was back in Wichita telling stories or asking questions, someone would explain to him the benefit of keeping his mouth shut around the Sinners.

"Well, Avery pointed the kid out. I was just going to carry him out and toss his dumb ass in the street, but fucking Toad came runnin' out of the dyno room when he heard all the screaming. His fuckin' belt wasn't buckled, and his baggy fuckin' pants were all around his thighs like Busta fuckin' Rhymes or one a those fuckers," Otis paused and started laughing.

"So this kid looks at Toad and his fuckin' pants and he starts laughing. I didn't hear it, but the fellas said he said some shit like, *what the fuck are 'you' gonna do about it?* Yeah, didn't end well for him. Toad jumped up in the air and did some fucking Bruce Lee shit. Kicked the kid in the head, and when he hit the ground, his head split open like a ripe melon. Funny part was when Toad came back down from the spinning kick deal. His fuckin' baggy pants hit the ground," Otis shook his head and started laughing again.

"Commando?" I chuckled as I looked up from my bloody knuckles.

"Yep," Otis nodded.

I shook my head and laughed, "Can't buy entertainment like this, can ya? Where's the girl?"

"In the Shop with Sloan. Think ya mighta scared her a little bit with the beatin' you gave that poor bastard," Otis shrugged.

I glanced down at my bloody hand. As I walked toward the shop I pressed my knuckles into my jeans. Avery and Sloan stood talking amongst a small group of Sinners. Without speaking, I walked to the cabinet, grabbed a rag and my lick 'n stick, and slowly made my way to my bike. Methodically, I wiped the dust off the rear fender, positioned the seat in the center, and pressed it into place. I tied the rag around my hand and looked over my shoulder toward Avery.

"Avery!" I hollered as I stretched my leg over the seat and rested my rag-wrapped hand on the right grip.

Her eyes widened as she spun my direction. It seemed as if she had no idea I was even in the shop. I reached behind me and slapped the lick 'n stick with my left hand. She smiled, nodded her head toward the fellas, gave Sloan a hug, and pulled her glasses from her purse. As she walked across the shop, rolled the hair tie off her wrist, and pulled her hair into a ponytail, I couldn't keep myself from smiling.

And I hate people seeing me smile.

Silently, she swung her leg over the fender, dropped down onto the seat, and placed her hands against my waist. I glanced down as she rested her feet on the pegs. After I twisted the throttle twice and pulled the choke, I flipped the ignition and hit the *start* button.

"See you fellas in the morning," I hollered over the sound of the exhaust.

"Ready?"

"Always," she responded.

I grabbed a handful of throttle, released the clutch, and pulled out onto the street. I knew Avery had no idea where we were headed; hell, she didn't care. As long as she was with me, she seemed to be satisfied with everything else around her. I turned and looked over my shoulder as we passed under a street light. She smiled a smile of complete satisfaction. The type of smile that washes over your face naturally and is never created for a camera; the smile you might see only a few times in a lifetime.

As I shifted my gaze to the road and out of her line of sight, I smiled the exact same smile.

# AVERY

There comes a time in every woman's life where she must decide whether or not she wants to take the next step with a man; to add him to the list of *other* men who have gone the distance with her sexually. Very few women, if any, stay with their first love for their entire life. Especially with girls my age, the lists of men continues to grow as we're drunk and make stupid decisions, are lied to by some smooth talking player, or fall into another trap of some married prick who gives us a false sense of security and really wants nothing more than a quick piece of ass.

A few months ago, I may have eagerly fucked a man who seemed at the time to be a challenge, an impossible task, or someone worthy of my advances. The difficult chase had always made the success taste sweeter. The more impossible the man was to obtain, the more justified the sex was in the end. Now, sitting in Axton's living room, I had one goal and one goal only.

To end the chase forever.

I would be a fool to believe at this point in time I was falling in love with Axton. To do so would be juvenile, and completely inaccurate. I'm not a foolish woman, and I don't fall into the typical patterns of wishful girls who fall in love with every man they meet. I did know one thing about Axton if I knew nothing else; being in his presence allowed me to exhale. When we were together, I relaxed. Nothing else around me mattered when he was by my side. After spending time with Axton, for the first time in my life I felt comfortable in my own skin. It wasn't necessarily what he said, because he was a man of few words. It was more of what he *didn't* say, and his ways of speaking which weren't necessarily vocal.

Maybe what I was feeling was the *onset* of love. I didn't know for sure, and would have no way of knowing; as I had no experience with being in love. Quite possibly it was Axton's alpha male presence combined with his *don't fuck with me* walk and handsome looks. It could very well be the fact that I *knew* in his presence I would never be harmed by another man. This certainly wouldn't prevent *him* from harming me, but I had a gut feeling as tough as he was, he would never be violent toward me.

Nervously sitting on the couch, I waited for him to get out of the bathroom. I looked around the house, surprised by the cleanliness. Everything was perfectly placed and the entire home appeared spotless. As I surveyed the contents of the living room, I realized everything in the home was symmetrical. The pictures hanging on the walls were all placed in a pattern. The lampshades were all perfectly positioned, none were out of place or titled. Two couches, a loveseat, and two chairs were in the living room. A coffee table in the center was decorated with two stone bookends and a dozen or so hardbound books that appeared to be no less than a century old. I stood from the couch and quietly walked toward the bedrooms. One room had a bed, nightstand, dresser, and weight lifting equipment. Again, everything was perfectly placed. I glanced in the other bedroom. One entire wall was a bookcase. After counting the spines of a few books and performing some simple math, it appeared there were over a thousand books in the case. A bed, nightstand, a sewing machine, and digital clock were the only other objects in the room. The bed, although made with a simple comforter and two pillows, was crease and wrinkle free. As I turned to walk from the room, I noticed a small cardboard box on the floor neatly placed by the door. I looked inside.

My cap, gown, diploma, and the gift box sat inside.

*You sneaky fucker.*

I tiptoed back into the living room and walked toward the coffee table and bent down. I carefully traced my index finger along the spine of the books, *A Bridge Too Far, Making of the President, The Blue and Gray, The Caine Mutiny, Midnight, Robin Hood, Closing the Ring, Cast the First Stone, Mark Twain's Works, The Days of McKinley, The Birth of Britain.*

As I heard Axton turn the faucet in the bathroom off, I fell backward onto the couch and rested my cheek in the palm of my hand. A few seconds later, he emerged from the bathroom.

"Your hands steady?" he asked.

"Huh?"

"Your hands, do you shake?"

"No, I mean not really. Why"

"Here," he said as he reached toward me.

I took a small plastic tube from his hand. As I looked at it curiously, he explained.

"Superglue. I need you to glue this back together," he sighed as he sat down beside me.

He pulled a dry washcloth from his front pocket and dabbed at the large cut across the knuckle of his middle finger.

He raised the washcloth slightly and fixed his eyes on mine, "I'll dry it up with *this*, and you squirt a little glue inside and pinch it together.

Don't *smash* it together, or it'll look like shit when it heals. You only get one fucking chance with that shit, you know."

I scrunched my brow, "Superglue?"

"Best shit ever," he nodded.

I glanced down at his hand. A cut which would probably require at least four or five stitches was across his middle knuckle and onto the back of his hand. As he dabbed the blood from it, I could see into the wound until it quickly filled with blood again. It appeared to be open clear to the bone of his knuckle.

"Uhhm. That looks like it may need…" I began.

"It *needs* Superglued. Give me that shit," he snapped as he reached for the glue.

I pulled my hand back sharply, "I'll do it. Jesus, Mr. stubborn. Press down on it for a minute."

"Does this stuff hurt?" I asked.

He raised both eyebrows and stared as he pressed the corner of the cloth onto the top of the wound, "Look at me. Do I really look like the type of guy that would complain if it did? And no, it doesn't hurt. Nothing hurts. It's only uncomfortable for a second. Ready?"

I pilled the cap from the glue and squeezed the tube until a small drop began to rise on the tip, "Go!"

As soon as he pulled the cloth from his skin, I lowered the tip of the tube to the wound and attempted to make a perfect line of glue along the cut. As I was finishing my masterpiece, the blood began to boil from the cut. I opened my mouth and lightly bit the tube, holding it in my teeth. Half frantic, I pulled the washcloth from his hand as I pinched the cut together. Almost magically, the wound closed and stopped bleeding. After a few seconds of blowing on it, I wiped the excess blood.

I sat back, placed the lid onto the tube of glue, and admired my handiwork.

"A regular Florence fucking Nightingale," he chuckled as he looked down at his knucles.

"Yep. Now all I need is for you to get the syndrome or whatever," I said as I handed him the tube.

He shifted his gaze from his hand to me, "What syndrome?"

"The Florence Nightingale syndrome," I said as I stood.

"Sit down," he chuckled.

"What do you know about that?" he asked; as if he were in shock I even knew who Florence Nightingale was.

I sat lightly on the edge of the couch, "It's where the caretaker develops a romantic interest for the…"

"I *know* what it is," he snapped.

*Well, if you've read all of those books in the back room, I'm sure you do.*

He studied his hand for a long moment and then glanced up and broke the silence, "I don't like sleeping in my bed if I'm dirty."

I gazed his direction and attempted to keep my face free of expression, "Okay."

He continued to stare at his hand, "So we're both going to need to shower. You'll be staying here tonight."

*Sweet Jesus.*

*Thank you Lord.*

I looked down and began to pick at my cuticles. I had no intention of allowing him to see my face.

"Okay," the word barely escaped my dry lips.

"So we can shower together or separate, but I'm exhausted," he said as he stood.

I glanced up and spoke almost apologetically, "Whatever makes you more comfortable."

"Look, don't think for one minute you're the first woman I've seen naked. *People* don't make me uncomfortable. If you're fine seeing my scars, come on," he said as he turned away.

I attempted to hide my excitement as I followed him to the bathroom. On this night I watched Axton beat a man half to death for attempting to claim me, learned he trusted me enough to allow me to tend to his wounds, came to his home for the first time, and now prepared to shower with him and stay all night.

*Progress.*

Axton and I were making progress.

# AVERY

With my head on Axton's chest, I waited quietly for him to fall asleep. As his breathing shifted to a soft effortless pattern, I relaxed and inhaled the scent of his soap on my skin. The first time I saw him naked was in the shower, and we didn't even have sex. Seeing his naked body and not greedily attacking him was not an easy feat, but it was a necessary one. It was crucial that the relationship proceeded at Axton's pace, not mine. Most women would be frustrated or disappointed with the return on their investment with Axton. I, on the other hand, was absolutely thrilled with what I had received from him. Dressed in one of his wife beaters and a pair of his extra-large sweat pants, the only thing absent was the low, scratchy rumble of his voice to comfort me.

I stared at the ceiling and attempted to count the times I had ridden on his motorcycle.

When we rode to the park and he asked me if I spoke Spanish. To eat in Wichita at the noodle place. Pizza downtown. When he dropped me off at work and went to make a *deal.* The ride home later. The other time he took me to work, and waited while I worked a two hour shift because Lori's fat ass was sick. To eat noodles again. To the coffee place in Riverside the first time. Down to the spot by the bridge where the big tree is. Riverside coffee shop again.

I started to fade in and out of sleep, and I wasn't a third of the way done. I began counting again at the most recent, and started working backward. There were too many to count.

To his house. To the barbeque. To get new shorts before the barbeque. The night we just went *to relax*. Graduation day back from Benton. To Benton. God, riding with all those bikes was so cool. When we rolled up to the restaurant at the airport, it sounded like a hurricane. Everyone turned and looked. It was so cool to be a part of that. When we walked into the bar, I was so proud to be with him.

When we left with the other group of bikers, God it felt so powerful. More than twenty of us, side-by-side at eighty miles an hour, following the curves together, staying a foot or so apart. It looked like a work of art as we flowed down the highway.

He said *slim and not at all* the day we met. Before long this summer will be over, and I'll have been on his bike the entire time.

*Pretty God damned slim, and not at all.*

Ha.

*Progress.*

Axton might be a big, mean, complex person, but to me, he's Axton. I wouldn't change anything about him, even if I had the chance.

What do I like about him the most?

Let me think...

# AXTON

It had been almost twenty years since I had seen a woman wake up in my bed. I stood in the doorway sipping coffee as I watched Avery slowly migrate from sleeping soundly to waking up. She shifted in the bed, closed her eyes tightly as she realized the sun was up, and yanked the comforter over her head.

"Are you going to wake up? It's almost eight o'clock," I said over the top of my cup of coffee.

She pulled the comforter down to her chest and blinked her eyes a few times, "Was that you grinding coffee beans at like six thirty?"

I nodded my head and took a sip of coffee, "Already worked out, showered, and made coffee. I'm ready to eat. What do you normally eat for breakfast?"

"What time is it again?" she groaned.

"It's ten before eight. I was going to make a bagel and cream cheese. Maybe some bacon if you want it. I eat a light breakfast," I explained.

"I don't eat pork. Uhhm, a bagel sounds good. A bagel and coffee," she said as she sat up in bed.

"Muslim?" I chuckled.

She shook her head and grinned, "No, pork's slippery and gross. I don't eat bacon because it's bouncy."

"Alright, *no bacon* coming right up. Well, I'll get a bagel toasted for you. Coffee's ready," I nodded as I turned toward the living room.

211

Avery was a very beautiful woman. Any fool could see it. What a man wasn't capable of seeing made her even more attractive. There was no doubt she was extremely intelligent, but she was also very perceptive. I've never been one to explain to someone what I expect of them or what I would like to see them change in their life. People are who they are and it certainly wasn't my place to be critical of them. I've always believed by the time we reach twenty-five years old, we are formed into the person we will live the rest of our lives as. Avery's age and lack of experience in living life allowed her to continue to learn from being exposed to her surroundings and make adjustments as she saw fit.

Her perceptive nature caused her to naturally pay attention to what my likes and dislikes were, and make modifications to how she acted and reacted in an effort to please me. The end result was her transformation into what I expected would be one of the best little Ol' Ladies a man could ever ask for. Whether or not she was the woman I needed to spend my days with had yet to be decided.

I dropped two bagels into the toaster, grabbed the cream cheese from the refrigerator, and two plates from the cabinet. As I was pouring Avery's coffee, my phone beeped, indicating I had received a text message. Typically, I didn't do a tremendous amount of texting or talking on the phone. To separate the text messages of the club from the text messages of customers, I had assigned different people different text tones. The tone of the chime on my phone was assigned to only one person.

El Pelón.

I sighed and reached for my phone.

*It's one of your own. Meet me in an hour at Cortez. Come alone.*

My heart rose into my throat. I snapped the rubber band against

212

my wrist a few times. Meeting at Cortez made me a little nervous. A joint known for violence, gang torture, and importation of illegal aliens, it wasn't a place where I would *ever* be comfortable. Knowing I'd be the only non-Spanish speaking person there made me even more uncomfortable. I wondered if the entire thing was a set-up. He said it was *one of my own*. My mind began to race, wondering who it may be, and the amount of value I would place on the information El Pelón provided me. To think of one of my brothers betraying the club was impossible. As I snapped the rubber band again, I looked up at the sound of Avery's footsteps.

"So, no bacon?" Avery asked as she walked into the kitchen.

I glanced up from my phone nervously, and held my index finger in the air, "I need to send a text."

Without speaking, she turned toward the living room, walked to the couch, and sat down. I pressed the keys on the screen, said what little I had to say, and pressed *send*.

*I'll be there at 9:00 but I won't be alone.*

If there were two people I knew I could *always* trust, they were Toad and Otis. For sheer intimidation purposes, Otis would be my best bet. I scrolled to Otis' number and pressed *call*. After ten rings with no answer, I hung up. I scrolled to Toad's number and pressed *call*. He answered on the third ring.

"*What's up?*" his deep raspy tone was proof enough he was clearly still half asleep.

"Need you to roll with me brother. We got to be in Wichita in one hour. Come to my place?" I asked.

"*Gimme twenty, Slice. Shit, I'm still in bed, bro,*" he responded.

I heard Sloan's voice in the background, asking him who he was speaking to. His response was what I would have expected.

"*Club business.*"

"I'll be here," I responded.

I hung up and tossed the phone across the countertop, "Listen. I'm going to eat this and then I have to run. Club business. You can stay here if you like, I should be back in an hour and a half, maybe two."

I reached for the toaster, pulled the bagels, and dropped them onto the plates. Avery stood from the couch and walked into the kitchen. Although she looked cute, she seemed somewhat out of place in my sweats and wife beater. I fumbled with trying to spread the cream cheese on the bagel as I watched her walk into the kitchen.

"You're a cute little fucker," I said as her gaze met mine.

She grinned as she ran her hands through her hair, "Thank you. My hair's probably a fucking mess. It was still wet when I fell asleep."

"Looks great," I said as I slid the bagel across the counter.

"You sure it's okay if I stay here?" she asked.

"I wouldn't have offered if it wasn't. I trust you," I responded as I bit into the bagel.

"I uhhm. I noticed a lot of books in the spare bedroom. Can I read while you're gone?" she asked as she stirred sugar into her coffee.

"Knock yourself out, there's plenty in there to read, that's for fucking sure. You always wake up looking like that?" I asked as I tilted my bagel toward her.

"Yeah, nice, huh?" she said in a sarcastic tone.

She lifted her coffee cup to her lips and hesitated. Her hair was a sculpted mess, as if she'd purposely attempted to make it look as shitty as she possibly could. I didn't have a mirror in my bedroom, and I didn't think she'd been into the bathroom yet, so I doubted she knew *exactly* what she looked like. To me, seeing her wake up looking like she did was all the proof I needed to know she was far more beautiful than ninety-nine percent of all other women who were on this earth. I stood silently with the bagel dangling from my fingertips as I admired her beautiful face and perfectly proportioned body. I lifted the remaining portion of bagel to my mouth and bit into it as she stood and sipped her coffee.

I gazed at her and snapped the rubber band repeatedly into my wrist as she nibbled around the circumference of the bagel. Standing across from me, unaware of my thoughts, feelings, or what I was about to go do, she looked innocent and beautiful as she gnawed at the toasted bread.

*You are a humble little bitch, aren't you?*

"You look great, babe," I responded as I swallowed the bagel.

*Babe?*

*Where the fuck did that come from?*

*Fuck, Slice, you're softening up.*

"Thanks. You always look the same. Hot as fuck," she said over her mouthful of bagel.

*God damn, I wish I didn't have to leave.*

As she stood beside the kitchen counter eating, I walked past her and into the living room. I couldn't stand to look at her any longer without making a move. I opened the small cabinet at the end of the sofa and pointed inside.

"There's a CD player in here, some CD's, and an iPod with a playlist on it. It's wireless to the speakers in the ceiling."

She glanced up from her bagel and toward the ceiling, "Cool."

The sound of Toad's bike pulling up reminded me of what I had to do. Getting the information about the robbery was high on my priority list, but the fact it included one of the club's own men wasn't what I had hoped for. Although I suppose I knew it was where the investigation was going to point, especially after talking to King, I had secretly hoped for another answer. I turned to face Avery, not really knowing what to say.

"Go. I'll be fine," she sighed.

As I walked toward the kitchen, she gazed down at her hand and continued to nibble at the small piece of remaining bagel. I reached for my phone, and hesitated; my eyes still fixed on her. With my right hand, I reached toward her face and lifted her chin slightly. As she glanced up, I leaned forward and kissed her lips lightly. As soon as our lips parted, I slid my hand to the back of her head and pulled her into me aggressively. I kissed her passionately, allowing our tongues to intertwine and my thoughts to rush places other than the potential violence which was before me. She dropped the remaining bagel onto the floor and gripped my ass firmly. After a long, impassioned kiss, I broke away, leaned back, and scanned her from head to toe.

I shook my head in an effort to clear it, "You sure as fuck do. You look great, Avery."

"Where the fuck did that come from" she whispered.

"That's progress, Avery," I said as I grabbed my phone and keys.

She nodded her head and glanced down at the floor at her piece of bagel.

"Five second rule, better hurry up," I chuckled.

"I'll make another?"

"Go right ahead. Whatever's here is all yours. I'll be back in a few hours," I said over my shoulder.

Kissing her just seemed like the right thing to do at the time; and considering where I was going, I didn't know if I was ever coming back.

# AVERY

Axton's kiss caught me completely off guard. I had no idea where he was going or what he had planned to do, but the fact he kissed me before he left led me to believe it wasn't something he really wanted to do. I walked into the living room wondering if what he had to do might be related to the attempted robbery. Feeling like some music might ease my mind; I fumbled through the CD's in the cabinet looking for something and not necessarily knowing what. After seeing nothing I recognized, I scrolled through the iPod. Again, nothing I had ever heard of.

I scrolled up to the top of the list of tunes on the iPod.

*Allman Brothers.*

Never heard of them.

*What the fuck, if he likes it, I better learn to.*

I pressed play. A soft organ and mellow guitar started playing. It sounded similar to country, but it was a little more bluesy and upbeat. I closed my eyes and listened to the piano. Eventually, a deep, soft voice began to sing. I opened my eyes and pressed *play* again. After listening to the song a second time, I immediately pressed *play* one more time, and listened to it a third time. As the song played the third time, it made perfect sense. The song was a story of an outlaw on the run from the law; or whoever it was that was chasing him. Obviously he was on a motorcycle, because he was *riding*. A man living life one day at a time, running from place to place and from woman to woman; owning no more than what was on his back and in his pocket. In the song, however, he never stops running. He never reaches a destination or gets away from the man chasing him. The only way he can stay free is to keep from hiding, to continue to run.

Running is riding.

In a sense, Axton was the Midnight Rider. Hell, all of the members of the club were. More accurately, most men who rode motorcycles were. Society, in a sense, is doing all of the chasing. To conform to society's expectations is to be caught. Riding, for me at least, allows me to feel free. I have no doubts Axton feels the same way. Axton calling my car a *cage* began to make sense.

I knew the rule, *no colors in cages*. It made a little more sense after listening to the song. The colors are a symbol of freedom. A cage is the opposite. It's absolute confinement. They contradict one another.

I found it strange how music has the ability to change our outlook on certain things. The song caused me to feel enlightened, more understanding, and considerably more appreciative of who Axton was and why he was so passionate about riding. I looked around the house, beginning to feel cramped and confined. I needed a ride, and I needed one soon. It had only been thirty minutes, and I was going stir crazy being locked up in the house. I flattened myself out on the couch, pulled a throw over my shoulders, and got lost in the memory of Axton kissing me. As I came to the realization Axton leaving and conducting *club business* was going to be common, I likened it to how a military wife must feel, knowing her husband was away, risking his life while she knew nothing of what he was doing or whether or not he was safe. A sacrifice, I suppose, to be in a relationship with a man who was unlike most other men.

A sacrifice I was willing to make.

# AXTON

We never know who we truly are until we have nothing. Losing everything and recovering from it causes a man to emerge from the tragedy a more understanding, humble, and appreciative soul. After having nothing, a man is appreciative of *everything*. For those who have everything, the fear of loss causes a select few to react in a manner contrary to what they or anyone else believed were their true moral beliefs.

Being faced with adversity and finding the courage to hold your chin high enough to see a life beyond the ruins defines a man who is satisfied with simply living life.

To think I voted a man into the club who I believed to be capable of laughing in the face of adversity, only to learn he would become an enemy, risking my life and the life of other brothers for a small potential monetary gain, was inconceivable.

"What was he riding? What color was his bike?"

El Pelón turned to the two men bound to the steam lines in the boiler room and jabbered some Spanish shit. After they responded an unintelligible answer, El Pelón glanced in my direction.

"They said he wasn't riding a motorcycle. He was in a red truck. A four door Ford with chrome rims," he said.

I shifted my gaze from the floor to Toad.

Toad shook his head and raised his hands to his face, "I know you don't want to hear it, and I don't either. But they picked out his picture off the website. They know what he drove. I hate it too, Slice, but it is what it is."

I spit on the concrete floor. The room was easily thirty degrees hotter than it was outside, probably at least 120 degrees of utter humid hell. I was covered in sweat, aggravated, and felt betrayed. El Pelón's scouts had found the two local Mexican gang-bangers who orchestrated the attempted robbery. Pelón's people heard the information through friends of friends of the two dead members of the gang, and the information was traced back to the two men now strapped to the steam lines. I guessed the Mexicans didn't adhere to the *club business is club business* belief. Hell, who was I to talk, one of my own brothers had stabbed me in the back and betrayed the club.

After a short interrogation of the men in Cortez's boiler room, they gave an accurate initial description of the Sinner, and picked him out of a photo off of the website on Toad's phone. Describing his truck and the chrome rims was icing on the cake. No one could possibly know what he drove short of someone who actually saw him driving the truck. He probably hadn't driven it a few hundred miles in the last year. As I tried to digest what happened, more questions came to mind.

"The split. I want to know what this cocksucker was going to gain. What were *they* going to get, and what were the two dead motherfuckers going to get? What was *his* fucking cut? My guy?"

After exchanging a few words, El Pelón spoke over his shoulder, "Thirty mil."

"What the fuck? It was a *sixty grand* deal?" I snapped.

"Thousand, my bad homie. Thirty grand," he said as he wiped his brow.

I smeared the sweat from my face with my forearm. After wiping my arm on my cut, I glanced at Toad, "Anything else"

Toad nodded his head, "Ask the motherfuckers what he was wearing when they met him."

I scrunched my brow and stared, "What the fuck for?"

"I want to know," Toad responded, "Ask 'em what he was wearing."

When they answered, they both nodded toward Toad and me. Pelón turned toward Toad and responded, "They said he was wearing a vest like yours with two crossed rifles, wings and a *calavera*. A skull."

"That motherfucker," I snapped.

"I knew it! That cocksucker! He disrespected the colors, the club, hell, he wore his fucking cut in a cage, he…" Toad paused and reached into his cut.

"What about these two fuckers?" Toad asked.

I gazed at El Pelón and shrugged, "Well?"

"These two? They're *mine.* Homie here and me are going to cut off their heads and play soccer with them on the playground where their kids go to school. They disrespected me, the MS, and their families. I'll take care of these two. You take care of yours. You got anything else you want from these two fuckers before I saw their heads off?" he asked calmly.

"Mother…fucker," I stammered, "No, I guess not. I just need to get out of this hot motherfucker. I'll be in touch."

He nodded his head once, and turned toward the two men. Thinking of what was next for them brought the reality of my own problems to the surface. As Toad and I walked out to our bikes silently, what bothered me more than anything was the fact Hollywood was Road Captain of the club. He was not only a member, but the fucking Road Captain. Hell, he helped put the gun deal together with Otis, acquiring the AK-47's.

Son-of-a-bitch probably knew all along he was going to steal the cash. As I sat down onto the seat of the bike, I felt absolutely sick.

"How you wanna handle this?" Toad asked as he dropped his pistol into the saddle bag of his bike.

"I don't know. Nothing's ever happened like this before. I want to keep it quiet, but I want everyone to know what happens when someone makes a move like this against the club. Let me think about it while we ride back to town," I responded as I fired up the bike.

Toad nodded his head and fired up his bagger. As he climbed into the seat, I sat, staring, as numbness washed over me. A brother willing to sacrifice the lives of two members of the club, two people who considered *him* a brother, all for a little money. The thought of it caused me to question the sincerity of many of the other members in the club. We needed a *come to Jesus meeting*, and we needed to have it quick.

As I glanced over my shoulder to check oncoming traffic, I noticed the lick 'n stick seat on the fender. Strangely, I came to realize the one person who I knew had my back in a life or death situation wasn't a brother, but a bitch.

And a damned good bitch at that.

# AXTON

"You still got that Glock 40 caliber? You know the one we got new out at Cabela's a few years back?" I asked.

He stared blankly, "Yep."

"I want to know if I can borrow it. Toad and I got an argument going on about 40 cal. versus 45 cal. Only one way to settle it," I shrugged.

"Yeah, hold on a sec. What are you gonna do?" he asked.

"He's got some ballistic gelatin or something. We're just going to fire a few rounds into it and see which one has more penetrating power," I responded.

"Hell you can get all that shit off the internet. Google is a powerful thing," he said over his shoulder as he walked toward his gun safe.

"Yeah, but you know me, arguments are only settled on facts. Not propaganda," I said flatly as I followed him to the safe.

"There you go, just cleaned it," he said as he handed me this pistol over his shoulder.

"Got an extra box of ammo?" I asked.

"Damn Slice. Sure, hold on," he said as he reached into the safe.

"Here you go," he said as he handed me the box of ammunition.

"Appreciate it. See ya in about thirty minutes when we get done.

# AXTON

I stood beside Toad's bike, "Alright, when we get there, I'll get him in the garage. Just stand by my side. Then, when he gives you an opening, but only after he opens the safe, pull some fucking Marine shit and get him in a choke hold so I can question him."

"I'm on it, Slice," he nodded.

I gazed down at the ground and shook my head thinking about what we were about to do. As I shifted my eyes to Toad, I crossed my arms and sighed, "I'll run into his house and get the pillow, just make sure you keep your fucking head out of the way. I guess it's a good thing this fucker lives out in the country away from a bunch of people."

"Let's roll," Toad responded.

Toad had proven himself over and over with the club. His ability to keep his mouth shut, willingness to participate in the more intricate club business, and for lack of a better term - downright toughness, made him a shoe-in for a seat on the board. I was proud to call him a brother. I hopped on my bike, flipped the on switch and hit the start button. As the motor began to rumble, I tossed my head forward motioning for Toad to lead.

As we pulled up to Hollywood's house, he did as I expected. He walked out into the garage by the gun safe. Having his pistol, which was registered to him, should allow me to shoot him with it and make it look like a suicide. Technically, he'd need blood splatter on his hands for it to pass a *good* investigation, but shielding his face with the pillow should assist with not needing to meet that necessity. The pillow would also, if checked, meet DNA requirements and sampling for being his. Whatever financial problems he was having should pass for motive.

As soon as we shut off the bikes, Toad made his way into the garage. I followed close behind holding the carrying case for the pistol. When I was a matter of a few feet from the garage, Hollywood opened the safe and began small talk with Toad. I slowed my stride and waited for Toad to make his move. Two more steps, and Toad had him in a choke hold. Now standing behind Hollywood, Toad had one arm around his neck, and another pressing the back of his head forward.

"Jesus Toad," I said as I placed the pistol on the garage floor.

I hustled through the garage and into the house. After grabbing a pillow from Hollywood's bed, I hurried back out into the garage. I tossed the pillow beside the pistol case and stood in front of Toad.

"Don't kill his ass, I want to talk to him Toad, Jesus."

Toad relaxed his hold on Hollywood's neck. As he gasped for breath, I began to speak.

"I need to ask you a few things, 'Wood. Now don't disrespect me again by trying to bullshit me and act like I'm some dumb fuck that doesn't know what I'm talking about. Why'd you set up the robbery with the Mexicans?"

Immediately shock washed over his face, followed by worry. After completely catching his breath and taking a short pause, he began to cry and attempt to explain.

"Slice, it got out of hand. I'm seventeen grand upside down on this place. You know it's been tough since the divorce," he coughed and started to blubber.

*Right now, I don't have a compassionate bone in my body. Crying like a pussy won't change a thing.*

"They're gonna foreclose on this fucker. I needed the money," he blubbered.

*Hell, I never thought it would be this easy to get you to admit it. Fuck. I still hoped it was all a lie, 'Wood.*

Still disappointed beyond comprehension, I stood in front of him with my arms crossed. Having him admit his participation allowed me to feel better about my own administration of justice. Not having him confess would never allow me any closure. As I stood and stared, still not quite believing he would betray the club, I started speaking my mind, "You know what? That Mexican motherfucker damn near killed Otis and I. I never said anything because I thought it originated in the club, and I wanted to find out for sure before I let the cat out of the fucking bag. And guess fucking what, motherfucker? That fucking girl that's been a fender ornament for the last month is the one who saved us. Not a brother, not even a *man*, but a fucking college girl. She shot both those fucking beaners and saved our asses."

"If you'd have asked, 'Wood, we'd have had a fundraiser. That's the sickening part. A poker run would have raised fifty grand. Hell, if you'd have asked me personally, I'd have flipped you twenty grand. Fuck this shit, you make me fucking sick, I'm done. Hold him, Toad," I growled.

As Hollywood tried to explain, Toad cinched his grip tighter on his neck. Hollywood relaxed and went limp.

"You know I ain't really a God fearing man, but on this earth, we got good and evil. Right and wrong. You know I read a lot to make me stronger in living life. Numbers 30:2 says," I paused, bent over and picked up the pillow and pistol.

*"If a man vow a vow to the LORD, or swear an oath to bind his soul with a bond; he shall not break his word, he shall do according to all that proceeds out of his mouth.* To me, that applies to us. So, if you're not a man who believes in the bible, you still took an oath to the *club*, and if you *do* believe in the bible, you took an oath with the club; but you're bound by the belief of God and the bible. However you want to look at it, but you're supposed to keep your fucking word. Either way, you fucked us. And you broke your word."

I lifted the pillow in front of his face, "Move your head to the side, Toad, I don't need both of your asses dead."

I held the pillow up to his face, and pressed the pistol into the pillow and against his forehead. I closed my eyes and pulled the trigger. Instantly, he fell limp into Toad's arms.

"Toss his ass beside the safe," I grunted.

I removed a round from the box of ammunition and bent down to where Hollywood lay on the floor. After pressing the bullet against his fingertips, I used his finger to push the round into the magazine.

I tilted my head toward the driveway, "Run and get those three phone books."

Toad quickly returned with the three phone books. After wiping the pistol free of my fingerprints and placing the pistol in Hollywood's hand, I cupped my hand around his and fired a round into the phonebooks. The brass casing fell to the garage floor.

I stood up and gazed down at a man I once admired and considered a brother, "Now his prints will be on the pistol, the brass, and he's got cordite on his hand from firing the gun. Safe's open, and it looks like he came out here, opened it, and shot his stupid self, using the pillow to muffle the sound. Hell, the fact they're foreclosing gives him all the motive in the world. Alright. Take the phonebooks and the *other* brass from when I shot him and load that shit up. And grab his cut off the bars of his bike."

As I wiped the fingerprints from the box of ammo and pistol case, Toad collected the phonebooks and the brass casing. Using my tee shirt, I opened the ammo box and placed it beside the safe. After doing the same with the pistol case, I turned toward the driveway. Toad sat quietly on his bike waiting.

In somewhat of a daze, I walked down the driveway to the bikes.

"Remind me to never piss you off," Toad said flatly as he started his bike.

Over the sound of his exhaust, I took exception to his comment, "What the fuck would *you* have done?"

He shook his head, then tilted it toward the garage, "I'd have just walked up and shot him. I was meaning all of the planting evidence. Shit, they'll rule this deal a suicide and close the book."

"Well, if there are any questions, I know the local cop, so it's all good. Fucking piece of shit, I'm glad it's over," I hissed.

"Let's roll," Toad said as he popped his neck.

I stepped over the seat and looked up the driveway at Hollywood's body. As I reached for the controls, I looked at my watch. It wasn't even noon yet, and I was exhausted mentally and physically. I needed something to calm my nerves and put my head in a peaceful place. There was only one thing I could think of that I knew would provide me with such pleasure.

And she was waiting for me at home.

# AVERY

It had been a little more than three hours since Axton had left, and I was on an Allman Brothers, Jonny Lang, and Ben Harper shuffle while reading *Alice in Wonderland*. Spending time in his home without him present gave me a false sense of being in a relationship with him. I realized in some respects, we were in a relationship, but it wasn't close to anything conventional, and it certainly wasn't sexual. Axton was a difficult man to get next to, but I felt if we ever did become intimate, he would be the type of person to provide me everything I needed in a relationship.

I turned the page to a new chapter as *Jonny Lang's When I Come to You* began to play. I closed my eyes and listened to his soulful voice and bluesy guitar. The sound of Axton's motorcycle caused me to jump to my feet and run to the window like an over anxious child. I watched from the corner of the pulled blind as Axton rolled up the street and into the driveway. I released the blind and flopped onto the couch and opened the book. As I was flipping to my current page, Axton opened the door.

"Nice day for a ride, huh?" I said over my shoulder.

"It's humid as fuck, but yeah. Actually, I was thinking of a shower and relaxing a little. You like Jonny Lang?" he asked over his shoulder as he tossed his phone and keys onto the kitchen counter.

"I do. I'm on a Lang, Allman Brothers, and Ben Harper shuffle," I responded as I arched my back.

"What are you reading?" he asked as he tossed his head my direction.

"Oh, *Alice in Wonderland*," I grinned.

He paused and gazed down at the floor. As he stared at his feet, he chuckled, "That's par for the course."

He lifted his head and gazed my direction, "*It would be so nice if something made sense for a change.*"

"Excuse me?" I said as I shifted in the seat.

"It's from the book. Let's see, how about, *it's no use going back to yesterday, because I was a different person then.* I like *that* quote, because to me, it's about making progress. And I've always felt like there was a part written for me," he sighed.

He placed his hands on his hips and stared up at the ceiling, "*Would you tell me, please, which way I ought to go from here?*"

"*That depends a good deal on where you want to get to.*"

"*I don't much care where…*"

"*Then it doesn't matter which way you go.*"

He glanced down from the ceiling and smiled, "Let's take another shower, I feel dirty."

I snapped the book closed and jumped from the couch. As I slowly walked his direction, I pushed the sweats down my hips and grinned. His eyes widened and his mouth opened slightly. Leaving the sweats half-way down my hips, I pulled my shirt over my head and tossed it on the floor beside him.

As I reached around and unclasped my bra, I quoted my new favorite line from the book, "*Actually, the best gift you could have given her was a lifetime of adventures…*"

"I hope you're ready for this," he sighed.

"I am," I responded as I pushed my sweats to the floor.

And I was.

# AVERY

Yet another sexless shower with Axton, and I was frustrated beyond comprehension. My sheer attraction to him, his gorgeous looks, and the fact he was hung like an absolute motherfucker made seeing him naked, and *not* having sex, all too difficult. As I walked to his room wrapped in a towel, I wondered what color baggy sweats he was going to give me to wear.

Standing beside the bed shirtless and dressed in pajama pants, Axton seemed out of place. All I had ever seen him wear were jeans, short of falling asleep with him the night before. And, on that night, he wore black sweats. They were close enough to the appearance of jeans it just seemed as if he were wearing black jeans. Standing in the well-lit room in plaid cotton pants was something new, and as much as I hated to admit it, I liked it. I liked it a lot.

As I entered the room, he turned his upper body toward me. His face seemed to harbor a hint or embarrassment or guilt. Probably from all of the scars, I figured. As drawn as I was to his muscular body, I made a conscious effort to shift my gaze away from him and not stare. As I prepared to ask him what he wanted me to wear, he reached for the bed and lifted up a black cotton spaghetti-strap summer dress.

"Put this on, I want to see you in it," he said as he dangled the dress in front of him.

*Seriously? I don't want to wear one of your former slut's clothes.*

I scrunched my nose slightly, "Uhhm, where'd you get it?"

"I bought it from the mall last week when I went to Wichita. I shoved the bag behind my Mexican blanket. Fucker flapped all the way here, I thought it was going to fly off, but it made the trip," he chuckled.

*You bought me a dress?*

Short of a gift from my father as a child, no man had ever bought me anything. I bit my quivering lower lip and held out my hand. As he tossed the dress over my outstretched arm, he smiled a genuine smile. As I admired his teeth, I silently wished he'd smile more. He didn't have the teeth of what I would have expected a biker to have; they were quite straight and considerably whiter than mine. I lifted the dress and glanced at the tag.

*Von Maur, size 2, $125.00. Holy shit, Axton. You didn't have to...*

"I was headed back from a meeting with a few other clubs and I stopped to see what they had. I thought you'd look cute in that little fucker. Hell, all you ever wear are shorts. Suppose you can't wear it on the bike, so you just as well put it on now," he shrugged.

I dropped the towel, and stood completely naked in front of him. I pulled the dress over my head, along my torso, and past my hips. It fit perfectly. After remembering he didn't have a mirror in his room, I held my index finger in the air excitedly, "Hold please."

I ran to the bathroom and opened the door. Standing in the opening, I looked into the mirror. Not only did the dress fit perfectly, it appeared I had gained a few pounds in all the right places. I turned, pressed the dress to my stomach and gazed in the mirror. I bend down slightly and stared at my reflection. I looked marvelous; I was braless and it looked like I actually had cleavage. My butt looked cute. As I felt Axton's presence behind me, I turned to face him. My mouth said the words *thank you*, but no sound escaped my lips. Overcome with joy, lust, a strong sense of self-worth, and an attraction to the man standing before me, I merely stood and stared.

"You uhhm. You look beautiful, Avery," he stammered.

Unable to speak without blubbering, I raised my hands in the air, smiled, and repeated my silent *thank you*. I watched curiously as he reached over, slipped one arm behind my legs, another along my shoulders, and picked me up from my feet. My head began to spin. I wrapped my arms around his neck as he carried me toward the room. As he lowered me to the bed, I realized I didn't care what his next move was. The dress, my newfound curvaceous body, his expression of my beauty, and the progress we had made so far was enough for me to survive the entire summer.

With my legs dangling over the edge slightly, he knelt on the floor at the end of the bed and raised his index finger to his lips. I lifted myself onto my elbows and watched as he pushed my thighs apart, raised the dress to my waist, and positioned his head between my thighs. Softly, his mouth kissed up the length of my thighs until I felt his tongue against my overly anxious pussy. My entire body shuddered as I felt his tongue against my clit.

*Oh God, seriously? We went from zero to a hundred miles an hour instantly.*

The slight pressure from his finger penetrating me caused me to inhale sharply. I bit my lower lip and craned my neck to watch as he slowly began to finger me and lick my soaking wet pussy simultaneously. The rhythmic motions of both his tongue against my clit and his finger working in and out of my wetness became expected and quite a pleasure. Anticipating each pleasurable move, my breathing began to be as predictable as his tongue and finger.

*If you expect me to last any length of time, we'd better slow down.*

I felt myself reaching a climax of new proportion. After Axton, my vibrator would become useless, and every orgasm preceding this one would be nothing short of some faint memory which would eventually fade into nothingness. As he continued to lick and slurp against my clit and work his magic finger in and out, l lowered my head and bit my lip.

I couldn't watch any longer. His two days growth of bad-boy beard and the muscles in his arms combined with his love for sucking and licking my pussy proved to be all too much. I wanted this to last at least another sixty seconds before I exploded into another atmosphere. My ears began to ring, and I felt itchy all over.

And.

I.

Screamed.

"Holy fucking Jesus fuck!" I screamed.

I felt as if I was going to die. The, *I'm headed to heaven* type of death, not the, *Oh shit I'm going to die* type. Knowing heaven had no place for a girl like me, I continued to scream as I opened and closed my eyes repeatedly. Visions of Axton came and went and he continued to flick his tongue against my now swollen clit. Combined with his finger's ability to find *whatever the fuck that spot is on the top of my pussy*, he extracted another earth shattering orgasm.

"Oh…" I bit against my lip.

I opened my mouth and stared at the ceiling, "My…"

I looked down at his face, still buried between my thighs, and blinked repeatedly, "Axton…"

My entire body shook from another five minute long orgasm.

240

Webster's Dictionary should have a picture of the face I made through the course of having it under the definition for *orgasmic bliss*. As I came back down to earth, I realized although I meant to say *Oh my God*, and I actually flubbed it into *Oh my Axton*. It was, however, a perfect expression for how I felt. Right now, Axton, to me, *was* God. He was my beginning and my end. My savior, my salvation, my bad-boy, and my alpha male biker, he was my...

*Holy shit!*

As he pulled down his pajama pants, I almost passed out. His cock was rigid and massive. From taking two showers with him, I knew it was huge, but I had no idea it would grow into what was between his legs. As he stood there stroking it, I realized I had no idea he'd even stopped licking me. I must have slipped away to some other distant place for a moment. Maybe it was the fact that deep down inside I wanted him more than I had ever wanted anything or anyone in my life.

As his knee pressed into the comforter, and I felt his full weight being added to the bed, I wanted to ask about protection, diseases, and at least tell him I was precautious enough to have been taking birth control, just in case. As he climbed into place on top of me, I stared down past his massive chest, chiseled stomach, flaring biceps, and focused on his rigid cock. I opened my mouth and inhaled a short breath.

"Fuck me," escaped my lips.

*I should really have him wear a condom.*

"Fuck me," I screamed.

"Now. Just fuck me. Please?" I pleaded.

His hand moved to his cock. I closed my eyes. Even though I was soaked, and my pussy was beyond willing, the pressure against my pussy was horrendous. His cock was huge and if pussies came in sizes, mine was without a doubt an X-Small. I bit my lip. I felt as if my hips became dislodged somehow. As soon as he finally penetrated me I opened my eyes in disbelief. The pain, although deep and dull, was pleasurable. As he slowly worked himself in and out, I began to feel more and more like this might actually work. I suppose, in a perfect world, a large cock and a small pussy are the perfect combination. The beginning, no doubt, is utter hell.

I'd always day dreamed about being with a bad-boy and having them do with me as they wished; tossing me around from room to room and maneuvering me through no less than half a dozen various sexual positions. Possibly held upside down while being eaten out, or being bent over the hand rail at a football game and being fucked from behind while the crowd cheered us on.

Having Axton on top of me exceeded any expectation whatsoever of crazy bad-boy sex. His weight against me, his chest pressed to mine, and his warm breath against my neck was far more of a turn-on than anything I had or would expect to ever experience. As his hands pressed into my shoulders, he worked his massive swollen manhood in and out of my wet, tight pussy. The flesh on flesh friction, combined with being completely filled with cock proved to be all too much, and I felt myself begin to return to my heavenly orgasmic place.

I felt the dress being lifted over my head. Momentarily, I opened my eyes and attempted to focus.

"I want to feel your skin on mine," he breathed.

I nodded my head and opened my mouth to say something in acknowledgement, but nothing happened. I was lost in his slow, methodical thrusts. As I felt his cock begin to swell, I bit my lip and prepared to explode myself. Slowly, he pulled himself from inside me.

I opened my eyes in disbelief.

As he stroked his cock and pointed it at my stomach, I continued to stare. Although I'd love to see him jack-off and cover me in his cum, I opened my mouth. This time words actually spilled from my lips.

"Inside me. I'm on the pill. God, please. Inside me!" I barked.

As I felt his cock against my wet mound, I sighed. Within a few seconds, I was back to where I was, tingling from head-to-toe, preparing to be launched into space. As I once again felt him begin to swell, I opened my eyes and stared at the ceiling. His cock continued to thrust in and out of me as if a man possessed was behind it.

As I heard him release a groan which would wake the dead, I joined in with my own scream of pleasure. Together, as we both reached climax, the sound of our voices was enough to cause any sane person within a mile to call the police. I shifted my gaze to meet his. His back arched, his hands held high above his head, and his fists clenched, he looked like a tattooed Greek God. As he unclenched his fists and ran his fingers through his short curly hair, he looked down and smiled.

A *new* smile.

One with white teeth gleaming, and the sides of his mouth curled up to depict what could only be described as…

Progress.

# AXTON

For as long as I grace the earth and am able, I will be an outlaw. Being in an Outlaw Motorcycle Club wasn't only where I belonged, it was who I was. This one thing, regardless of any other changes in my life, would never change.

Allowing Avery to enter my world caused me to feel a sense of accomplishment in my life I had never felt. She allowed me to exhale and believe, at least in her presence, I was not only an outlaw, but an outlaw *and* human. Having never felt like much other than a criminal, keeping her by my side would certainly prove effective in making me feel better about myself, and making me a more effective president. In some way or another, everyone in my life would benefit from what Avery provided me.

"You know I'll always be an outlaw," I said without looking up.

"Uh huh. I wouldn't want it any other way," she responded.

I glanced up from my bowl of noodles, "I could end up in prison for some bullshit charge, and you may never see me again."

"They allow visitors," she grinned.

"The club always comes first, Avery. Always," I explained.

"As they should," she said as she stirred her chopsticks through her soup.

"You realize there isn't really a law or a commandment I haven't broken. Think about that," I said as I laid my chopsticks across the bowl and pushed it toward the center of the table.

She looked up from her bowl and raised her eyebrows, "Seriously? I'll be caught up with you in no time. You're not going to scare me away."

"Well, I'm just making sure you know who I am for sure," I shrugged.

"Well, it's a little late for starting to introduce yourself, but yeah, I know who you are," she said as dropped the chopsticks into her bowl.

"Guess that's all I've got for now. You got anything?" I asked.

After a short hesitation, she raised her hand to her mouth and tapped her index finger to her lips, "Yep. One thing."

"Well?" I sighed.

"Can I like say whatever, and you won't get mad?" she asked.

I nodded my head, "Sure."

"Okay. Well, I think I've been doing a good job of being respectful and stuff. You know, keeping my smart-ass mouth shut and not saying shit. Like don't speak unless you're spoken to," she paused and leaned into the center of the table.

"I never told you *that*, but yeah, I'll agree. You've been pretty good," I nodded.

She pressed her elbows into the table and rested her chin in her hands, "Well, I figured it out on my own, you know, from reading and stuff. So, anyway. What I was wondering is this. When it's you and me, just us, can I like speak a little more freely? Not be disrespectful, but like say what I want without you getting mad?"

She sat up and leaned into her chair as she waited on my response.

I raised my hands in the air slightly and shrugged, "Sure. But from you or anyone for that fucking matter, I won't be disrespected."

"And I won't disrespect you. Agreed," she said as she extended her hand to the middle of the table.

I shook my head and rolled my eyes as I leaned over and shook her hand, "Agreed."

"Okay. Well, I have always dreamt of having a guy like you. I know I don't *have* you, but you know what I mean. A bad-boy, an alpha male, a biker; all of those things are my perfect dream. So, I get you, and then we finally have sex. Now don't get me wrong, I loved the sex. I *loved* it. But, I uhhm. I was kinda wondering if we could like go all crazy once in a while. You know, like pull my hair and shit. Have some of that wild shit like people always tell stories about and stuff. What do you think about that?" she said without so much as taking a breath.

Avery always spoke a hundred miles an hour whenever she chose to speak. Hearing her say all of what she just said as fast as she said it made me take a moment to digest it all. As I watched her face change from a look of confidence to worry, I sighed.

I leaned forward, pinched my chin between my thumb and forefinger, and nodded my head, "You like it rough?"

She shrugged, "I don't know. I like *thinking* about it. But not just rough. You know, rough and adventurous."

I raised one eyebrow, "You want me to fuck you harder than I did?"

She shrugged again, "Oh God. I don't know. Maybe after we bone for a while. Your cock's huge and I've got a little hoo-hah."

I shook my head, "Don't ever call it that again. A fucking hoo-hah? You can add that to the list of shit not to say. It's a pussy."

She leaned into the table and whispered, "I have a tiny pussy."

"That you do," I agreed.

"Well, we'll see. I think you'll be satisfied with what you get from me. We've had sex one time. Well, one and a half if you want to include the shower sex after the bed. But you didn't last long."

She widened her eyes and gasped, "It was hot as fuck, humid, and you'd already fucked me senseless. What did you expect?"

"Hell, if it was up to me, we'd still be fucking," I said as I stood.

I pulled my wallet from my pocket and threw thirty bucks on the table. As I glanced across the table, she stood from her seat and stretched.

"You might want to do the splits a couple times before we saddle up. Where we're headed it might come in handy," I said as I walked past her and toward the door.

"Where are we headed?" she asked excitedly as she ran to my side.

I pulled the door open and held it for her to pass through, "You'll find out soon enough. But if we get caught, I can tell you this, we'll both probably go to jail."

Standing in the open doorway, her eyes widened. I grinned and walked past her, knowing our perceptions of events would never quite match. Satisfying her, however, was strangely on my list of priorities.

As I stepped over the bike and lowered myself into the seat, I glanced toward the entrance. Still standing at the door with her mouth open, she stared back at me.

"Saddle up, we've got some fucking to do," I hollered.

As she slowly walked toward the bike, I figured she was attempting to dream up all of the possibilities of what might be next. She was without a doubt an intelligent girl, but she would never figure out what I had planned.

Not in a million years.

# AVERY

Be careful what you wish for. I've heard it. I've preached it. I had a sinking suspicion just to prove a point Axton would attempt to make me regret ever telling him I wanted rough and adventurous sex. Axton wasn't much of a practical joker or a prankster of any sort. He was all business. As I was wondering exactly what I signed on for, he pulled his bike along a side street in Winfield and parked it alongside the curb.

"Well, get off," he insisted after he parked.

He turned the ignition to *lock*, and put the keys in his front pocket, "You hear me?"

"I'm getting off," I said as I stepped off the bike and looked around.

"Follow me," he said as he began walking down the sidewalk.

"You kind of like *really* stand out. You're fucking huge, covered in tattoos, and you're wearing a 1%er cut. Someone's going to call the cops," I sighed as I attempted to catch up with his long stride.

He continued to walk silently.

"I fit in. I'm a cute college girl wearing roll-hem jean shorts and a *Pink* tee. Hey, slow down," I said between breaths as I tried to catch up with him.

"You're a college *graduate* who talks too fucking much. Be quiet," he said flatly.

As we turned a corner and began walking down another residential side street, I stopped and stared. A police cruiser was parked in the street two houses down from where we were.

"Cops," I said as I pointed toward the car.

"No shit," he sighed as he continued walking.

As we walked up to the car, it became apparent what he had planned. At least *where* he planned to fuck me was clear.

"Watch for the cop, I'm going to look for a spare key," he whispered as he lowered himself to the ground.

I scanned the street in both directions, "You're going to steal a fucking cop car?"

"No, I'm not going to *steal* the motherfucker. Now be fucking quiet. They always keep a key in one of those magnetic key holders on the frame of the car, just in case they get locked out. Just stand there and look pretty," he said as he slid under the car.

As I listened to him groan and grunt, his feet moved along the outside of the car, indicating where he was looking for the key. Honestly, I had no desire to have sex in a cop car. It would be exciting I suppose, but we would definitely go to jail if we were caught. I'm sure in a small town like Winfield it would be written up in the local newspaper as well. My professors would certainly have a long laugh at my expense.

*Please, don't find it.*

I looked up and down the block for pedestrians, neighbors, and of course, the cop. It was nine o'clock at night in the summer, and it had only been dark for fifteen minutes. No one was in bed yet; everyone was up and watching television or cleaning up the mess from dinner. As I attempted to look innocent, he said the three words I had hoped he wouldn't.

"I found it!" he whispered.

As he slid out from under the car, I inhaled a shallow breath and sighed heavily.

"When I open the door, the interior light is going to come on. If I don't start the car, it'll stay on for ninety seconds or so; and I don't intend to start it. So, during that time, you little smart-ass, you're going to suck my cock. That way you'll be hidden. When the light goes out, we'll figure it out from there," he said as he held the key in front of him.

I glanced up and down the block. The street lights illuminated the street rather well. As a girl, I had always felt the city's streets were dark and scary at night. Now, standing beside the cop car thinking of sucking Axton's cock, the street seemed to be illuminated all too well.

"Do they like *add* street lights on the blocks where the cops live? It's like day time out here," I complained.

He pressed the button on the key and unlocked the door. As he glanced up toward the house, he nodded his head toward the car and gave me his command, "Get the fuck in."

He pulled the door open and slid into the seat, "Come on."

I rolled my eyes and slid in beside him. As he had guessed, the light stayed on long after he shut the door. I sat in the car with my heart beating through my chest, hoping I didn't see a cop walk up and beat on the window. As I planned my escape route *just in case*, he unbuckled his belt.

"Get down so they don't see you," he whispered as he pulled out his cock.

"Jesus, Axton. You're already hard as fuck. I thought you had problems with that?" I chuckled.

He was far from amused. The look on his face was one of sheer disappointment and anger. Although I've never really been one to actually *want* to suck a dude's cock, I immediately planted my face into his lap and began to lick and suck his huge cock. On about the third slurp, the interior light went out. I slowly lifted my head from his lap.

"You're nowhere near done," he grunted as he gripped my head in his hands.

Reluctantly, I began to work my mouth up and down his cock. I was kind of starting to get into it, and it was turning me on no matter how much I disliked doing it. One advantage, I suppose, was that for the entire time, my eyes were closed and I didn't think of where we were or what might happen if we were caught. After sucking and stroking it for some time, my jaw began to get sore. I lifted my mouth free of his massive rod, and began to stroke it as I opened my eyes.

He was sitting upright in the seat, looking down at me as if I were crazy.

"Take off your shorts," he grunted as he tossed his hand toward my waist.

"Off off? Like Off?" I asked as I wiped my mouth on the back of my hand and looked out the window.

"What other kind of *off* is there? Yes, fucking *off*, Avery. I'm going to fuck you, and it'll be a real bitch if you leave those fuckers on," he growled as he pulled his jeans down past his thighs.

I looked out the window and gazed up and down the block.

*Nothing.*

I turned and looked the other direction.

*Nothing.*

I leaned back into the seat, and stretched my legs out as far as I could. Half scared, and with my heart pounding, I unbuttoned my shorts and slid them to my ankles. After a second's thought I decided to leave my shoes on, and pulled the shorts past my shoes. Not knowing where to put them, and considering there were all kinds of cop radios and shit everywhere, I tossed them onto the dash. After a quick survey of the front of the car, I reached into the floorboard, picked up my clutch, and placed it on the dash beside the shorts.

"Jesus jumped up Christ. You ready?" Axton sighed angrily.

I nodded my head eagerly although I was scared to death.

"Get up here and ride me," he said as he began stroking his cock.

"Holy shit. Seriously?" I gasped as I looked down at the ten inches of throbbing flesh.

He raised his hands in the air and spoke crossly, "I swear, you went from *fuck me hard and be adventurous doing it* to a complete scared ass little fucker in a matter of hours, didn't you? If you're scared, go to fucking church."

I climbed across the seat and lifted my leg over his thighs. After resting for a moment on his upper legs, I raised myself into the air and hovered over his cock, holding my ass over him with what little arm strength I had. Half in fear of his cock killing me in this particular position, and half in fear of the cops shooting us or arresting us, I slowly lowered myself onto his cock. As I felt it begin to penetrate me, I exhaled loudly and attempted help relieve myself with my quivering arms.

I leaned forward and looked between my legs. The street lights shining in through the window confirmed my suspicion. I had roughly a fourth of his cock in me. I felt like I was being impaled by a sword. I closed my eyes, raised myself up and lowered myself again. Slowly, I repeated the process. Each time, I took a little more of his cock inside of me. I bit my lip and lowered myself onto it again, taking a little more of the shaft inside me. It came as no surprise as I relaxed on the down stroke, I had a miniature orgasm. I raised myself and lowered myself again.

Another orgasm.

I opened my eyes.

"Having fun?" Axton sighed.

"Uhhm. I forgot where we were. It feels weird. I keep having like mini orgasms. You're fucking huge," I shrugged.

"I know I'm huge. It's *my* cock. I've had it for a while, so I'm well aware. You ought to try walking around with this motherfucker hanging between your legs for a lifetime. Now," he paused and reached under my ass with both hands, "we're going to *fuck*."

He lifted me off of his cock and released me. As I literally fell down the entire length of his shaft, he raised me again. Again he lowered me down the shaft, then up, down, up. I began to breathe heavily. He moved his hands from my ass to my hips and began slamming me up and down his cock.

About thirty seconds into it and I was a literal wreck. I bit my lip and began to have what I knew would be another earth shattering orgasm. When I realized where we were, I began to look around nervously as I felt myself reaching climax. As if embarrassed to be seen having an orgasm, my muscles tensed. After seeing no one peering inside the car, I relaxed onto his cock.

As I exhaled a breath, Axton shook his head, lifted me off his cock, and tossed me to his side.

"What?" I gasped.

"You nervous little motherfucker. You're done driving this train. Get out," he demanded.

"What?" I stammered.

"Out. It's the opposite of in. *Get. Out*," he growled.

Not knowing what I had done or what to do, I sat and stared, sad that I hadn't satisfied him. He reached over me and pulled against the door handle, opening the door, and turning on the interior light. He pointed out toward the street.

"Get out and put your hands on the fucking trunk. I'll fuck you in the street," he grunted.

Nervous, but not willing to risk making him angry, I stepped out of the car naked from the waist down and walked nervously to the trunk. Right behind me, Axton shuffled his way to the rear of the car with his jeans around his ankles and his boots still on. As I glanced up and down the well-lit street, he pushed me against the trunk and kicked my legs apart.

"Long-legged little bitch. Get that little pussy down here where I can get to it," he said under his breath.

I pressed my hands onto the surface of the trunk and closed my eyes. As I felt his hand against my butt, I flinched nervously. His still swollen cock now in his hand, he guided it into my wetness. I gasped at the angle of his cock inside of me; it was hitting spots that had never been hit. Never having felt anything like it, I spread my hands across the trunk and planted my face against the cold metal. After a few short, slow strokes, he grasped my hips and forced himself inside me completely.

"Ready?" he asked.

"Always," I whimpered.

He began to forcefully fuck me with all his might. His hips slapping against my ass, and my thighs banging against the edge of the trunk, he continued to fuck me steadily and deeply. I opened my eyes and stared into the back of the car in shock as he continued to fill me with his ten inch swollen dick. His balls slapping against my clit with each stroke were enough to cause me to close my eyes and attempt to focus.

"Tight pussied little fucker," he grunted.

Being fucked in the street of small town USA wasn't necessarily what I had in mind when I said I wanted adventurous sex. Although it wasn't as scary as I expected, having him pound me into the back of a cop car wasn't anything that made me various shades of comfortable either. As he slid his stiff cock in and out of my soaking wet pussy, I opened my eyes and began to moan.

*Whack!*

His hand slapped my ass.

*Holy fuck.*

Initially startled, I was immediately turned on by his hand slapping me. As the stinging on my butt cheek heightened, he slapped me again.

*Whack!*

"My hair," I gasped as I lifted my head and tossed my hair over my shoulders.

"Pull it."

"Fuck yeah I will," he breathed against my neck.

He gathered my hair in his hand and pulled it steadily. As my scalp began to sting, I arched my back and rose up onto my tip-toes.

*Fuck yes, this is what I was talking about.*

"Fuck me," I whimpered.

The sound of his hips slapping my ass echoed up and down the block. Lost in the feeling of his cock filling me, I began to moan louder and louder. I arched my back and moaned in pleasure as his swollen balls banged against my clit. Knowing I was mere seconds from exploding, I opened my mouth and groaned.

"I'm..."

He pulled my hair with a little more force.

"I'm going..." I closed my eyes and focused.

My entire body began to tingle. Again, just as before, my ears started ringing slightly.

"I'm going to fucking cum. You sexy little bitch. I'm going to fill that tight little pussy with cum," he growled.

As I listened to his breathing change to heavily labored choppy breaths, I relaxed my arches and lowered myself off my tip-toes. Immediately, I exploded into an earth shattering orgasm. As my legs began to collapse, he thrust himself into me and held his cock still. I felt him explode inside of me, filling me with his warm cum. I relaxed and exhaled into the darkness, satisfied that I had satisfied him. As he stood still, I felt my inner self quiver into another orgasm. I closed my eyes and sighed into another orgasmic bliss. As my knees bent and I almost collapsed, he reached under my hips and held me upright.

"Holy shit, that's one tight little pussy you've got, Avery. God damn, we're going to need to work up to an all-nighter. No way I can last all night in that little fucker right now," he sighed.

"Can you stand?" he asked as he pulled up his jeans, forced his half stiff cock inside, and buckled his belt.

"Doubt it," I moaned.

"I'll grab your shorts and little wallet," he said flatly.

As he opened the door to the car, I heard a voice from my right side.

"What the fuck are you doing on the trunk of my car?" a deep voice hollered from the front porch of the house.

I immediately stood straight up. As I heard the car door close, Axton screamed, "Come on. Hurry the fuck up."

As Axton passed me, in a full on dead run toward the corner, I turned and began running toward him, naked from the waist down except my Chuck's. My legs and hips on fire, and cum falling from my sopping wet pussy, I slowly began to catch up. As we ran, we both began to laugh heavily.

As our laughter filled the night air, I knew one thing for sure.

Being with Axton would never produce a day of boredom.

Not a single one.

# AXTON

I sat at the sewing machine, staring down at the cut. Something about sewing a cut myself had always pleased me. A sense of accomplishment filed me as I carefully placed the patches in their respective locations, held them in place, and worked the material through the machine. Watching the red thread unravel as the patch became one with the leather made me feel as if I was breathing life into the vest, and in turn, the vest would breathe life into the new addition to my family.

Pride in craftsmanship, and pride in the materials used allowed me to look through the ranks of my club and see the men in their cuts with a deep sense of pride. I reached down and carefully cut the excess thread from the last patch. I stood up, lifted the finished cut from the machine and shook it in the sunlight of the room.

It was perfect.

Now.

It was time to make my move.

# AXTON

Making changes in the way we live our life is to admit something was wrong, or we had been living a life filled with mistakes. When natural changes occur through the course of merely living, it can only be described as progress. Progress is change over time; a step or steps in the right direction, one at a time, making simple improvements which one day might lead to a brighter future, a better way, or a life with less complication.

Progress. Equals. Improvement.

Somewhat nervously, I studied her as she sat quietly across the table from me, "We've made quite a bit of progress in only a few months. I never thought I'd give two fucks about a woman for as long as I lived, but I'll be the first to admit I was wrong. You're one hell of a woman, Avery."

She smiled and tilted her chin downward slightly, "Appreciate it."

"You know, I'm not one for flowers and cards, or any kind of shit like that. And for me to think of marriage," I paused and inhaled a short choppy breath.

"Well, it just doesn't make any fucking sense. For me to conform to the rules and regulations society establishes as law? I can't do it. A piece of paper is required by the court to show how I feel about another person? I can't wrap my mind around that. But Avery, there are other types of commitment," I paused and stood from my seat.

261

I reached down and pulled my keychain from the clip on my belt. Methodically, I walked to the cabinet and pushed the key in the lock. A lone cardboard box sat amongst the cuts and patches in the cabinet. I removed it, walked back to the table and sat down.

I laid the box in front of me on the table and placed my hands on the top as if protecting it from harm, "You know when you're a teenager you ask a girl to *go steady*. You get older, you say you're what is it? People say *we're exclusive*. You get a little older or maybe a little more committed and you buy a ring and say you're *engaged*. If you get her another ring, you're *married*. My life isn't like that. Sure as fuck isn't. Here, in the world of the MC, things are much different. The commitment might be the same or deeper, but the means of expressing it is different."

I gazed at the floor, inhaled through my nose, and shifted my eyes to meet hers, "Avery, I need to ask you something."

She lifted her chin and glanced up, "I'm listening."

*Short breaths; just take it easy, Slice. You can do this.*

I slid the box across the table and held my right hand on the top as I swallowed heavily, "I want to know if you're interested in this."

I removed my hand from the box and sat back in my chair.

She narrowed her eyes, opened the box, and peered inside. Carefully, she reached in and removed the leather cut. After placing it on the table beside her, she unfolded it and stared down at the back of the cut. Her gaze never shifted upward.

A little more nervous than I expected, I stammered as I attempted to speak, "I uhhm. I stitched it myself. I know it ain't much, but I think having my hands involved in actually making it gives it a little more importance, you know? Makes it that much more, hell I don't know what I'm trying to say. Meaningful. Yeah, more meaningful."

I stood from my seat and crossed my arms, "Before you answer, let me explain a few things. Wearing it means more than you think. When two people get married, the woman gets a ring, and with that ring she gets a sense of ownership and a feeling of commitment from her husband. He, in turn, wears a ring showing his commitment to her. When you see them together, and they're *each* wearing a ring, there's no doubt they belong together and they're committed to each other. If they're apart, however, all you know is that each one is committed – because of the rings they wear, but you don't know *where* the commitment lies."

I nodded my head toward the cut, "Now with *that*, it's obvious where the commitment lies. *My* name is on the back of it, and *you're* wearing it. Anyone see's that cut on you, and they know you're mine and I'm yours. There's no question."

"You know, most people don't understand the *Property Of* patch. Not only am I claiming you, but it's worn as a warning to others outside the club that the Ol' Lady wearing the patch is to be respected the same as a fully patched male member, and that she warrants the same protections as her male member counterpart. That patch, Avery, says *don't fuck with this girl*, in more ways than one. You'd be the President's Ol' Lady, and nobody, and I do mean *nobody* will fuck with you."

"So," I uncrossed my arms and turned my palms up, "Will you be my Ol'Lady?"

She stood from her seat, slipped her arms through the cut, and snapped each button carefully. She glanced up at the motto posted on the wall and swallowed heavily. As she rubbed her bracelet with her thumb and forefinger, she inhaled a shallow breath and shifted her gaze down to meet mine.

*God damn, woman, say something...*

# AVERY

To understand a woman or women's thoughts would be impossible. I am convinced there are more personalities in the female population than grains of sand on the beaches of the world. To attempt to comprehend the intricate thoughts and behaviors of a woman would be impossible for a trained psychiatrist, let alone an average man. Most women, including me, don't necessarily know what we want until it arrives on our doorstep.

Diamond rings and wedding dresses may be for *some* women, and I always believed they were one of my main goals in my life. I had learned over the course of the summer I wanted so much more than a conventional wedding. I wanted a man, not just any man, but a man who was satisfied with what he had in life, and didn't need a woman to complicate things.

I wanted Axton.

We never really know where we belong for certain until we get there. This summer, I landed where I belonged, and I now stood grateful for being delivered to my final destination. Axton may not *totally* agree, but his asking me to be his Ol' Lady and allowing me to wear the *Property Of* patch meant more to me than an engagement or marriage ever could.

I removed the cut from the box and stared, afraid I was going to lose my composure and begin crying. I pressed it into the table, unsure of what he had specifically done. A simple *Property Of* patch would have meant one thing. But a *Property Of* patch with *Slice* on the lower rocker meant so much more.

*We were committed to each other.*

*And the club had my back.*

I pulled the cut over my shoulders and buttoned it up. Axton stood across from me with his arms crossed in his *what the fuck are you looking at* pose. He didn't realize it, but when he did that, he was one scary motherfucker. As he turned his palms upward and spoke, I bit my quivering lip.

"So, will you be my Ol'Lady?"

I knew the answer, but I was incapable of speaking. Still biting my lip, I shifted my eyes upward and lowered my chin in a half-assed nod. I swallowed heavily and for the first time in my life, spoke slowly.

"I won't embarrass you or the club, Axton. And yes, I'll be your Ol' Lady."

"Go saddle up, we got to make a run to Wichita. El Pelón needs to talk," he nodded, "I'll get the lights."

Standing taller, feeling prouder, and knowing no matter where I went or who I was with I would always have the confidence I previously only had in Axton's presence, I walked out to the shop.

*Progress.*

*I made it.*

*Mission accomplished.*

# AXTON

The only family I had ever claimed were the men I rode with; my brothers. Adding a new member to the family had always been an exciting thing for me. Adding Avery? Well, that was a totally different feeling.

Having her as my Ol' Lady was a huge step for me. Her wearing the cut was even a bigger commitment. I offered it to her knowing I was ready for the responsibility, and I'd never disappoint her. Feeling more proud than I had in my entire life, I walked to the door, looked up at the motto, and flipped out the lights. As I stepped through the door and pulled it closed, I realized there was one more thing I needed to do.

I shook my head and grinned at the thought.

*The unthinkable.*

I opened the door, flipped on the lights, and stared at the membership board. No doubt about it, one thing was missing. I walked to the board, picked up the pen, and without hesitation, marked a big black "X" beside my name in the *Ol' Lady Allowed* column.

I stood back and crossed my arms as I gazed at the board.

*God damned right, fellas.*

She's mine.

And I'm proud to admit it.

Made in the USA
Lexington, KY
19 August 2017